the
sweet
ness
of
salt

ALSO BY CECILIA GALANTE

The Patron Saint of Butterflies

the sweetness of salt

CECILIA GALANTE

BLOOMSBURY

NEW YORK BERLIN LONDON SYDNEY

First published in the United States of America in November 2010
by Bloomsbury Books for Young Readers
www.bloomsburyteens.com

For information about permission to reproduce selections from this book, write to
Permissions, Bloomsbury BFYR, 175 Fifth Avenue, New York, New York 10010

Lyrics on page 170 from "Folsom Prison Blues" by Johnny Cash

Library of Congress Cataloging-in-Publication Data
Galante, Cecilia.
The sweetness of salt / by Cecilia Galante. — 1st U.S. ed.
p.   cm.
Summary: After graduating from high school, class valedictorian Julia travels to
Poultney, Vermont, to visit her older sister, and while she is there she learns about
long-held family secrets that have shaped her into the person she has grown up to be.
ISBN 978-1-59990-512-9
[1. Secrets—Fiction.   2. Sisters—Fiction.   3. Family problems—Fiction.
4. Self-perception—Fiction.   5. Poultney (Vt.)—Fiction.]   I. Title.
PZ7.G12965Sw 2010   [Fic]—dc22   2010003477

Book design by Donna Mark
Typeset by Westchester Book Composition
Printed in the U.S.A. by Quad/Graphics, Fairfield, Pennsylvania
2 4 6 8 10 9 7 5 3 1

This book is dedicated to Josie, Therese, and Margaret:
my sisters, my heart, my life.

"We dance round in a ring and suppose;
But the Secret sits in the middle and knows."
ROBERT FROST

"Sometimes the best laid plans of mice and men go awry."
ROBERT BURNS

part
one

chapter
1

"Julia!" Mom leaped up from the couch as I walked through the front door. "I was wondering when you'd get back. What took so long?"

I glanced down at my watch and sidestepped my way over to the stairs. "Mrs. Soprano is in charge of graduation practice this year. She made us all line up and then walk across the stage *three* times. Like we're in kindergarten or something."

Behind Mom, I could see my bright gold graduation robe spread out over one arm of the couch, the hem folded back neatly. No, no, no. There was no time for this now. Milo was probably already in the window seat, a book resting on his knees. His worn-out Converse sneakers would be pushed comfortably up against the corner wall, while his honey-ribboned hair flopped across his forehead. I had to get up there. Now. I lunged up the steps, two at a time. "I'll talk to you later, Mom, okay? I have some stuff I have to do."

Mom took the needle and thread out from between her teeth.

"Wait a second, will you?" Mom turned around and grabbed my robe off the couch. "Just try this on for me real quick. I hemmed the bottom where it was loose, and I want to make sure it's even all the way around."

I paused at the top of the steps. "Later, okay? I got this great idea on the way home for the end of my speech, and I want to write it down before I forget."

Mom paused, her small blue eyes crinkling around the corners. "Oh. Well, why didn't you say that? After dinner, all right?"

"Great." I turned, ready to head into my room.

"Oh, and Julia?"

"What?"

"You have it memorized, don't you? Your speech, I mean?"

"Yes. I have it memorized, Mom. Don't worry."

She ran a hand through her short brown hair and then rested it on the hip of her purple sweat jacket. Beneath the hall light, I could see the tiny cord attached to the hearing aid in her left ear, something she'd had to wear even before I was born. As the founder of the neighborhood walking club, Mom was fit and strong, but sometimes, like then, when I caught a glimpse of her hearing aid, she looked a little fragile.

"I'm not worried, honey," she said. "It's just... well, the valedictorian has to be prepared, you know? When all is said and done, it's kind of your day, Julia. You have to make sure you sound really professional. I mean, to the hilt."

I sighed. "I won't sound like anything, Mom, if you don't let me work."

"Go!" she said, tapping the step. "Work away! I'll call you when dinner's ready."

I closed the door carefully to my room and then locked it. Mom had a habit of forgetting to knock sometimes, barging into my room with an armful of clean laundry or something she'd brought home from the florist, where she worked a few days a week. Some days I came home to find arrangements of sunflowers or dried seed pod wreaths arranged on my desk. I didn't need that today. Not right now.

I walked over to my window and drew back the curtain ever so slightly. Oh God, there he was, right there, in the window across the street, just like he was every afternoon at this time. I withdrew a small notebook from the bottom drawer of my dresser, positioned my chair in front of the window, and opened the curtains. With everything in its place I set my feet against the windowsill, rested my tablet against my knees, and began.

Milo was easy to draw, not just because he was beautiful, but because he sat still for so long. At least during this time of the day. During school he raced from person to person, laughing and joking, always in on—and usually a part of—whatever new thing was happening. Just last week, he'd been voted Mr. Personality by the senior class. The nickname, I thought wistfully, fit him. But I wondered how many people knew this side of him, this secret-reader side. Every once in a while he would put his book down and just stare out the window. Those were the times I lived for most, when his profile turned suddenly, revealing the whole of his face: the long Roman nose, widely set green eyes that looked out from behind a pair of brown glasses, and the dimple in his left cheek, an indentation so deep that when his sister Zoe, his younger sister, told me she had been able to fit a peanut M&M into it, I'd actually believed her.

The pencil moved across the page swiftly, my hand knowing where the slope of Milo's cheekbone began and how the curve of his chin dipped narrowly in the center. Soon, his eye appeared, the lashes framing an almond-shaped lid. I shaded most of the iris, leaving tiny speckle-points of white where I knew the lightest points were, and started on the other one.

My mind began to drift in the easy way it always did when I drew, wondering what book he was immersed in today. This morning, on the way to school, I'd watched from the backseat of Zoe's car as he opened *Carrie* again. Lately he'd been reading a lot of Stephen King, which surprised me because his head was usually buried inside a book of poetry. Milo read poetry the way Zoe drank Dr Pepper, first thing every morning on the way to school and then steadily on the way back home. Walt Whitman. Anne Sexton. Sylvia Plath. Ralph Waldo Emerson. He read poets I hadn't even heard of, like Mary Oliver and W. H. Auden, Billy Elliot and Sharon Olds, writers he called the "scary truth tellers." Every once in a while he would look up and recite some line he liked. He'd just say it—whether Zoe and I were listening or not—and then leave it hanging there, like a tiny cord of stars strung on the dashboard.

Did he do that kind of thing for Cheryl Hanes? I tried to picture him at the foot of his girlfriend's staircase, arm outstretched as he recited Emerson or Whitman up to her. The thing was, I could not imagine Cheryl—who, despite being the most beautiful girl in the senior class, had a brain like a bag of rocks—actually sticking around long enough to hear it. Cheryl didn't get poetry—or literature of any kind. It bored her. Once, in ninth grade, she'd actually asked our English teacher if Mark Twain was related to Shania Twain. I doubted Milo had heard about that one.

But I guess it didn't matter. The rules of high school dating were the same everywhere: the prettiest girls always got the pick of the lot. The rest of us had to make do—whether we liked it or not. And so I made do with watching Milo from afar.

Then, a few days before Christmas, while we were waiting in the parking lot for Zoe to come out of the building, Milo turned and handed me a small, stiff piece of paper. I had been staring at the freckles on the back of his neck, which were arranged exactly like the Little Dipper, and wondering what he would do if I reached out and touched one. Actually, I thought, he probably wouldn't even notice. Half the time he seemed surprised when he caught sight of me in the backseat, as if he had forgotten completely that I tagged along in his sister's car every day. "Here," he said, talking to my knees. "I thought you might like this. Merry Christmas."

I glanced down at it. There, in tiny cramped handwriting, was the line: *"nobody, not even the rain, has such small hands."* Around the words, like a frame, were curly vines and leaves of all different sizes. They had been drawn with a felt-tip marker, and some of the edges were smudged.

"I didn't write it," Milo said. "It's by a poet named e. e. cummings. He's one of my favorites. One of the scary truth tellers."

I didn't understand what the words meant.

How could rain have hands?

But it was for me.

From him.

And I knew it meant everything. "I love it," I whispered. "Thank you."

He looked up at me and smiled, the dimple in his left cheek deepening. For a split second, I wanted to lean forward and put both of my lips over that dimple. But of course I didn't.

At the beginning of May, Cheryl and Milo broke up. There were lots of rumors going around—Cheryl was getting too clingy, Milo was flirting with other girls—but Milo himself never said a word about it. He didn't say much at all actually, until one day, when he turned around again in the car and asked me if I wanted to go to the prom with him. Just as friends, of course. Just to go, since we were both seniors.

I didn't sleep for two days. Mom took me shopping for a dress, and I listened with half an ear as she yammered on about delicate necklines—nothing V-necked, nothing cleavage-baring—and long white gloves. To me, the dress—and even the prom itself—was secondary. It was Milo I wanted. Just him. Nothing else.

He spent most of the night dancing like a crazy person out on the dance floor with his buddies, but he'd rested his hand on my arm twice. Once, just before he'd asked if I wanted something to drink from the soda bar, and then again, when he asked me if I wanted to slow dance. Both times, a heat had traveled through my arm, straight to my stomach, until I felt like my whole body was glowing.

And then, in the car on the way home, as we parked in front of my house, he'd said that he wanted to tell me something. The street light behind us threw a shadow over his face. He'd taken off that silly red tuxedo tie, and a faint sheen of perspiration gleamed along his jaw. I didn't wait for him to say anything more. Instead, that same longing I'd felt in the car at Christmas reared its head again. This time, I leaned over and kissed him. *Really* kissed him. Like, pressed myself against the front of him, flattened both my hands against the lapels of his tux, and leaned in with my whole weight, kissed him. I could taste Certs against the heat of his tongue.

But he'd pulled away, looked at me with liquid eyes that I could not read.

I held my breath, waiting.

"I'm sorry...," he started, shaking his head a little. "I just..."

I turned and bolted, mortified that I'd misunderstood.

That was in May.

Today was June fourth.

He hadn't said another word to me since.

I closed my sketch book, stood up, and walked over to my dresser. Taped in the corner was Milo's little cardboard note. I ran my fingertips lightly over the words: "*no one, not even the rain...*" and closed my eyes. I would give up anything, I thought, even being introduced tomorrow in front of a crowd of eight hundred people as the valedictorian of Silver Springs High School, if I could kiss Milo again—and have him kiss me back. For real this time.

"Jules?" My doorknob rattled softly, followed by a light knock on the door. "Are you in there?"

I threw the sketch pad in my bottom drawer again and snatched my speech from off the top of my desk. "Yeah, I'm here. I'm working, Mom." I rattled the papers loudly for good measure.

She sighed. "Okay. Dad just got home. We're eating in ten minutes. Swiss steak with buttered noodles. Your favorite."

"All right. Be right there."

I stared back out the window.

But Milo had disappeared.

chapter
2

Sitting in the back of Dad's car the next morning, I took a slow, deep breath. My anxiety, which was already on a steady incline, shot up as I caught sight of my reflection in the rearview mirror. A gold graduation cap was set neatly on a head of straight brown hair, parted in the middle, and tied back in a ponytail. My white face, accentuated by a high forehead, half-circles under my eyes, and chipmunk cheeks, had a deer-in-the-headlights kind of look to it. Even my lips, which I had painted with a light pink gloss, had a sad, ridiculous sort of quality to them, like I was trying too hard.

God. How could I have ever thought that Milo would be attracted to me? I was the quintessential nerd, the exact opposite of his free-spirited, poetic whatever the heck he was. School was my thing. School and grades. To perfection. And I had done it. In less than an hour, Principal Bellas would introduce me as the valedictorian of my whole class. Out of three hundred and seventy-seven students, I had come out on top. First. The head cheese, as Dad liked to say. Numero uno. It was definitely something to be proud of. The first of many larger steps to come.

I closed my eyes, whispering the first line of my speech in my head. "Fellow graduates, Superintendent Ringold, Principal Bellas, Vice Principal Elias, family and friends, welcome."

Mom and Dad came racing out of the house then, Mom in front, Dad turning to double check the door and straighten the welcome mat.

"Hurry, John!" Mom called, getting in the front seat. "She can't be late!"

"Here I am," Dad said, collapsing into his seat. "We're all set."

Mom had put on too much perfume. The cloying scent, combined with the mid-morning air, already thick with heat, was starting to make me nauseous. On the seat next to me was an enormous assortment of red and pink roses, which Mom had put together just this morning at the florist shop. I rolled down my window and closed my eyes. Underneath my gown my phone started buzzing.

"Where r u?" Zoe's message read.

"Just left," I texted back. *"Be there in 10."*

"Dad," I said, leaning over his shoulder. "Can you hurry? I was supposed to be there five minutes ago."

"I'm going as fast as I can," he said, stepping on the gas again. "I think the whole damn town is going to the same place. Hold on."

Mom braced herself as Dad made a hard right on Walnut Street, and sighed deeply as he settled back into traffic. "It's so nice that Sophie's coming, isn't it?" she asked.

Sophie was my older sister. She was eight years older than I, and had left Silver Springs when I was in fifth grade. She lived somewhere in Vermont now, working as an aide in an old persons' home. Every so often she graced us with a sudden appearance, descending on Silver Springs amid a flurry of demands, cigarette smoke, and her perpetual negative attitude. Her departures were just as abrupt, leaving Mom and Dad (and me, back when I cared) in a state of complete disarray. I was not exactly looking forward to seeing her.

Mom turned to look apologetically at me. She had accidentally let Sophie's secret out of the bag, letting it slip last night at dinner. "Please don't let on that you know she's coming, Julia. She really wanted to surprise you."

"Mom." I cocked my head, trying not to let my annoyance show. "You've told me that at least ten times already. Don't worry. I won't let on that I know."

"All right." Mom smoothed down the front of her dress. "Just making sure."

I rolled my eyes. Mom always tiptoed around Sophie. She had forbidden all of us, for example, from referring to the "Milford years"—ever—in Sophie's presence. Milford was the little town she and Dad and Sophie had lived in before I was born. Apparently, those seven years or so hadn't been the happiest in our family history. Dad's law firm hadn't been doing well and he had been drinking too much, which led to a lot of arguments. Now, twenty years later, Sophie never let a visit slip by without some sort of reference to that time. She just couldn't let it go—no matter how much Mom and Dad begged her to. It was this insistence of hers—this immaturity, really, to keep punishing Mom and Dad like she did—that made me so wary and resentful of her.

"Why isn't Goober coming?" Dad asked suddenly.

"Sophie said it was Greg's weekend, but that she was going to try to get him to switch," Mom said.

Goober was Sophie's four-year-old daughter. Her real name was Grace, but Sophie had started calling her Goober in the hospital, and the nickname had stuck.

"I hope she does," I said. "Sophie always acts more human when Goober's around."

"Julia!" Mom turned around, looking disapprovingly at me.

"It's true!" I said. "And you know it! When Goober's here, *she's* the baby. There's no room for Sophie to throw one of her temper tantrums."

Mom glanced over at Dad and then settled back in her seat. "No one will be throwing any temper tantrums," she said quietly. "It's going to be wonderful."

I caught Dad's eye in the rearview mirror. He winked at me.

"And even if the baby can't come, it will be so nice just to have the four of us all together again," Mom said. "I can't even remember the last time we were under the same roof."

"Christmas, Arlene," Dad's voice sounded far away. "The two of them were just here at Christmas."

"Actually, it was last Christmas," I said.

Dad had a way of blocking out a lot of things when it came to Sophie. Time was one of them. I didn't blame him, though. Sophie put him through a lot of crap whenever she was here. I probably would've figured out a way to block it out too.

"Well, it doesn't really matter..." Mom's voice drifted off the way it did when she had stopped talking to anyone in particular. She turned around suddenly and put her hand on my knee. "Oh, Julia. We're just so proud of you."

"Thanks, Mom."

"And I know I've already said this a million times," Dad said, looking at me in the rearview mirror again, "but I'm thrilled that you're going to my alma mater."

Wellesley had been my first choice for college and I'd been accepted, but the University of Pittsburgh had offered me a full ride. There was no way I was going to put up a fuss about not attending Wellesley, which had only offered partial scholarships and would have required Mom and Dad to pay thousands of extra dollars a year. Especially since after Pittsburgh, there would be law school.

"I know," I said. "It's gonna be great."

Someone in the line of cars began to honk, which sparked a flurry of more honking. I glanced at the digital clock above the radio. Ten thirty-nine. I was supposed to have been in line at ten thirty. The ceremony was going to start at eleven.

"I gotta go," I grabbed my speech and shoved the door open. "I'll just walk the rest of the way."

"In the eyes!" Dad yelled, using one of his attorney mantras. "Remember to look 'em right in the eyes! And don't let 'em see you sweat!"

I broke into a run as I spotted the line of yellow gowned students ahead.

There was no turning back now.

It was showtime.

chapter
3

I led my class out of the auditorium as the last stomachache strains of the orchestra faded behind us. My speech had been flawless. Not a single *uh* or *um*. No unnecessary pauses, no word stumbles. It was like I'd gone on autopilot. From start to finish. The crowd had approved too, cheering wildly when I finished. A few people even jumped up and pumped their fists in the air. One of them had probably been Sophie. I sat back down in my chair on stage, folded my hands, and felt my stomach plummet.

We were graduated. Done with Silver Springs High. Forever.

It was a slightly amazing feeling. I slowed as the foyer came into view, trying to absorb it.

"Jules!"

My heart flopped like a fish as Milo walked up to me. "Hey!"

For a split second, I wondered what he would do if I buried my nose into the front of his gold gown. "Hi," I said.

"I tried to find you before, to wish you luck," Milo said, "but I didn't see you."

"Oh, I was late. I was kind of hiding from Mrs. Soprano, and then I had to get in line…"

Wait. How were we talking like this all of a sudden? We hadn't exchanged this many words since… well, since that horrible night at prom.

Milo nodded. "You did great," he said. "Your speech, I mean. It was incredible."

"You think so?"

"The Auden quote was perfect."

"That was for you," I wanted to say. "I researched all the scary truth tellers until I found a quote that you might notice."

"Yeah, my dad found that," I said. "He loves Auden."

"It was brilliant," Milo said. "Especially right at the end like that. It really made it stand out. Gave everyone something to chew on, you know?" There were little specks of gold in the green of his eyes, and his hair had just been cut. A tiny dot of dried blood sat just under his nose, where he had cut himself shaving.

"Thanks," I said. "I'll make sure to tell my dad."

People were pushing past us on all sides, trying to get outside. Off to the right, Melissa Binsko, who had just gotten a boob job and was voted Most Likely to End Up on a Reality Show, was screaming and clutching a gaggle of girls. But at that moment I was all alone, standing in front of Milo. "Please," I thought to myself. "Please, Milo."

He opened his mouth as if he wanted to say something else, but then his eyes shifted as the girls in the corner squealed again. "Okay, well, I'll see you around," he said. And then, "Hey, Melissa! Melissa! Wait up!"

I stood there for half a second, just blinking.

"Julia!" Milo's vacancy was filled suddenly by Zoe and Sophie and my parents, all of whom draped themselves over me. "Oh, Julia, congratulations! Your speech was perfect. We're so proud of you. Look who's here, Julia! Look who it is! It's Sophie! She came all the way down from Vermont just to see you. We need pictures! Come outside where the light is good. Where's the camera? Who has the camera?"

I could hear their voices, see their bright faces bobbing up and down like so many buoyed lights. But the only thing I felt as they dragged me outside onto the front steps and arranged me like a paper doll in their arms was that I was moving farther and farther away from the only person I wanted to be with at that moment; and who, once again, had disappeared right in front of my eyes.

We split up after pictures, Mom and Dad going to their car, Zoe and I scrambling into Sophie's old green VW Bug. I got in the passenger seat next to Sophie and rolled down the window. A few of the roses Mom had given me were already wilting, and my armpits were starting to sweat. A pop sounded in the backseat as Zoe cracked open a Dr Pepper. "Woo-hoo!" she yelled, as a little foam spilled out of the top of the can. "Here's to Julia! The smartest chick in Silver Springs!"

I turned around and glared at Zoe. "Chill!" I mouthed the word soundlessly, tilting my head in Sophie's direction.

Zoe nodded, unfazed, and took a swig of soda. She sat forward a little in between Sophie and me, and yanked at her T-shirt, the front of which said IT'S LONELY AT THE TOP, BUT YOU EAT BETTER. Zoe had a thing for weird T-shirts. "Thanks for giving me a lift, Sophie. My parents are parked all the way in the back. It's gonna take them over an hour to get out of here. The parking here sucks."

"No prob," Sophie said. She had twisted her usually free-flowing blond hair into a knot and was wearing a pale pink slip dress that displayed both of her upper arm tattoos prominently—something Mom was sure to comment on. Her toenails were painted an electric blue, and she had a thin silver toe ring on her left foot. She waved a package of Camels in the air. "Anyone mind if I smoke?"

"Yes," I said emphatically.

"Actually," Zoe giggled, "could I have one?"

I gave her another look, but Zoe just shrugged.

Sophie laughed and pulled two cigarettes out of the pack. "That was a kick-ass speech you gave."

I opened my window as Sophie lit both cigarettes with the button lighter in the car. She handed one to Zoe, who took it, inhaled, and immediately began to cough. Her eyes, already as large as zinnias, grew to planet proportions.

"Open your window," I said, glaring at her. "It's bad enough up here."

The car moved forward another foot. Sophie clenched the wheel. The muscles under her arm tattoo were tight. "Seriously, Jules, that speech was fantastic. You were so clear, so concise. And you spoke with such conviction. Everyone in the whole place was just holding their breath."

I looked at her out of the corner of my eye. It was hard to know sometimes when Sophie was being sincere. "Thanks," I said cautiously.

"And can you even believe Melissa Binsko invited everyone to her party tonight? Including me?" Zoe leaned forward conspiratorially. "I'm just a lowly junior. Un-friggin'-believable."

"Who's Melissa Binsko?" Sophie asked, looking at me.

"Just a girl in my class." Melissa Binsko had said all of maybe three words to me in the four years we had gone to school together. The last time I had seen her in the hall, she'd been draped all over Milo. "We're not even friends, but Zoe is going to have a heart attack if we don't go."

"Dude!" Zoe said. "Who cares if we're not friends? Do you know how much money that girl's family has? Come on! It's gonna be the coolest party of the entire year!"

"So you're just interested in going because she has money?"

"Money, great food, a pool, and a hot tub." Zoe ticked off the items on one hand. "Um...*yeah?*"

"Whatever." I turned to look at my sister. "So why couldn't Goober come?"

"Greg wouldn't switch weekends. You know how he can get."

Actually, I didn't know how Greg could get. I didn't know Goober's father at all. Neither did Mom and Dad. He and Sophie had split up early in her pregnancy and had never gotten back together. "Well, tell her I miss her," I said. "To Pluto and back and around again to infinity." That was Goober's and my pet phrase. Goober had made it up. We said it all the time before we had to say good-bye.

Sophie made a gesture with her chin. "Will do."

"So, Sophie." Zoe brought her cigarette to her lips and inhaled, a little more confidently this time. "How's Vermont?"

"Actually, I just moved," Sophie said.

I glanced over at my sister again. This was news.

Sophie pushed a piece of hair out of her face. "Not very far from where I used to be in Rutland, though. I bought a little place in a town called Poultney."

"Is that still in Vermont?" I asked.

"Uh-huh. Right on the New York border."

"Do Mom and Dad know?"

Sophie shrugged. "No. But I just moved a few weeks ago. And I was going to tell everyone tonight at dinner."

"Why'd you move?" Zoe asked.

"Well," Sophie said, taking another drag from her cigarette, "I'm opening a business."

I stared at her. "You *are*?"

"Awesome!" Zoe gushed. "What kind of business?"

"A bakery," Sophie said. "Just a little one."

"A bakery?" I struggled to suppress a wave of annoyance. It was embarrassing that I only knew as much about my older sister as my best friend did.

"Yeah," Sophie said. "I've always wanted to open a bakery. And I've been saving for years. So when things finally started coming together, and I saw this place, I decided the hell with it, I was just gonna do it." She took a drag on her cigarette. "It's not in the best of shape right now, but I have the rest of the summer to work on it. I'm planning on opening for business in September."

"What does Goober think?" I asked.

"Oh, she loves it!" Sophie said. "Seriously. She's so excited."

"Do you have to learn how to bake?" Zoe asked. "I mean, you're the one who has to make everything, right? Or are you going to hire someone to do that for you?"

Sophie smiled slightly. "No, I can bake," she said. "Right, Julia?"

I stared straight ahead, annoyed suddenly by something I couldn't name. "Yeah."

She nudged me with her elbow. "Remember all that stuff I used to make in high school?"

"Mm-hmm."

"I've been working on my muffins for years," Sophie said. "And I want to sell fresh bread and pies. Maybe some cakes too."

"That sounds like a lot of work," I said.

"It is," Sophie replied promptly. "That's the fun of it."

"What's it called?" Zoe asked.

"I haven't decided on a name just yet," Sophie said. "I'm open to suggestions."

"Cool." Zoe sat forward, holding on to the back of my seat again. "I'm gonna think of something good."

"Yeah." I felt tired all of a sudden, as if the morning's events had just caught up with me. "That's great."

For a second, like a balloon floating by, I wondered where Milo was, what he was doing. And then, as the car began to move, the balloon disappeared, floating up past the trees until it was just a pinpoint of color against the sky.

chapter
4

When Sophie was sixteen she had a boyfriend named Eddie Waters. We all loved Eddie. He was tall and dark haired, and when he came to dinner he always brought my mother a bouquet of flowers. But Sophie was mean to him. Cruel, even. She spoke down to him as if he were stupid, and often ended their long, drawn-out phone calls by slamming the phone back into the receiver. One night, after a particularly loud argument between them, I tapped softly on Sophie's bedroom door. She hadn't come down for dinner, and didn't touch a thing on the plate Mom brought up. "Soph?"

No answer. Sophie usually let me in when I knocked. I would sprawl out over her bed, drawing in my doodle pad while she did homework. After tonight's fight with Eddie, however, maybe she had other ideas.

I tapped again. "Soph?" I said, a little louder this time.

"Yeah?" Her voice was stuffy with tears.

"Can I come in?"

There was a long pause. Finally, "Okay."

I pushed open the door gently. Sophie sat in the middle of her bed, which she had pulled out from against the wall and centered in the middle of the room. She was reading a magazine. Dirty clothes and pieces of paper littered the floor, and her desk was scattered with pens, pencils, and empty coffee mugs. I climbed up amid the perpetual tangle of rumpled sheets and blankets and crossed my legs. "Are you okay?"

She nodded and turned a page of her magazine without looking up. "Why aren't you in bed yet? Isn't it past nine?"

"Yeah, but…"

"Listen, if you're here about me and Eddie fighting, then you can leave," she said. "Because it's none of your business."

I stared at her for a minute. It felt as though she had just slapped me. "You're mean to him," I said, before I could stop myself.

Sophie looked up from her magazine. "What did I just say?"

I held my ground. This was for Eddie, not her. "He's so nice to you all the time, and you're just mean." My lower lip began to wobble. "You're mean and nasty and everyone…"

"Out." Sophie cut me off abruptly, and then looked down at her magazine. "Out," she said again when I didn't move. "Now."

My eyes began to fill with tears. "You're mean to everyone!" I shouted.

"Whose side are you on?" Sophie asked. "You're tired, Julia. Go to bed."

It might have helped things if she had gotten worked up. Maybe if she had yelled back at me or shed a few tears, the big block inside my chest might have split open. But the boredom in her voice made me furious. "I won't go to bed." I was speaking through gritted teeth. "Not until you call Eddie and apologize for being so mean to him."

"Oh. My. God." Sophie tossed her magazine to one side and rolled off her bed, all in one fluid motion. She caught me around the top of the arm, dragged me from her room, and while I stood there yelling at the top of my lungs, she slammed and locked her door.

Mom came running upstairs, "What in the world is going on here?"

I was sobbing by then, incomprehensible as I tried to explain what had happened.

"Sophie?" Mom knocked on her door. "What's going on?"

"Leave me alone." The words were heavy and solid, spoken with finality.

"Come on, sweetie," Mom said, taking my hand. "Come with me."

Mom sat with me while I took a warm bath and then she dried me off, helped me into clean pajamas, and tucked me into bed. My breath was still coming in little hiccups.

"Don't let Sophie get to you," Mom said, sitting on the edge of my mattress. "She's going through a lot right now."

"What's the matter with her?" I asked.

"She's a teenager," Mom said. "And she has a boyfriend. You'll see when you get there. There are a lot of emotions involved."

"She's mean," I said stubbornly. "I hate her guts."

"No, you don't."

I ignored her. "And she's not even nice to Eddie."

Mom tucked her hearing aid wire behind her ear. "Well, Eddie and Sophie's business is for them to worry about."

I pouted for a few seconds, and then reached up to finger the tiny springy cord attached to her hearing aid. When I was really little, still drinking out of a bottle, I used to drift off to sleep with one hand attached to the delicate rubber tubing. As I got older, I pretended that the wire was a pet baby caterpillar. Now, I just touched it because it was there.

I reached up with my arms. "I love you, Mom."

She bent down and kissed me. She smelled like Ivory soap and charcoal smoke from the grill. "I love you too, sweetie. Good night."

———

Later that night, I felt someone crawling into bed with me. I turned, half asleep, to see Sophie's tear-streaked face staring at me from across the pillow. Her big blue eyes were lined with little veins of red, and her nose was running.

"I'm sorry I'm so awful," she whispered. "I don't mean to be." Her voice broke on the last word and a new sob worked its way out of her mouth. I snuggled in under her neck as she wrapped her arms around me. She cried softly for a few more moments. After a while, I could feel her settle her chin on top of my head. She breathed in deeply and then exhaled with a soft shudder. "I love you, Jules," she murmured.

"I love you too," I whispered.

We fell asleep like that, until morning.

chapter
5

I went upstairs to change when Sophie and I finally got home. Zoe had rushed across the street into her house, but there still wasn't any sign of Milo. Mom and Dad were busying themselves in the kitchen: Mom setting out a platter of cheese and fruit, while Dad struggled to open a bottle of sparkling water. The radio was on in the background, tuned to the soft-rock station Mom always listened to.

I had just kicked off my shoes when a light knock sounded on my door. Before I had a chance to say anything, Sophie opened it and walked into the room. "Hey." She had already changed out of her slip dress into a Tweety Bird T-shirt and a pair of soft, worn-out jeans that hung low on her hips "Mind if I hang out for a minute?"

"Sure." My heart pounded as she meandered around, studying the room the way she always did when she came back home. This had been her bedroom before she left and sometimes as I watched her inspect it, I felt nervous, as if I wasn't holding up my end of some unstated bargain. Now she paused in front of my dresser, staring down at Milo's little cardboard card taped to the top of it.

"Unhook me?" I turned around so I could back my way to Sophie.

Sophie unhooked the tiny clasp and then turned back to my dresser. She leaned in, moving her lips soundlessly as she recited the words that Milo had written. "Is this your handwriting?" she asked, pointing. "It's so tiny."

"No. Milo gave it to me. For Christmas."

"Milo?" she repeated. "Zoe's brother?"

I nodded.

Her face lit up. "The one you were talking to after graduation? Oh my God! He's so cute! Are you guys dating?"

I stepped out of my robe and arranged it on a hanger. "No, we're not dating. We're just friends."

"Well, this is a pretty—what's the word I'm looking for?— personal gift to give a *friend*."

I blushed, glancing briefly out my window. The tiny window seat across the street was empty. "What do you mean?"

"*nobody, not even the rain, has such small hands.*" I bit the inside of my cheek as Sophie read the quote aloud. For some reason, it didn't sound quite so magical coming from her. "Are you serious?" Sophie asked. "That's practically intimate."

I shrugged. "It's about hands. What's intimate about hands?"

"Julia." Sophie sat down on the bed with her knees open wide. "That is an incredibly intimate line. Think about it. The person who wrote it was obviously deeply in love with someone. People don't write things like that for just anyone, you know. There's meaning behind those words. He's trying to tell you..."

I rolled my eyes, cutting her off. "Okay, so maybe Milo and I sorta, I don't know, tried something." (Or whatever taking me to the prom was.) "But it didn't work. We're better off as friends." (If we were even that.) "Believe me."

"Oh." Sophie paused. "Why?"

"We just are." I shook my head. "It's not really something I want to talk about."

Sophie got up and walked over to me. She pulled one of my hands out and studied it for a moment, like she was examining it under a microscope. "I never thought of you as having small hands," she said finally.

I pulled away uncomfortably and headed for the closet. "I don't. That line's not literally about me. Milo just likes that poet."

She paused for a few beats. "That's e. e. cummings, right?"

"Yeah." I paused, hanger in my hand. "How'd you know that?"

"I know a lot of things you don't know that I know." For a split second, she held my eyes with hers. "Anyway, whatever the situation is between you and Milo, the boy's got good taste. In girls *and* poetry."

I exhaled as I realized the moment had passed, hung up my robe, and began to unbutton the front of my dress.

Sophie looked amused as I shimmied out of it and made a beeline for my dresser, clutching the dress against the front of me. "Can I ask you a question without you getting mad?" she asked, flopping down on top of my bed.

"Maybe."

"Are you still a virgin?"

I whirled around, still holding the dress against me, and looked at her, aghast. "What?"

She rolled up along her back so her legs stuck up straight above her. "I'm just saying. You look so uncomfortable getting undressed in front of me, and I remember that I used to be like that too, until I started sleeping with Eddie."

"You and Eddie . . . ?" I let the sentence trail off.

Sophie let her legs fall back down. "Had sex?" she finished. "Well, yeah. You ever get a good look at him? Jesus, I think even the *boys* in our school wanted to sleep with him."

I turned back around, yanked open my dresser drawer, and rummaged inside for my favorite jeans. This little bit of unwanted information had just sullied the golden image I still had of Eddie. Sophie watched me intently, still in her upside-down position, as I pulled on a black camisole and a V-neck T-shirt edged with tiny sparkles. I didn't know what Zoe was planning on wearing to Melissa's party, but this was about as fancy as I got when it came to going out.

"So, are you then?" she asked. "A virgin, I mean?"

I reached down and snatched my dress off the bed. Of course I was still a virgin. "You know what, Sophie? That's really none of your business."

"Oh, I know." Sophie rolled back down, stood up, and walked over to look at my shot glass collection. "God, Mom would be horrified, wouldn't she?" She picked up a shot glass Dad had bought me from Wellesley when we had gone to visit the campus last fall. It said GO BLUE on the front. "Where's Pitt?" she asked finally, turning around.

"What?"

She pointed to the shot glass collection. "The one from Wellesley is front and center, and it looks like you have one from every other place in the country, but nothing from Pitt. Don't you think it's weird that you don't have a shot glass from the school you're going to?"

I shrugged. "It's there. I think it's toward the back."

Sophie set the shot glass back in its place. "What's your major going to be there, anyway?"

"Political science," I said. "I'm doing the whole prelaw thing."

Sophie stared at me. "Prelaw?" she repeated. "As in becoming a lawyer? Like Dad?"

I nodded, pushing down another flutter of annoyance. "What's wrong with being a lawyer?"

"Nothing's wrong with it." Sophie sat back down on my bed. "I mean, if that's what you want to do." She looked at me. "Is that what you want to do?"

"Of course it's what I want to do." I picked up a folded T-shirt, shook it loose, and then began folding it again.

"Why? Because Dad's a lawyer?"

I gave her a look. "Don't be annoying, Sophie. Why would Dad being a lawyer have anything to do with what I want to do with my life? I do have my own brain, you know."

"You think so well on your feet, Julia, which is exactly the kind of trait you need to become a good trial lawyer." Dad had said that to me in ninth grade, solidifying my decision once and for all.

Sophie sidestepped my question by asking another one. "Okay then, why do you want to be a lawyer?"

"Because I think it's interesting, okay? And I like it."

"What's interesting about it?"

I sighed exasperatedly. "Everything's interesting about it. It's... the law. You know. You get to uphold our constitution every day, protect people's rights. See that the accused get a fair and honest trial. It's a noble profession, Sophie. Maybe one of the noblest. "

"Since when have you been interested in being noble?" Sophie drew her head back as if she had just tasted something bitter.

I put a hand on my hip. "Why do you always have to be so critical?"

"I'm not being critical," Sophie said. "I'm just trying to understand. What is it about being an attorney that excites you, Julia? What gets your blood pumping? Helping people? Is that it? Or do you have some kind of burning desire to keep law and order in Silver Springs? I mean, what is it?"

Excites me? Was she kidding? This wasn't about being excited. It was about getting things accomplished. Creating a career that would lead to bigger and better things. Assistant district attorney maybe, or even the district attorney, if I created a sharp enough record. Maybe even a judgeship somewhere in the future. "You know what?" I said. "You're being a real jerk."

Sophie looked away. "Well, I'm sorry. I don't mean to be. I just never would've thought you'd go that route. You were always so creative, Julia."

"Creative?" I repeated. "I don't have a creative bone in my body!"

"You do too!" Sophie insisted. "What about all those adorable little fruit people you used to draw when you were little? Remember?

Mr. and Mrs. Apple? The Twin Bing Cherries? With their tiny striped arms and legs. Mr. Lima Bean even had a little fedora. They were so cute!"

I cocked my head. "Sophie, I was like *six* when I did that stuff. It was doodling. You can't make a career out of doodling." I tossed my head. "I'm getting a chance to see things up close up this summer too. Dad got me an internship at the DA's office."

"So you're gonna tail the district attorney around all summer?"

I shrugged. "Probably not the district attorney himself. But definitely the assistant DAs. Dad said I'll probably be able to sit in on a few trials too."

Sophie got up from the bed and went over to my shot-glass collection again. "Well, I hope you have fun," she said, picking up the Harvard glass. "That's what it's all about, Julia."

Fun. This was only one of a gazillion things that separated my sister and me. She insisted that life was meant to be lived in some weird, constant state of amusement, even if it meant not making enough money to pay for heat in the winter or falling behind on her rent. It was probably the reason why she was leaving a steady, good-paying job at the nursing home to go open a bakery. Fun was for weekends, I wanted to tell her now. Fun was for later. After the hard work. "I'll have fun. I always have fun."

"I don't know about that," Sophie said. "It seems to me you haven't—"

"You don't know anything about me," I said, cutting her off sharply.

She turned, absorbing the blow of my statement, and then put the shot glass back on the shelf. For a moment she just stood there, aligning it neatly with the others. Then she nodded, as if accepting the ugly fact.

"You know, I used to have a collection," she said finally.

"Of what?"

"Condoms." She grinned slyly. "Unused, of course."

"Sophie…," I started, but she pulled on my arm and sat me down on the bed next to her.

"I'm serious! I did!"

I extricated myself from her grip. "Whatever. You're acting really weird."

Sophie's eyes narrowed. "Why? Because I'm talking about things like sex?"

"No, because you're talking about things like sex with *me*. We've never talked about stuff like this, Sophie, because we don't talk more than two or three times a year, and when we do, it's about school or grades or the weather. I mean, I don't even know how I'm supposed to respond when you tell me things like that."

The expression on Sophie's face changed from amusement to annoyance to confusion—all in five seconds. "What do you mean, how you're supposed to respond?" she asked. "It's just a conversation, Julia, not a test."

"Well, it makes me uncomfortable," I said firmly.

"Okay. Fine. I'm sorry I brought it up."

I headed for the door. "I'm going down. You coming?"

Sophie sighed. "Yeah," she said, dragging herself off the bed. "I'm coming."

chapter
6

Dad was sitting at the dining room table drinking a glass of seltzer when Sophie and I came downstairs again. "It's the head cheese!" he said, slipping an arm around my waist. I kissed the top of his head. Sophie stood behind one of the dining room chairs, cracking her knuckles. Mom walked in from the kitchen, placed a salad down on the table next to a vase of pink tulips, and nodded to Sophie and me. "You girls have a seat. I just have to finish up the pasta, and then we can start."

Sophie eyed Dad, who was staring into his water glass, and then reached for her own. Taking a long, slow swallow, she wiped her mouth with the back of her wrist and set the glass back in its place. "You guys don't have that silly no-smoking rule in this house anymore, do you?"

"We sure do." The ice cubes in Dad's glass rattled as he brought it to his mouth. "If you need to smoke one of those things, take it outside."

Sophie took another sip from her water glass. Above the rim, her eyes had formed two dark slits. Suddenly, she held it up. "Julia, here's to you." I bumped my glass clumsily against hers. Dad extended his glass toward Sophie and me. We clinked and then set them back down. Sophie pushed back her chair. "I was going to wait until later but…" She raised her eyebrows, looking first at Dad and then at me. "Well, I guess I can do this now."

I watched carefully as she leaned down and retrieved an envelope from her back pocket. She held it against her chest for a moment and looked at me. "I'm really proud of you, Julia, for everything you've accomplished." She took a deep breath and then let it out, cocking her head as she did. "This is for you," she said, leaning over the table and handing me the envelope. "From me and Goober. For all your hard work."

I took the envelope gingerly, giving Dad a sidelong glance as I ran my finger under the flap. He was holding his breath. Literally. My cheeks felt hot. "You didn't have to do anything," I said. "Really."

Inside the card were two tiny envelopes. One was pink. The other was blue.

"Open the blue one first," Sophie said.

Mom came back in, setting a large platter of shrimp and linguine down as I opened the envelope. She put her hands on the back of her chair and watched us, smiling. Inside the envelope was a large silver key. The letters *VW* were printed on the rubber edge. I held it up and looked over at Sophie, confused.

"It's yours," she said, calm as daylight. "The Bug. Sitting outside. It's yours, Jules. I'm giving it to you."

I swallowed. Closed my eyes tight for a moment and then opened them again, as if the words I knew I should say would appear suddenly in front of me. They did not.

"She's speechless!" Sophie laughed. She got up from her chair and came around the back of mine, putting her arms across my shoulders. "What do you think? Are you excited?"

I nodded. There was no way I could take it. The gift totally outdid Mom and Dad's, which had been a Prada briefcase for my internship at the courthouse.

"Wow," Dad said softly. He cleared his throat. "That certainly is generous of you, Sophie."

Mom's eyes were still roving over the key. She sat down and pressed her hand against the base of her throat. "The car?" She looked at Sophie. "You're giving her your car?"

Sophie nodded gleefully. "She's gonna need one anyway, right? Getting to and from Pittsburgh, driving God knows where else." She grabbed my shoulders with both hands and squeezed. "You gotta hit the open road, girl. Spread your wings. Take a road trip now and again."

Mom's face had paled considerably. "I just…" She glanced over at Dad for help. "It's just… such a …"

"Big responsibility?" Sophie finished.

Mom nodded, and fiddled with the cord on her hearing aid. I knew responsibility was not her main concern at all. Mom's main concern was my safety, which no car—however well built—would be able to live up to. Every morning, she watched from the front window as I got into the back of Zoe's rusty Ford Taurus, waiting until I fastened my seat belt. Once, I had forgotten, and she dashed outside, arms waving, shouting, until Zoe slowed again. I was mortified.

Sophie shrugged. "I got it covered," she said. "I just paid this puppy off in April. Julia won't have to worry about car payments at all. Just insurance."

Mom looked over at Sophie. "It's a wonderful gift, Sophie. You're very generous, honey." She glanced down at the large serving dish. "We really should eat before everything gets cold."

Sophie grinned. "Hold on, Mom. There's one more thing."

"Oh?" Mom's voice was faint. "What's that?"

Sophie nodded at me. "Open the pink envelope, Jules."

I looked inside it again, shaking another, much smaller key out of the side corner.

"What's that?" Mom asked, making her way around the table with the bowl of linguine.

"It's a key to my place," Sophie answered. "I want you to take a trip this summer, Julia. To Vermont. Come visit me for a few days. I'll show you around Poultney. It'll be great."

Dad set his water glass down. "That sounds terrific, Sophie. We've never been to Vermont and I'm sure..."

"Just Julia." Sophie did not take her eyes off me. "You guys can come another time."

Mom exchanged a quick look with Dad. "Well, I don't know about that," Dad said. His voice was much too loud, as if he was trying to regain control of the situation. "Julia's never driven such a long distance before. It's not an easy drive. And she'd have to do it alone."

"This is Julia's gift," Sophie said. She had started eating, shoving enormous forkfuls of the long, oily pasta into her mouth. "It should be her decision."

I held Sophie's gaze as long as possible before dropping it again.

Sophie put her fork down and swallowed. "You don't want to go, do you?"

I shrugged helplessly, fingering a lone piece of linguine that had drooped over one side of my plate. Mom and Dad's eyes were burning a hole on one side of my cheek; Sophie's eyes on the other. "Of course I do. I mean…"

"Then why do you look as if I've just asked you to donate an organ?" Sophie asked.

"She's not…," Dad started.

"Can you let her answer a question for herself?" Sophie turned on him, eyes flashing. "Just once?"

"Sophie." Mom wiped her mouth with her napkin. "Let's go for a walk around the block. Cool down a little."

"I don't need to cool down," Sophie retorted. "And I don't need to go for a walk. What I need…" She paused, turning back to look at me. "What I need is for Julia to answer me. Herself."

"I'll come," I said, flicking my eyes at her quickly, wanting to get this over with. "Okay? I will. Sometime."

Sophie inhaled deeply and then took another sip of water. The heavy *clink* of silver against Mom's good china echoed throughout the room. Dad chewed violently, the sides of his jaw flexing in and out, while Mom ate in small rabbit bites. I speared a wilted piece of lettuce and snuck a look at Sophie, who was busy twirling another forkful of pasta. "I hate you," I thought to myself. "You ruin everything."

Suddenly Sophie set her fork down on the side of her plate. "You know what? This is going to be my last visit to Silver Springs."

"Sophie." Dad's voice had assumed the exhausted-impatient tone reserved strictly for her. "Please. Don't start."

Sophie held up her hands, palms out, as if surrendering. "I am not starting anything. On the contrary, Dad, I guess I'm ending something."

"What?" Dad's lips had begun to twitch. "What are you ending?"

"This." Sophie encompassed the table, the living room, the entire house with a swoop of her wide-open arms. "All of this. It's a lie. And you know it's a lie. Until you tell her the truth about what really happened in Milford all those years ago…"

Three hours. It had only taken her three hours to bring up Milford. If there was one thing I could say about my big sister, it was this: she did not disappoint. Not when it came to Milford.

"Sophie, come on!" I said. "I already know what happened—"

Sophie cut me off with a stab of her index finger. Her eyes were still boring down on Mom and Dad. "And I'm talking about the stuff she *doesn't* know about…"

"Can you stop?" Mom begged. "Please, Sophie. You're ruining Julia's whole celebration."

Sophie stared at Mom. "When are you going to stop living on another planet?" She shifted her eyes toward Dad. "And you… what alternate universe have *you* settled down in? When are the two of you going to stop pretending like everything is so perfect in this family, and start…"

"God Almighty!" Dad cut Sophie off, throwing his napkin on top of his plate. "I cannot believe you're seriously thinking of getting into all of this right now."

"Yes," Mom said. "Please stop it. You really are being selfish."

Sophie looked down at the word "selfish." She began to work her lower lip with her teeth.

Dad's teeth were clenched. "You want to talk about Milford, we'll talk about it. But there is no need to do it right now. Right now, we are celebrating Julia's graduation and..."

Zoe's signature three-beep alert came blaring from the street. I stood up hurriedly, gratefully, and pushed back my chair. "That's my ride. I have to go."

I practically ran for the door, taking my first real breath as I pushed it open.

"Ten o'clock, Julia!" Dad's voice followed me. "No later than ten!"

The door slammed behind me, loud as a gunshot.

chapter
7

I had already decided, while running out of the house, that if Milo was not in the car, I wouldn't go with Zoe to the party. I just didn't have it in me tonight. But there he was in the passenger side, one elbow resting on the window. Just like always.

"Hey, guys!" I tried to sound excited as I got in the backseat, as if I had not just left a train wreck behind me. Milo nodded at me. He looked weirdly handsome in a white button-down shirt and pair of green swim trunks dotted with red lobsters. Only someone like Milo could pull off an outfit like that. He'd slicked his hair back too, and I could make out the faint scent of soap as he leaned his arms over the top of his seat.

"You guys ready to party?" Zoe had done her eyes up in some kind of glittery purple eyeliner. Her own outfit was a study in dichotomy: black leggings paired with a hip-length T-shirt that said I LIKE CATS; I JUST CAN'T EAT A WHOLE ONE BY MYSELF, and a bright red pair of cowboy boots.

"Chill, rock star," Milo said. "And keep your hands on the wheel."

"Oh, you're such a fart," Zoe said. "Relax."

"I'll relax when you get us there without getting into an accident."

Milo turned and looked out the window. He stayed that way too, as Zoe yammered on about the party, not so much as even turning his head in my direction for the entire trip. It was as if the whole conversation we'd had after graduation had never even happened.

Like we were strangers all over again.

———

Melissa's backyard looked like something out of MTV's *Spring Break*. Dark purple material had been draped canopy style over the pool umbrellas, while disco balls, spinning tiny coins of light, swayed lightly underneath. A rap album blared from the outdoor speakers, and tiki torches, standing well over seven feet, blazed against the lengthening shadows. Then there was the food. Aside from the usual pretzels and chips, there were two tables filled with platters of triangular pita toasts, seeded crackers, bowls of strangely hued dip, and small phyllo-dough pockets. Whole sides of ribs were buried deep inside a charcoal pit across the yard, and pieces of chicken sputtered and sizzled on a large silver grill on the patio.

Off to the right was a kidney-shaped pool, complete with a diving board and circular steps. It was filled to capacity with students from Silver Springs High, including Melissa, who was sitting like a queen on the top step, surveying her subjects, and Cheryl, who was sitting in a lawn chair next to a few other girls.

"You guys coming in?" Milo asked, pausing at the front gate as Zoe and I peered out from behind him. "Or are you just going to watch everything from back there?"

"Of course we're coming in!" Zoe stepped forward, pushing her brother out of the way, and made her way over to the food table. Milo cleared his throat loudly as Melissa came toward us. She had tied a sarong around her hips, and she was spilling out of her bikini top. Behind her, I could make out the slightest tilt of Cheryl's head as she watched us from her chair.

"Hey, guys!" Melissa draped a hand casually on Milo's shoulder. Her eyes took in every inch of Zoe's appearance in the span of three disgusted seconds. "I'm so glad you could make it! Did you just get here?"

"Just now." Milo shoved his hands in his pockets, rose up on his toes. "Wow, Melissa. Your place is great."

"Thanks!" Melissa still hadn't moved her hand from his shoulder. "Did you get anything to eat yet?"

"We were just admiring all the options," Zoe said, waving a hand at the phyllo-dough pockets. "There's a lot of stuff here."

Melissa rolled her eyes. "God, that is *so* all my mother. She belongs to some culinary group down at the country club, so of course she decided to try out all her freaky recipes for my party." She tossed her head. "Whatever. I mean, just eat what you want. There's chips and stuff too. You know, real food." She squeezed Milo's shoulder, looking at him slyly. "How about drinks? Did you get something to drink?"

"A drink would be great," Milo said.

Melissa bumped him with her hip. "There's soda in the silver buckets over there, or we have punch in the pool house." She used her fingers to make air quotes around the word "punch." "Just get one of those big red plastic cups and fill it up, okay? My parents are upstairs, so don't even worry about it. Seriously."

I glanced over at Milo. He was staring directly at Melissa's chest. "Cool," he said. "Thanks."

Melissa tossed her hair and looked at me. "Oh, and you guys too, of course. Help yourself." She tilted her head toward the party. "Okay, well I'm gonna get back in the pool. Come on over when you're ready."

She bounded off across the lawn, running lightly on the balls of her feet. I tried not to stare, but I couldn't help it. There was no way any part of my body looked—or moved—like that in a bathing suit. Cheryl was still watching Milo from her seat.

"Hey, Milo!" The three of us turned as a guy inside the pool house yelled his name. "Come on, man! Get your ass over here!"

Milo glanced at me and then Zoe.

"We'll be fine," Zoe said.

"I'll come find you in a little while." He looked at me. "You gotta be back by ten, right, Jules?"

I nodded and looked away.

"Okay." He pointed at Zoe. "*You*, behave. See you later."

"See you, *Dad*!" Zoe called out behind him. I watched him lope across the lawn, his hair unmoving and stiff on top of his head. "Hey, Julia." I turned around. Zoe had stuck two baby carrots into her mouth, inserting them at such an angle that they looked like enormous buck teeth.

I laughed. "You're such a dork."

She let them fall from her mouth one by one. "Listen, are you okay? You hardly said a word in the car."

I selected a cucumber spear from an exotic vegetable plate and nibbled on it slowly. "Yeah. Everything's fine. Guess what Sophie got me for a graduation present?"

"Um…" Zoe looked up at the sky for a moment. "A hundred bucks."

"Nope."

"Two hundred bucks."

I leaned in. "A car."

Zoe's eyes bloomed wide. "A car?"

"Yup. And not only that, but it's the Bug."

"The Bug?" Zoe squealed. "Oh my God, Julia!" She hopped up and down, holding onto the side of my arm. "That's so cool! Did you try it? Do you love it?"

I shook my head. "I haven't taken it out yet."

Zoe stopped jumping. "You just got a car for graduation and you haven't taken it out for a spin yet?"

"There was a lot going on. There wasn't really time." I paused as Zoe studied me curiously.

"You need to talk?" she asked.

I looked away.

Zoe nudged me. "Julia?"

"Yeah," I said. "I do."

Zoe and I slipped out from the patio, circled back around the side of the house, and sat on the front steps. It was much quieter out here, and more private. A set of pale bricks formed a semicircle of stairs that lead up to the front door. Next to us, two stone lions rested on their haunches, heads up and alert, as if guarding the house.

Zoe took a long drink from a can of root beer and then gasped, wiping her lip with the back of her wrist. "Who drinks this shit?" she asked. "And how can they even think of serving it at a party? It's garbage."

"Zoe. It's root beer. It's the same stuff as Dr Pepper."

Zoe's face darkened. "Take that back!" she said. "Take it back! Now!"

"Fine." I shook my head, giggling a little. "I take it back. God, you're such a nut."

"Nothing is the same as Dr Pepper," Zoe said. "*Nothing*. Especially root beer." She set the can off to the side. "Okay. So now that we've cleared that up, tell me what's going on."

I plucked a piece of grass from the lawn and tried to sound nonchalant. "Oh, Sophie just got into another fight with my parents. I don't even know why I'm upset about it. They're always pissed off at each other. This is nothing new."

"What were they fighting about?"

I shrugged. "What they always fight about, more or less. All the horrible years in Milford before I was born." I paused. "I'm just so sick of it. Sophie's always jumping down my father's throat about it. My mom's too." I stared down at the space of brick between my feet. "I'm not saying they're perfect. I know they're a little overprotective."

"Um...*yeah*." To her credit, Zoe stopped there.

"But they still don't deserve all this drama every time my sister comes home. It's so freaking annoying. And totally uncalled for."

"Have you ever asked your Mom and Dad what happened in Milford?" Zoe asked. "I mean, to make Sophie so mad?"

"Well, yeah. My dad used to drink back then. And I guess my parents fought sometimes. But Sophie always makes it sound like she grew up in a war zone or something. And my dad has been sober for fifteen years now! That's gotta count for something, right?"

"Yeah," Zoe said. "Fifteen years is pretty good."

A long silence followed. Zoe and I stared at Melissa's beautiful front lawn. A row of narrow cypress trees separated one side from the neighboring house, and the grass was lush and green. Twilight had begun to descend, and the summer air was fragrant with the purple scent of lilac blooms.

"Except..." The words came out barely over a whisper. "I might be crazy, but something sounded different this time."

"What do you mean?" Zoe asked.

"I'm not really sure. Something she said about Milford." I smoothed my palms down the sides of my hair. "She said there were things I didn't know about. Stuff my parents hadn't told me."

Zoe took another swing of soda. "Well, maybe you should find out," she said.

I closed my eyes.

I didn't want to find out.

Zoe shook my shoulder. "Listen, let's go have fun. It's your gradu-ation! You can worry about all this stuff later. Right now, you just need to chill and enjoy yourself."

"Okay." I got back up slowly. She was right. Nothing I did right now was going to fix anything.

The music had been turned up to a startling decibel, the bass thumping above the trees like a gigantic heartbeat. Kids danced and shrieked, running around with red cups in their hands and jumping into the pool. I followed Zoe, who was making her way over to the pool house, but stopped when I caught sight of Cheryl, who had moved from the lawn chair to the side of the pool. Milo was next to her, dangling his feet in the water, holding a red cup in his hand. His shirt was off, and his head was bent toward her. As she whispered something in his ear, Cheryl ran a finger slowly over the curve of his bare shoulder.

Just then, Milo looked up. Our eyes locked.

"Oh God," I said.

"Where you going?" Zoe asked, as I turned around.

"I don't know," I said over my shoulder. "Anywhere but here."

chapter
8

A slow thrumming had started to make its way behind my eyes, quickening with every step. Despite the heat, my arms prickled with cold and I shuddered, crossing them tightly over my chest. The houses in this part of town were breathtakingly beautiful. For as hard as Dad worked on our yard, it would never in a million years look like these did, with their acres of landscaped property and exotic bushes. But I did not stop to look at any of them. Instead, as the air around me ached under a relentlessly floral smell, I put my head down and ran as I hard as I could.

"Julia!" Milo's voice shot out behind me. He ran soundlessly along the sidewalk, his rubber slides gripped tightly in both hands, getting closer with every step. I kept running. "Julia! Wait up!" He caught up to me all at once, grabbing me by the elbow and spinning me around.

I jerked my arm away, panting. "What?"

Milo leaned over, holding on to the front of his knees, struggling to catch his breath. "What…happened? Why'd you leave… like that?"

There was no way I was going to add insult to injury by stroking his ego. "No reason. I just wanted to go."

Milo straightened back up. His gelled hair had flopped out of shape; small pieces of it stood up awkwardly, like grass.

"Zoe said you had some stuff going on at home," Milo said. "With your parents and Sophie and all."

"And?" I started walking again.

Milo fell in step next to me, hopping awkwardly as he struggled to get his slides back on. "And...I don't know, do you want to talk about it?"

What? Was he really saying this?

"Not really," I said.

"All right." He shoved his hands into his pockets.

I kept walking, fuming inside. Why would I talk to him about my family's most private details? Why would I talk to him about anything? We didn't *talk*. We didn't do anything. He barely even acknowledged my presence most days, unless he felt like it. Or unless things weren't going so great with Cheryl or Melissa or whatever other girl he was interested in that week.

"Are you..." Milo looked down at the ground. "Are you upset that Cheryl was talking to me?"

I felt nauseated just hearing him say her name. "Why would I be mad that you were talking to Cheryl? You can talk to whoever you want. I don't *own* you, Milo. We're not dating. Actually, I don't think we ever went on a date. Prom was just a favor you did for your sister's geeky friend so she wouldn't have to spend it alone in her room, wasn't it?" I laughed harshly.

Was I really saying these things? Where were they coming from? And how could I take them back?

"I didn't ask you to the prom as a favor to Zoe," Milo said. He was squinting, as if trying to decipher something. "And you're not a geek."

I chewed the inside of my lip.

"Listen, Julia, I know we're not dating…" He struggled. "But come on. It's me."

"Don't flatter yourself," I said coldly. "Not *every* girl at school wants to throw herself at you, Milo."

Milo stopped abruptly and pulled on my sleeve. "You're the one who kissed me, Julia. Not the other way around. That poem at Christmas…it wasn't meant to be romantic or anything. It was…it was just something that made me think of you. And that's what I was trying to tell you that night, after prom. But then you just leaned over and kissed me and…"

"And I'm also the one who said I made a mistake!" I shook my head against the flush of memory, remembering the note I had slipped him the next day in which I tried to explain away my behavior. "Do you remember the note? Or do you want me to say it again? It was a mistake, Milo. A big one, okay? It was a complete and total lapse of judgment. So don't worry. I don't want to be with you. I've never wanted to be with you. Not now. Not ever. Leaning over and kissing you like that…honestly, I was actually thinking about someone else."

Milo blinked. "You were?"

"Totally!" I tried to laugh. "I mean come on. Do you seriously think I would be dumb enough to want to get involved with my best friend's brother?"

Milo looked stunned for a moment. He blinked a few times, and shook his head gently, as if settling something inside. "Yeah," he said softly. "I know. Right."

I turned and kept walking, waiting for the slap of his flip-flops to follow me. But they didn't come. And when I reached the end of the block and turned my head just the slightest bit, there was no sign of Milo at all.

chapter
9

It was completely dark outside by the time I got home. The last remnants of the graduation dinner had been erased from the dining room table. Only the tulips remained, their pink heads drooping heavily against the sides of the vase, as if exhausted from the day's activities.

"Julia?" Mom's anxious voice drifted out of the living room.

I walked in. "Yeah, it's me." Mom was sitting on the couch, staring at the television, which was muted. She had changed finally into her sweat suit, and taken her sneakers off. One leg was tucked under her. Dad was sitting in the big easy chair, his arm draped over his eyes. He lifted it when he heard my voice.

"What're you doing home so early?" he asked.

I looked around. "Where's Sophie?"

Mom and Dad exchanged a knowing glance. "She left, honey," Mom said softly. "She went back to Vermont."

"What do you mean, she went back? She was supposed to be here until tomorrow. How'd she get back?"

"She took the train," Mom said. "Dad took her to the station a little while ago."

I felt a stir of panic. Had there been a scene? Something worse than when I left? "Why'd she leave?" I asked. Because of what happened at dinner?"

Dad sighed heavily. He reached down along the side of his easy chair and pulled the handle so the footrest closed back up. Then he folded his hands. "Yes," he said simply. "Because of what happened at dinner."

"But why?" My panic was folding in on itself, turning into some kind of confused rage. "Why do things always come down to this? Why's she always so mad at you?"

Dad put his head in between his hands.

"Dad," I started. "Sophie said at dinner that there were things that I didn't know about..."

His voice came out from under him like an echo. "Yes."

"Can you..."

"Listen to me, Julia." Dad lifted his head. His voice was so grave and so serious that for a moment I was frightened. "Before I say what I am about to say, I want you to know that being loyal to this family is the most important thing in the world. Your mother and I would do anything to protect you, Julia. Anything. And we may not have done everything perfectly, but we've tried our best." He stared at me with a piercing look. "Being loyal to your mother and your sister and you has been my whole life. Do you understand what I'm saying?"

I nodded, trying to push down the fear rising inside my chest. My heart beat unsteadily with a lopsided kind of rhythm: *ba-dum-ba-dum-ba-dum.* I rubbed my hands up and down my arms again, trying to get warm. Dad cleared his throat.

Mom looked up. "You have to start at the beginning, John." Her voice was as faint as fog. The clock in the kitchen ticked slowly. My insides were churning.

"Dad?" I pressed.

He swallowed. "There was another..."

"Woman?" I said softly. "There was another woman?"

His head snapped up. "No! Of course not." He ran his hand down the length of his neck. "A child. Another child."

Mom pressed her fingers against her mouth. Her nails, which she had gotten painted at the salon, were chipped and worn at the edges.

"What are you talking about?" I demanded.

"Your sister," Dad said. "Maggie."

Mom shut her eyes at the mention of the name.

"Maggie?" I echoed.

Dad nodded. "She was born three years after Sophie. In Milford." He paused. "She died when she was four."

Wait. Was I imagining this? Was this really happening? "But why...haven't you ever told me about her?"

"That was a decision your mother and I made a long time ago," Dad answered quietly. "We were trying to protect you."

"Protect me?" I repeated. "From what?"

Mom opened her eyes. They were dull and glassy looking, as if a thin film had descended over the iris. She reached up behind her ear and fingered the cord attached to her hearing aid. "Oh honey, Maggie died so...tragically. It wasn't something we ever wanted to revisit, let alone make you part of."

My legs folded themselves beneath me until I was sitting on the floor. "How did she die?"

Neither of them answered.

"Dad?" The worst possible scenarios began to unfold behind my eyes: She was murdered. Kidnapped. Killed in a terrible, unspeakable way. "What happened to her? Tell me."

"She had asthma," Dad said. His face contorted, as if something beneath it was pulling strings in opposite directions. "She couldn't breathe..."

"It wasn't anyone's fault," Mom said. "She got worked up one day, and couldn't stop crying, and..."

"Oh my God." My hand flew involuntarily to my chest, as if to steady the violent beat of my heart. "She suffocated? When she was four? Goober's age?"

A muscle flexed in Dad's cheek. He nodded.

"And Sophie?" I asked. "She was there? She knew about it? She saw...?"

Dad nodded again. "She saw everything, Julia. And she's never gotten over it. She was only seven when it happened." He raised his head again. "We thought maybe if we just didn't talk about it, if we put it behind us, that Sophie would be able to do the same thing. And when you came along..." He caught the tiny noise that escaped from between his lips with the edge of his fist. "It was like we'd been given another chance, another shot at life. At...starting over."

"We didn't want to involve you in any part of that time," Mom said. Her eyes were rimmed with tears. "Of all that terrible sadness, honey. We wanted it to be different for you. The best it could possibly be."

"You should've told me," I whispered.

"Julia…," Dad started.

"You should have told me!" My voice was rising. "I can't believe you've kept all of this—my *sister*!—a secret from me. For seventeen years!"

"Julia," Mom said, wiping her eyes. "Honey, we just told you…"

"You told me what? That you were trying to protect me? From your sadness? What does that even mean? What about *my* sadness? What about the sadness I feel now, knowing that you've kept my own sister hidden away in some drawer all my life?"

Dad stood up. "Do you want to see a picture of her?" he asked. "Is that what you want? We have…"

"I don't want you to do anything! Just leave me alone. I mean it! Do not talk to me!"

"Julia," Mom cried. "Please!"

"No!" I screamed, running up the stairs. "There is nothing you could say right now that would fix this. Nothing! Just leave me alone!"

chapter
10

Inside my bedroom, I held on to the wall and tried to envision breathing slowly, but the strangling sensation became even worse. It was as if all the air in my room had been sucked out by some enormous vacuum. Beneath my shirt, I could feel my heart hammering, rapid as a woodpecker, and the palms of my hands grew slick with sweat.

I stumbled over to my dresser, balancing myself against the top of it with the flats of my palms. *"no one, not even the rain, has such small hands."* I repeated the phrase over and over again, waiting for the usual warmth to settle my trembling, but nothing happened. Instead, a coldness unlike any I had ever felt before began to sway and then move, little seaweed fingers pushing up through my stomach and along my arms. I began to cry, pushing my head under my pillow so Mom and Dad wouldn't hear.

"Julia?" Mom's voice sounded distorted, as if she were calling to me underwater. "Julia? Let us in!"

Dad rattled the doorknob. "Open the door!"

"Go away!"

"Please, Julia!" Mom's voice was breaking. "Are you okay? Just open the door."

I brought the tops of my knees to my chest, feeling the thing inside lessening, leaking out of me like a slow drip. My shoulders sagged around me and my feet slid down heavily. "I'm fine," I murmured. "I want to be alone."

"Come on, Arlene," Dad said in a low voice. "She just needs some time."

I could hear Mom hesitate, as if she was about to say something more, and then the soft sound of their footfalls as they made their way back downstairs. I lay down flat on the floor and stared up at the ceiling. A pulse inside my head throbbed like a wayward electrical cord. My chest hurt. Even my fingertips hurt. I closed my eyes, as if the action might ward off the pain, but it did nothing except make the room darker. I kept them closed. Dark was what I wanted.

———

When I opened my eyes again, it was black outside. I glanced at the clock next to my bed. 4:45 a.m. A wind rustled through the leaves of the trees outside, making a low, whistling sound against my window. My cell phone blinked and buzzed on my dresser. I picked it up and flipped it open. Seventeen missed calls. All from Zoe.

I pushed the off button and threw it on the floor.

Outside, the wind blew mournfully, trying to get my attention. Purple light, fragile as an iris petal, hovered behind the trees outside. The throbbing in my head had dimmed to a dull ache. I got up to get a drink. The floor creaked beneath my feet. Just the sound of the rushing water made me wince. The water itself felt like a thick sliver of ice inside my parched mouth. I drank for a long time, and then went back to bed.

Maggie.

I hadn't dreamed that, right? Had they really told me I'd had a sister once, years ago, who had died? A real person they'd somehow— and purposely—kept from me for seventeen years?

"When you were born, Julia, it was like we'd been given another chance at life. We wanted to make things as perfect for you as possible."

Perfect for me?

Or perfect for them?

Was there a difference?

Maggie. I couldn't get the name out of my head. Maggie. Short for Margaret, I guessed. There was no face to attach to the name, no visual to flood my head. The only baby I'd ever known in my life was Goober. Little Goober, who had a face as red and wrinkled as the skin of a pomegranate when she'd been born, whose blue eyes were so dark they were like looking into deep water.

What had Maggie looked like when she was born? Had she been a peanut like me? Tall and skinny like Sophie? Black hair? Blue eyes? Maybe she had looked like Goober. I didn't know.

I didn't *know*!

I hadn't been told.

I'd been kept out for some reason, left outside the inner ring.

Maybe that was what some people called protection.

Me, I just called it lying.

A sharp rapping on my door a few hours later woke me up.

"Julia?" It was Dad. "You have a visitor. Please get up now and come downstairs."

I peered at the clock. 11:06 a.m. "Who is it?"

"Zoe," Dad answered.

"Tell her I'll call her later."

The sound of Dad's footsteps descended down the steps. I could make out just the faintest sound of conversation between Mom, Zoe, and Dad. God only knew what they were telling her. Probably that I got food poisoning or something at the party last night, which was why I was still in bed. There was the sound of pounding footsteps suddenly, and then a sharp banging on the door.

"Julia!" Zoe yelled. "Let me in! I have to talk to you!"

I slid out of bed, wincing as my feet touched the bare floor, and opened the door a crack. Zoe was dressed in blue jeans that she had cut off at the knee and a bright yellow T-shirt, emblazoned with the question WHAT'S YOUR PROBLEM? on the front. A tiny gold butterfly barrette cinched a lock of hair against her forehead. She raised her eyebrows as I opened the door a bit more, and then strode into the room.

"What?" I asked.

"What do you mean, what?" Zoe glanced around slowly, as if looking for contraband.

I lifted my arms and then let them fall heavily against my sides. "Zoe, you just came running up the steps, yelling and screaming that you had to talk to me. What's wrong?"

"I want to know why you ran off last night." Zoe planted herself on top of my bed, crossed her flip-flops at the ankles, and leaned back on her palms. "I texted you like eighty times, but of course you didn't answer. Now what happened?"

"Nothing happened." I grabbed my robe off the back of the door and tied it tightly around my waist. "You know I hate parties like that. I just wanted to leave."

"That's bullshit, and you know it." Zoe lifted her knee and began to examine her toes, which were painted the same bubble-gum pink as her fingernails. "Come on, Jules. Spill."

"Can you please leave? It's…" I looked around, bewildered. "God, what day is it?"

"Friday," Zoe said nonchalantly.

"Right, Friday. One of the few days I have left to sleep in before my internship starts. Can we please have this discussion later?"

Zoe bounded off my bed. "No. Listen, I have to go run a few errands for my mom. But I'll be done in a half hour. I want you to meet me at Charles Street Park at 11:45 sharp so we can talk. Then I'm taking you to lunch."

"No way." I shook my head. "I'm going back to bed."

Zoe put her hand on her hip. "Your parents already know you're up. If you don't leave they're going to bug you until you come out of your room. You won't get any sleep anyway."

I bit my lip. "Fine."

"Don't be late," Zoe said, pausing at the door. "And dude?"

"What?"

"Drive the new car."

chapter 11

The hot water felt good against my skin, but it did nothing to ease the ache that was beneath it. Still, I stood under it for so long that clouds of steam began to make the walls sweat. When I opened the door, the blast of cold air shocked me. I wrapped a towel around myself quickly. Except that I couldn't do anything quickly, it seemed. Everything felt as though it took an enormous effort—even breathing. The towel scratched against my skin like sandpaper, and the muscles in my calf muscles were tight as knots. I got dressed, pulling on my soft jeans, a white T-shirt, and flats, and knotted my wet hair into a loose ponytail.

"Hi," Mom said softly, getting up from her chair as I came down to the kitchen. Her green stem-stripper gloves were on the table, next to her coffee. "How are you feeling?" I didn't answer, reaching instead for my purse, which was hanging on the back of one of the chairs. Mom's eyes were taking in my appearance, but slowly, as if she didn't want to frighten me.

"Are you going to work?" I asked, nodding at the gloves.

"I thought I would," Mom said. "It'll be slow at the shop today, though. If you need me to..."

"No. I'm leaving."

"Where're you going?"

"I'm meeting Zoe for lunch."

"Don't you want to dry your hair first?" Mom came around behind me, surveying my ponytail. "It's soaking wet, Julia. The whole back of your shirt is..."

"It's fine," I said curtly. "It'll dry on my way over. I have to go."

"Well, hold on a minute," Mom said. "You haven't eaten anything yet, honey. I made you some scrambled eggs and toast."

"I'm not hungry." I swung my purse over my shoulder and headed for the door.

"Julia." Mom rested her hand on side of the stove. "You father had to run out to get a few things but we want to talk to you. Honey, please. Could we just talk before you leave?"

I slammed the door behind me with a sharp *thwack*.

I spotted Zoe immediately, sitting on a swing next to a little kid, who was pumping his feet furiously. "Come on!" she yelled to him. "You gotta get super high first. Come on! Pump!" Pieces of the boy's brown hair blew backward as he threw back his head and strained his legs. "That's it!" Zoe said. "You're almost there! A couple more! Keep going! I'll tell you when!"

The swing shook as it flew forward and then back again. Even from where I stood, I could see the boy's eyes scanning the patch of ground up ahead of him. He looked terrified.

"Okay!" Zoe yelled as the swing began another upward ascent. The boy's face was white. At the apex of the swing, Zoe stood up. "*Now!*" she screamed. The boy let go all at once, his eyes the size of quarters. He soared through the air, arms and legs flailing like a kite unleashed. Just for a moment, it seemed, he hung there—suspended against the fading light, almost as if he had been pinned up against the sky somehow—and then he came crashing back down, a tangle of elbows and knees, rolling in the dirt. He skidded a few feet and then lay still, flat on his back.

Zoe rushed over to him and got down on one knee. "You okay?"

The little boy sat up. He blinked a few times, and then grinned. "I want to do it again."

"That was friggin' awesome," Zoe said. "You were flying! Gimme five!" She held up both hands. The boy slapped them hard and raced back to the swing set.

Zoe spotted me coming up behind him. She trotted over quickly and slowed as she got closer. "You still look like crap."

"Thanks."

She interlocked her elbow into mine and led me over to the small cluster of trees that overlooked the pond. Arranging herself along one of the thick roots, she settled in, tucking her legs under her. I leaned against the side of the tree, poking the grass with my toe. "I really don't feel like talking."

"Just sit, okay?" Zoe squinted up in my direction. "Please. Humor me."

I sighed heavily and sat down.

Zoe stared out across the park at the little boy who was still working his way up to jumping height on the swing. "I'm worried about you," she said quietly.

"Don't be. I'm fine."

She swiveled her head, looking at me sharply. "Don't give me that. The only thing I know that would make you stay in your room for twenty-four continual hours would be a college rejecting you. And since you got accepted to not one, not two, but all *ten* of the colleges you applied to, I'm assuming it's not that. So what is it?"

"I don't want to talk about it."

"Why not?"

"I don't know. I just don't."

"I don't know why you always shut me out," Zoe said. "I told you about my mom. You're the only one too."

I thought about this for a moment. It was true. The real reason Zoe and Milo's parents had moved across the country so abruptly two years ago was because their father had discovered their mother was having an affair. The move was a last-ditch effort to keep their marriage together, but things were strained. The last time they had fought about it, Zoe said, her mother had started crying and said that she felt as though she was living in jail. Milo had never said anything to me about it.

"I know," I said, stalling. "This is just... I don't know. I guess I need a little time."

Zoe plucked a blade of grass out from between her toes. "Does it have anything to do with Melissa's party? With Milo and Cheryl, I mean?"

My stomach twisted at the sound of his name. "No."

"Have you talked to Milo?"

"No," I lied.

"There he goes," Zoe said, pointing at the swings. I looked up. Zoe held her breath as the boy became airborne once again and then hurtled back down to earth. "Yes!" she whispered. The little boy scrambled back up to his feet and looked over in our direction. Zoe stuck her arm out, thumb up. "Awesome!" He grinned and clapped, and ran over to the swings again.

"He'll do that jump a million times," Zoe said. "Because now he knows he can."

Neither of us said anything for a minute.

Then Zoe turned and looked at me. "What about the internship? Are you worried about that? I mean, is hanging around inside that courthouse something you really want to do all summer?"

I shrugged. "Yeah, it'll be fine."

"Fine." Zoe said the word slowly, rolling it around in her mouth like a marble. "You say that a lot, you know that? What does fine mean, anyway?"

I stood up. "Listen, I gotta go."

Zoe stood up too. "Don't blow me off."

"I'm not!" I turned my hands up. "Seriously. I just have things to do at home."

"Like mope around in your room? Feel sorry for yourself?"

"Whatever." I shrugged her off. "Because you know everything."

Zoe stopped walking. "I know some of this is about Milo," she called. "You should just tell him the truth, Julia."

Now I stopped walking. "The truth about what?"

"How you feel." Zoe crossed her arms. "I mean, how long are you two gonna go on like this, pretending that there wasn't—and still isn't—something between you?"

I could feel the blood rush to my neck and then spread across my cheeks. "What are you talking about? Did he say something?"

"Milo?" Zoe snorted. "Milo doesn't say two words to me unless you're around. But he doesn't have to. God, it's so obvious you guys are crazy about each other. Why don't you just..."

"Stop, okay?" I said. "Could you just *stop* for ten seconds? As usual, you have no idea what you're talking about, but you just talk and talk and talk anyway. It's not what's bothering me anyway."

"So what *is* bothering you?"

"I don't want to talk about it." I turned around again, walking toward the entrance of the park.

Zoe grabbed my arm. "Julia."

"God!" I shouted. "Lay off, will you? It's like you just like to hear yourself talk and most of the time you're talking about nothing!"

Zoe steadied her bottom lip with her teeth.

"I'm tired of listening to nothing, okay, Zoe? I'm not built that way. I need quiet. I need to think. I like to be alone. So if you want to be my friend, do that for me, okay? Just leave me alone. Let me have some peace and quiet. For once."

I strode away from her, looking straight ahead.

"You're just afraid!" She called after me.

I winced as the words hurtled through the air between us, and then subconsciously raised one shoulder, as if to ward them off. But they rang in my ears as I kept walking, and then settled in beside me, an unwelcome passenger, as I got back into the car.

chapter
12

I drove around for a long time after leaving Zoe at the park. My destination was anywhere but home. I knew as soon as I set foot inside the house that Mom and Dad would be all over me. I didn't know *what* I wanted right now, but I knew I didn't want to talk to them. They would insist on a discussion about Maggie, pushing the issue until every last question had been raised and then answered. Dad would insist on "resolving the matter," as if it were just another court case that he had to sift through, complete with an appeal to the jury. Except that the appeal would be to me this time and I knew he would not stop—he would not rest his case—until I assured him that I understood.

Well, I didn't understand. I doubted if I would ever understand. And nothing they could say or do was going to change that.

I already knew Mom and Dad and Sophie had had a whole life before me in Milford. Even the revelation about Maggie wasn't what was ripping away inside of me right now. It was that they'd kept it from me. All three of them. For seventeen years. Mom and Dad said it was to protect me. But what was Sophie's reason? It was her silence that really bothered me, I realized, making a right on Amsterdam Avenue. I'd never known Sophie to be silent about anything.

What would happen if I reversed things? If I went up there and confronted *her* the way she'd confronted Mom and Dad all these years? She'd been there too, after all. Dad had said she'd seen everything. Why shouldn't she be the one to tell me? What would happen if I went up to Poultney and asked her to tell me her side of the story? Would it help anything? Or just make it worse?

I pulled into a gas station on the way home and asked the attendant to fill up the tank. Then I had him check the oil level, which was low, and the tires and windshield wiper fluid too. I packed as soon as I got home, tucking three full outfits—underwear, shirts, matching pants—into my suitcase, along with an extra pair of sneakers, socks, my toothbrush, floss, and cell phone. I stayed in my room to avoid conversation with Mom, printing out a map and step-by-step directions from my computer instead. It was not until I heard the front door slam, followed by Dad's "Hey! I'm home!" that I finally came downstairs, bag in hand.

"Hi," Mom said, obviously startled by my appearance. She had circles under her eyes. "You hungry? Dinner's almost ready."

"No," I said.

Dad was holding the mail. He glanced at my bag and raised his eyebrows.

"I'm leaving." I talked loudly, hoping it would make me sound confident. "I'm going to Sophie's for the weekend."

Dad put the mail down slowly. "You're going to Sophie's? Right now?"

I nodded.

"Julia, it's already five o'clock. Do you have any idea what a long drive it is?"

"I already printed out the directions. If I leave now and take some breaks, it won't be too bad. Sophie'll be up."

"You can't drive in the dark, Julia!" Mom said. "It's too..."

"I'll be okay," I said. "I've driven in the dark before."

They both stared at me for a few seconds, eyes wild. If I had the ability to look inside their heads, I thought briefly, I would see gears and cogs moving at the speed of light.

"You're going up for a visit?" Dad asked finally.

"Yeah. I need same time away." I shrugged.

Mom turned suddenly, wiping her hands on the edge of a dish-cloth. "Well, let me at least pack you something to eat..."

"No, it's okay," I said. "I'll just stop at a Burger King or something."

Dad dug into his back pocket and extracted his wallet. He pulled out three twenty-dollar bills and held them out to me. "Take this too."

"I'm fine, Dad. Really."

He strode over to me and pushed the money into my hands. "I know you're fine, Julia. But take the money anyway. You never know..." He left the sentence unfinished, hanging in the air between the three of us like a storm cloud.

I took the bills and shoved them into my pocket. "Thanks."

"Be back on Sunday." Dad said.

I nodded. "I'll call before I leave."

"Hit the road earlier rather than later," Dad said. "You'll want to be fresh for your internship on Monday."

I pushed past him and headed for the door.

"Julia?"

"I know!" I turned, my hand on the doorknob. "I will be back for my internship, Dad. You don't have to worry."

He dropped his eyes. "Okay," he said. "All right, then."

Mom stepped forward, her hand on his arm. "Make sure to call us as soon as you get there safely. I mean it. As soon as you get there."

"It'll be late," I protested.

"I don't care what time it is." Mom's eyes flashed. "Just call me when you get there."

"Okay." I pushed the door open. "I'll call you when I get there. Bye."

I got into the car and shut the door. Mom and Dad stayed in the open doorway, watching as I inserted the key into the ignition and reversed the vehicle out of the driveway. I gave them a small wave as I put the car back into drive and surged forward.

At the stop sign, halfway down the street, I glanced briefly in the rearview mirror.

They were still there, watching from the doorway, Dad's arm encircled around Mom's thin shoulders, the tips of Mom's fingers pressed against her lips. Sophie and I used to do this thing sometimes, just for fun, where we positioned objects at a distance in between our thumb and index finger. It was a trick of the eye, of course, an optical illusion, meant to make us feel bigger, I guess, than the things that actually were. And this was what I did now, fitting both of my parents—still reflected in the rearview mirror—in between my slightly parted fingers.

They were so small, I thought. Like dolls. Little kids, even.

I stepped hard on the gas and did not look back again.

part
two

chapter
13

Mom was right. Driving such a distance in the dark was probably not the smartest thing to do. As the light began to sink behind the hills and fade entirely from the sky, I tried not to let my nerves get the best of me. The good thing was that the majority of the trip was on the highway. A straight highway. In fact, the first hundred miles, along Route 84, was so boring that I had to turn the radio on loud so I wouldn't fall asleep. Cyndi Lauper wailed in my ears as I pulled onto the New York Thruway and settled in for eighty more miles of silent road, but after a while, I turned the radio off. The silence, strangely enough, was comforting.

I still wasn't 100 percent sure what my motivation was for doing this. I did know I wanted to hear Sophie's version of things. I wanted to stand in front of her and ask her why she had kept Maggie from me. But why I was driving three hundred and fifty miles to ask her—right now, with everything else going on in my life—wasn't really clear. Why was I letting this weird sense of urgency take over instead of the usual straightforward, calculated way I did things?

And how was it that I had just graduated at the top of my class two days ago and now felt as if I didn't have a clue about anything at all? Maybe in an ironic sort of way it would turn out that Sophie was the one who had a handle on things; after all, she'd spent seventeen years keeping a secret. And a massive secret at that. I'd done a lot difficult things in the last few years—getting a 1680 on my SATs (after taking them six times), receiving the highest score ever on Mr. Phillips's ridiculously grueling chemistry final—but I'd never done anything like that. And as much as it angered me that she had done it, I couldn't help but feel a strange kind of awe about her too.

The occasional punctuation of a few red taillights broke up the vast blackness in front of me. A lopsided moon moved overhead, gossamer clouds separating in front of it like milkweed strands. By the time I reached the end of the thruway, it had scuttled to the front, like an enormous blinker pointing the way.

Every time I tried to imagine the impending scene between Sophie and me, I felt sick. I'd seen enough blowouts between Sophie and Mom and Dad over the years to know that arguing with Sophie was not for the faint of heart. Sophie, if it could be said, was pretty damn good at arguing. I had never known her to back down. She held her ground the way a bullfighter waited in front of a bull, fluttering that red cape until the last possible second. And then, just before the charge, she would move, so swiftly that Mom or Dad or whoever it was she was baiting did not even have time to blink. By the time they were ready to face her again, she had settled into another fighter stance, red flag waving all over again.

It was not something I was looking forward to. But maybe, when things finally got said, when details were spread out before us, an argument would not be necessary. Maybe we could just sit there and . . . talk.

I closed my eyes for a second, trying to imagine it. And then I opened them again.

We were talking about Sophie here, a girl who had once been dubbed by Dad as Miss Darrow, after Clarence Darrow, possibly the most famous trial lawyer in history. He was known for his powerful closing arguments.

Who was I kidding?

chapter
14

When I was nine years old I won the Acahela Summer Camp Spelling Bee. It had come down to a final round between me and Hannah Reed, who stumbled on the word "octopus." I clutched my little plastic trophy on the bus ride home, wriggling with excitement at the thought of showing it to Sophie. Mom and Dad always made a fuss over my good grades, but getting Sophie's approval was like hitting gold. Once, after I had shown her a perfect math test—complete with three gold stars—Sophie asked if she could hang it in her room. Seeing my paper there every time I came into her room afterward sent a swell of pride through me.

It was unseasonably cool that day in July. Leaves on the maple trees whipped to and fro under a sharp wind, and the sun peered out faintly behind a film of clouds. The air smelled like rain. I had just passed the kitchen window when I heard someone shouting. The window was cracked slightly and I stood under it, listening with my heart in my throat.

"They've been saying shit behind my back since the end of last year," Sophie said. "They just haven't been as vocal about it until now. Seriously, Mom, I don't care. It doesn't matter."

"What kinds of things? About your weight?"

"Yes, about my weight!" Sophie exploded. "Like it's a big deal that I put on twenty pounds!"

"Well, what are they saying exactly?" Mom asked.

"You want to know what they've been saying? When I got up from my lounge chair at the pool today, some asshole friend of Eddie's made oinking noises. And when I walked over to the snack bar to get a soda, I heard Marissa Harrington call me a lard-ass under her breath. Okay? That's the kind of shit I'm dealing with."

"Sophie, please." Mom was begging. "Don't use that kind of language."

"Jesus Christ," Sophie yelled. "Me using bad language isn't the point here, okay? You asked me what was wrong and I told you what was wrong." I flinched as the sound of something being slammed filtered through the window. "I don't know why I ever think I can talk to you about anything!"

I counted slowly to ten, then went inside.

Mom looked bewildered as I walked through the door. "Julia," she said flatly.

"What's wrong with Sophie?"

Mom blinked. "Oh, nothing. She's having a rough day is all. She'll be fine." She glanced down at my trophy. "What's that?"

I held it up. "I won the spelling bee at camp today." Somehow, the news didn't feel that exciting anymore.

But Mom squealed and clapped her hands and kissed me. She

placed the trophy on the kitchen counter so she could admire it, and then said, "How about a snack?"

"No thanks." I grabbed the trophy and began to climb the stairs.

Mom came after me. "Honey? Don't bother Sophie right now, okay? She's not feeling that great. You can show her your trophy later. Don't bug her now."

"I won't *bug* her." Insulted that Mom would even suggest such a thing, I sat in my room for a while, staring at the little prize in my hands.

Little drops of rain began to pelt my bedroom window. I put my trophy down and went over to the chair behind my desk. I drew a fat pear with arms, legs, a hat, and a skirt. Then I drew a pair of cherries, connected by a single stem, holding hands. All of them wore striped socks, bows in their hair, and had little red cheeks. I put my colored pencils down. Sophie had to see my trophy. She just had to. If anything could make her feel better right now, it would be this. I knew it.

I tapped very gently on her door. "Sophie?"

"Go away."

I paused, pressing my forehead against the door, and squeezed the trophy in my hand. "Sophie, I just want to show..."

The door flung open and I stepped back, surprised. Sophie's hair hung around her face, as if she had turned her head upside down and shaken it. Black eyeliner had been drawn thickly around the bottoms of her eyes, and her lips were painted a garish red color. "What do you want?" she screamed. Even her voice, hoarse and shrill, sounded as if it didn't belong to her. But it was not until I looked down and saw the hair—a large, massive clump of it—clutched in her right hand, that I began to cry.

I took another step back and bumped into the wall. The sound of Mom's footsteps running up the stairs echoed somewhere faintly in the background, but she was not fast enough. Sophie had already snatched the trophy out of my hands and was glaring at it. "This?" she yelled. "This is what you wanted to show me?" I tried to flatten myself even more against the wall as Sophie leaned down. Her weird eyes leveled with mine. The red lipstick had begun to smudge around her bottom lip, and her breath, hot and metallic smelling, made me wince. "You think getting first place all the time will make them like you a little more?" she hissed. She held the trophy to my face, as if I might forget what it looked like, and then threw it down the hallway. I stared, horrified, as it scuttled noisily against the hardwood floor, and then spun into a corner. Suddenly, Sophie's hot breath was in my ear. "Well guess what? Being perfect won't change anything. Believe me. I've already tried."

Mom burst out from the steps, racing toward us. "Don't touch her!" she screamed, arms waving out in front. "Don't you *touch* her, Sophie!"

Sophie straightened up. She stepped back as Mom grabbed me and held me against the front of her. Mom's breath was coming in little spurts, as if she couldn't catch it fast enough, and behind me I could feel her legs shaking.

"Don't worry," Sophie said in a strange voice. "I'm not going to hurt her."

I could hear her behind me as she turned and walked back into her room.

And then, inside the safety of Mom's arms, the slam of her door.

chapter
15

I got lost in Albany after stopping at a Burger King for dinner. "Stupid, stupid, stupid," I thought, driving aimlessly along a mile-long street before realizing I was probably going in the wrong direction. It was almost two in the morning. A few street lights here and there broke up the darkness, but it was hard to make out much of anything. Finally I pulled over at a twenty-four-hour gas station. It was empty except for a lone gas attendant, an older man with a graying beard. I locked my doors as he approached and then rolled down the window just an inch as I asked for directions. "Oh, you ain't too far off." The man scratched his head with diesel-stained fingers. "You gotta go back down this road…"

"Can you hold on a second?" I dug around in my purse for a pen. "I want to write this down." The man slowed his speech as I wrote and when I went over it, repeating his words back slowly to him, he grinned and nodded his head. "You'll be fine," he said, tapping the side of the car. "Just drive it like I said it."

He was right. Twenty minutes later, much to my relief, I was back on course.

The sun was just starting to rise, dismissing the moon with a slow bleed of horizontal light, when I finally spotted the sign for Poultney. I pulled the car off to the side of the road, put my head down in the middle of the steering wheel, and took my first real breath since the trip had begun. It was 4:47 a.m.—eleven hours and forty-seven minutes after I had left Silver Springs.

Sophie hadn't told me where on Main Street her place was, but since the street itself was no longer than a football field, I drove up and down several times, looking for some kind of clue. It was a sweet, sleepy stretch of road, scattered with black lampposts and neat lawns. Green Mountain College sat at the north end of it, a tiny campus dotted with brick buildings, paved pathways, and a multitude of maple trees. I slowed the car down as I passed a Mobil station, Perry's Family Eatery, the Poultney House of Pizza, something called the Red Brick Café, Tot's Diner, a red-brick church, and finally, around a slight curve, Poultney High School.

Interspersed between the business establishments were regular houses, all in various states of duress. Most of them were neatly maintained, with picture-perfect lawns and pristine front porches. One or two of them, however, looked as if they had been forgotten about entirely. I passed by them with my heart in my throat, hoping that I wouldn't find some semblance of Sophie behind the peeling paint and rickety frames.

My phone buzzed inside my pocket. Damn. I'd forgotten to call Mom again. She'd called as I'd been trying to find my way out of Albany and I'd lied, telling her that I had an hour or so more to go.

I'd turned my phone off, but she'd probably been up the rest of night, pacing around the house. Dad too.

"Mom," I said. "I literally just got..."

"You said you would *call*, Sophie. You promised!" Her voice was a combination of rage and tears.

"I got lost, Mom. But I'm here now. I just this second drove into Poultney. I'm here, okay? And I'm fine. I'm totally fine."

She inhaled shakily. "Okay."

"I'm going to get Sophie now. I'll call you in a little while."

I tossed the phone back into my bag and let my head fall back against the seat. Out of the corner of my eye I spotted something moving. A man wearing baggy black pants and a Red Sox baseball cap was strolling down the opposite side of the street. I watched as he stopped suddenly, stooped to the ground, and picked something up. He studied the object for a few seconds, turning it around with his fingers, and then inserted it into the side pocket of his jacket.

I rolled down the window. "Excuse me?"

The man looked over at me and adjusted the brim of his cap. Tufts of white hair poked out from the sides.

"Hi," I leaned across the seat, close to the window. "I'm from out of town. I'm looking for my sister. Sophie Anderson? She lives somewhere here on Main Street. She's opening a bakery. Have you ever heard..."

The man cut me off with a point of his finger, indicating the house directly behind me. I turned around, taking in the two-story, ramshackle structure with a slow dread, and then looked back at the man. "This...this one? Are you sure?"

He nodded, closing his eyes for emphasis, and pointed at it once again.

"Okay," I said miserably. "Well, thanks."

To be honest, 149 Main Street looked as if it had once been a pretty decent-looking house. About a hundred years ago. Now it had the unsettling appearance of having been uprooted by a tornado, whirled around a few times, and then flung back to earth. A good chunk of the roof on the left side was missing entirely. Bare wooden beams, thick and pale as elephant ribs, indicated that something up there was in the process of being restructured, but I could not tell what. The other half of the roof, miraculously enough, looked okay, except for an old dilapidated chimney that stood stubbornly upright in one corner. Curls of peeling brown paint dotted the sides of the house, and the front porch had an enormous hole in the middle of it. The porch railing, full of missing spokes, looked like a mouthful of teeth that had been punched out.

This was Sophie's place? The soon-to-be bakery?

I ran my hands through my hair, put the car back in gear, and made a hesitant turn into the driveway. Clusters of dead, rotting bushes cleaved to the side of the house, and the lawn—if it had indeed ever been a lawn—was a mess of brown dirt. A side porch, leading up to a small narrow door, held a green watering can and a white wicker rocking chair. Maybe the man had been mistaken. This place didn't look or feel like Sophie at all.

Suddenly the side door opened, and as if she knew I'd been thinking about her, Sophie appeared, dressed in denim overalls and a white T-shirt. The cuffs of her overalls had been rolled up around the ankles, and her sneakers were spattered with paint. The edges of a red bandanna, folded and tied around the top of her head, stuck out like little ears, and her blond hair was scooped back into a ponytail. She looked confused for a moment, her eyes taking in the green Bug, and then they opened up wide. "Julia?" She ran over, tapped on the window glass and then yanked open the door. "Julia? Oh my God! You're here! I can't believe you're here!"

I giggled with relief, forgetting the state of the house for a moment, or even the reason I had come up to see her in the first place. "Believe it," I said, getting out of the car. "I'm here."

She grabbed me and held me tight against her. The smell of turpentine and cigarettes drifted out from her hair. "You *drove?*" she asked, pulling away again. "The whole way? By yourself?"

I nodded, realizing for the first time as she said it, that in fact I had. "I got lost in Albany, though. That place is like a maze."

Sophie looked down at her watch. "It's not even five yet. What'd you do, drive all night?"

I nodded again.

"Aha!" she chortled. "That's my girl!" She frowned suddenly. "Wait. Is everything all right? Are you in trouble?"

"No!"

"Mom and Dad? They're all right?"

"Yeah. They're fine." Now was definitely not the time to get into things. "God, Sophie. You always think the worst."

"So then, you just…felt like coming?" Her voice was soft. "To see me?"

"Well, yeah. Just for the weekend though. I have to leave Sunday. My internship starts Monday."

For a split second, Sophie's face fell. Then she flung an arm around my shoulder. "Oh, Jules, I'm so sorry about that whole scene. At your dinner, I mean. I was gonna call and explain everything to you, but then I felt weird about it, and I don't know…I just feel so bad about the whole thing. Especially leaving without saying good-bye." She scratched her upper lip. "I really am sorry. I hope I didn't ruin your big day."

I shook my head. "You didn't. It's okay."

She studied my face for a minute and then laughed out loud. "I just can't believe you're here! In Vermont! And that I get you all to myself for a whole weekend!"

"What about Goober?" I asked suddenly, looking around. "Where's she?"

"Oh, she's still with Greg. He took her camping. It's her favorite thing to do in the summer. They go up to Lake Bomoseen and stay the whole weekend."

"Oh." I was disappointed. "She's not even gonna remember what I look like the next time she sees me. When'll she be back?"

"Not till Monday."

"Shoot. I'll be gone by then."

"We'll call her." Sophie grabbed my arm. "Listen, have you eaten yet?"

"You mean breakfast?" I shook my head.

"Leave your things in the car," Sophie said, pulling me down the driveway toward the street. "Right now, I'm taking you to breakfast at the best place in town."

chapter
16

Perry's Main Street Eatery was a small, brightly lit place directly
across the street. Several glass-topped tables set with paper place-
mats and silverware had been placed neatly throughout the room,
and green-checkered curtains were draped over a single front
window. A long counter complete with six swivel stools lined the
opposite side of the restaurant. The kitchen could be seen at one
end, while various muffins the size of softballs sat underneath a glass
dome at the other.

Sophie looked around quickly and then pointed to a small table
next to the window. "Over there," she said. "Right behind the Table of
Knowledge."

"The what?" I repeated, following her across the small expanse
of restaurant, being careful not to bump into anyone.

"The Table of Knowledge!" Sophie announced, stopping next
to a table where three men were sitting. I recognized the one with
the Red Sox baseball hat, but he did not look up. She slapped the
shoulder of the largest man, a ruddy-looking guy with small

hairs protruding from the end of his nose. "How're you doin', Walt?"

Walt grinned and tipped his head back a little in Sophie's direction. "Just dandy, Anderson. Just dandy. You finish the upstairs bedrooms yet?" Walt's blue-checkered shirt with bright orange suspenders exposed a vast stomach underneath. His hands were as wide and rough as baseball mitts, and he had a wad of chewing tobacco shoved inside his left cheek.

"Almost," Sophie said. "I have a little bit more sanding to do in the first one. But listen, we can talk shop later. I want to introduce you to someone." She put an arm around my shoulder. "This is my little sister, Julia. The one I told you about, remember? Who just graduated?"

Another man, sitting opposite Walt, made an "Oh ho!" sound. A scruffy beard covered the lower half of his face, and he had a piece of egg on the front of his red hunting shirt. "Valedictorian, right?" He extended his hand.

I shook it and looked away, embarrassed. "Sophie!"

Sophie beamed at me and squeezed my shoulder a little more tightly. "She's just shy, Lloyd. She's always been that way. But yes, this is our valedictorian."

"Congratulations," Walt said. "That's quite an accomplishment."

"It sure is." Lloyd scooped a piece of runny egg up with the edge of his toast, and popped it into his mouth. "Nothing to be shy about."

The man in the Red Sox cap looked up at me briefly but didn't say anything. Sophie held out her palm in his direction. "This is Jimmy," she said. "Jimmy, this is my little sister, Julia."

Jimmy acknowledged me with a nod of his head, and then dropped his eyes once more.

"These guys," Sophie said, addressing me now, "are known in Poultney as the Table of Knowledge. They're called that because they know the answer to just about every question under the sun."

"We've also got our finger in everyone's business around this place," Lloyd said. "You want to know what's really going on in Poultney? Pull up a chair and sit yourself down."

Sophie guffawed. "They're also the best carpenters around. I wouldn't be halfway as far along with my place right now if it weren't for them. They've taught me everything."

"Wow. That's great."

Walt waved off Sophie's compliments. "We just give her suggestions," he said. "She's the one doing all the work."

"That's not true and you know it," Sophie said, leaning in closer to me. "Walt just put up half that roof last week, and Jimmy's done most of the kitchen himself." She straightened back up again. "Besides, I couldn't do any of the work I'm doing without your suggestions. What do I know about redoing a house?"

Walt made a snorting sound. "You know a lot more than you give yourself credit for. I never seen no one come down here outta the blue like you and just wing it." He nodded. "I keep telling you. You got guts, girl."

It was weird listening to a stranger say things about Sophie. House-building skills? Sophie?

Sophie moved in a few steps as a waitress holding a pot of

coffee above her head tried to angle her way in behind her. A pencil stuck out menacingly behind her ear, and her mouth was set in a thin line.

"You two go on over and eat now," Lloyd said, gesturing toward the waitress with his chin. "You keep blocking Miriam's way, she's gonna get all ornery on me, and slip some regular in with my decaf."

Miriam, pouring coffee at the next table, raised a thin eyebrow in Lloyd's direction. Sophie laughed. "Okay. Talk to you later, guys."

"Later," Lloyd said.

"Make sure you get the special," Walt said, leaning back in his chair. "It's excellent."

"What is it?" Sophie asked.

"Creamed chipped beef over biscuits, plus two fried eggs."

Sophie and I exchanged a look. "We'll think about it, Walt," Sophie said.

We settled ourselves at our table as Walt turned back around.

"You know, I saw that other guy—the one with the Red Sox hat—this morning," I kept my voice low as I opened my napkin and put it in my lap.

"Jimmy?" Sophie asked.

"Yeah, he was walking along the street and I asked him for directions to your place. He didn't say anything, though. He just pointed to it."

"Yeah, that's Jimmy," Sophie said. "He doesn't talk much."

"He's shy?"

"No, he's not shy. I've seen him talk with certain people. Like Goober. He loves Goober. He'll talk up a storm with her." She shrugged. "I don't know. He lost his wife a while back. And he's . . . particular, I guess." She reached out and rubbed my hand. "I still can't believe you're here. It's just so great!"

Miriam appeared next to us suddenly, holding her coffee pot directly over my cup. She had an elfish-looking face, with small green eyes, a pointed chin, and round cheeks. "Coffee, girls?"

"Please." Sophie and I both pushed our cups forward.

"Know what you want?" Miriam asked.

"Oh, you have to get the pancakes," Sophie said to me. "They use real maple syrup here that they tap themselves. Wait'll you taste it. It's incredible."

I glanced over as a burst of laughter exploded from the Table of Knowledge. Walt slapped the sides of his belly and then leaned over, spitting a brown substance into a cup. Lloyd tilted his head back and laughed again. Even Jimmy smiled—into his coffee cup.

"So all of them have been helping you?" I asked. "With the house?"

Sophie leaned forward, her fingers balanced on the rim of her cup. "Julia, let me tell you something. I don't know where I would be or what I would be doing right now if it weren't for those guys." She glanced down. "It was kind of stupid, really, when I think about it now—just buying a place with no real knowledge of how to fix it up or anything. I mean, look at it!" We both stared out the window at the house across the street, which managed somehow, despite the distance, to look even worse. "And that's with work done," Sophie said. "You should've seen the place when I first bought it."

I stared at the structure, trying to imagine it looking worse than it did now.

It was difficult.

"So...why are they helping you?" I asked. "I mean, it's nice of them and everything, but it just seems kind of weird. You buy this place, move to this town where no one knows you, and suddenly three strangers just..."

"The house used to belong to Jimmy's family," Sophie said. "It's kind of a cool story, actually. The three of them—Walt and Lloyd and Jimmy—have been best friends since elementary school. Apparently Walt and Lloyd used to hang out over there when they were growing up. I guess back then it was a really beautiful place. But as Jimmy's family passed away, it started to fall apart. No one's lived in it for years."

"So the three of them have a vested interest in getting it fixed up again," I concluded.

Sophie nodded. "Exactly."

"That's nice of them," I said softly.

"It is nice," Sophie echoed. "And don't get me wrong when I say this, because I'm more than grateful for everything they've done. But I want to do some on my own too. It's one thing to have help. It's another to have three different opinions breathing down your neck all day, every day."

I glanced over in their direction. Lloyd had finally spotted the egg on his shirt and was brushing it off. Walt was beckoning to Miriam for another coffee. And Jimmy was looking at something outside. They looked okay to me. And I liked the whole part about them having a stake in getting the house fixed up. But it still felt a little weird. And I hoped Sophie knew what she was doing.

chapter
17

When she lived at home, Saturday mornings were sacred to Sophie. That was when she rolled up her sleeves, donned an apron, and began to bake. Cookies mostly at first, until she moved on to things like bread and fudge and pies and cakes. Even if I slept in late, I always knew it was Saturday because the smells of melted chocolate and sticky vanilla, buttered cookie sheets and roasted walnuts, would fill the house like perfume, punctuated every ten minutes or so by the tiny *ding* of the timer on the stove.

I was not allowed anywhere near Sophie on Saturdays; she demanded to be alone. Even Mom and Dad cleared out, eating breakfast early and then making themselves scarce so Sophie could have free reign in the kitchen. But I loved to be around Sophie when she baked. I sat on the bottom step in the living room, which gave me a nearly perfect view of my big sister while still hiding me from her sight.

Sophie's ability to create things in the kitchen was unlike anything I had ever seen. It was a skill that came naturally, an innate knowledge that only she possessed, with an end result that was nothing short of magnificent. In the span of half a day, the blue kitchen counter would be covered with whole vanilla cakes, the edges moist and slightly crumbling, bowls of fudge frosting accented with a splash of espresso, zucchini bread studded with pineapple and carrots and walnuts, even peanut brittle made with a combination of brown sugar and toffee. She created everything from scratch; each recipe an original, tried again and again until the proportions were perfect.

And she worked hard. There was no doubt about that. Her shoulders would droop as the day went on, her cheeks would flush pink. But the exertion didn't seem to bother her. On the contrary, it seemed to inspire her even more. She would finish with some sort of cream puff or biscotti and then, staring at it for a minute, say something like: "I wonder would what happen if…" The next moment, she would start all over again, throwing ingredients into a bowl, and whipping something else into a frenzy. Everything she made went to Eddie and his family, though. We never got a chance to try any of it.

I struck gold only once, when Sophie looked up in the middle of making her dark-chocolate chip cookies with walnuts, oatmeal, and toffee, and grinned at me. I ducked behind the wall, but I was too late. "I know you're there," she said. "You want to help?"

"Me?" I peeked out around the step.

She laughed. "Yeah, dork. You."

I scrambled from my seat and ran into the kitchen. Sophie made me turn around as she tied an apron around my waist and scooped my hair up into a ponytail, and I was glad I wasn't facing her, because my mouth was plastered with an idiotic smile. I washed my hands and rolled up my sleeves, ready to be let in on Sophie's magical world of baking.

But there was not as much magic as I imagined. Not nearly as much. I'd conjured up visuals of Sophie adding secret ingredients here and there—maybe some sort of exotic extract that brought out the taste of the dough. Instead, I tried to hide my disappointment as she placed boring old butter, sugar, eggs, flour, and baking soda on the countertop, and then pulled out the mixer.

"That's it?" I asked. "Isn't there anything else?"

"What do you mean?"

"That's all that goes into your cookies?"

Sophie shrugged. "Well, we have to add the chocolate and walnuts and toffee at the end, but yeah, all this stuff makes up the base of the dough." She reached for a tiny white dish on top of the stove. "Oops, and salt. I almost forgot salt."

"Salt?" I wrinkled my nose, and then widened my eyes. "Is that your secret ingredient?"

Sophie laughed. "Salt isn't a secret ingredient, doofus. Besides, you just add a pinch. Salt brings out all the flavors." She paused. "It's weird, isn't it? How something so opposite of sweet can make things taste even better?"

"How does it do that?" I asked.

"I don't know," Sophie answered. "It just kind of brings everything together in its own strange little way."

The cookies came out of the oven twenty minutes later. Sophie poured each of us a tall glass of milk, placed two cookies apiece on Mom's rose and ivy teacup saucers, and drew up a chair at the kitchen counter. I stood on the chair while Sophie rested her elbows on the counter, and we dug in. The cookies were warm and soft, a perfect contrast to the heavy, weighted centers, and the edges were crisped only slightly.

"You know, getting to eat what you make is the second-best thing about baking," Sophie said, sinking her teeth into another cookie.

"What's the first thing?" I asked.

"Being in the kitchen with a head full of ideas." There was a tiny smear of chocolate on her chin. "Right before you start—when anything is possible. That's the best thing."

chapter
18

After breakfast, Sophie showed me around the house. She took me upstairs first, leading me into two small bedrooms. Except for a single bed and dresser in one of them, both rooms were completely bare. Despite their sparseness, they didn't look half as bad as I expected them to. Their pale walls, freshly refinished floors, and undressed windows, however, indicated that some work had already been done to them. The scent of clean wood filled the air, and light streamed in from the wide windows on both sides.

"Where is all of Goober's stuff?" I asked.

Sophie waved her hand. "Her things are still in the garage until I finish all of this. I don't want them to get dirty. And technically she doesn't even need her bed. She still sleeps with me."

She led me back downstairs, into a large, very wide room in the front of the house. The floors were rough and unfinished, and while two of the walls were bare and smooth, the other two were pocked with cracked plaster. Unlike the woodsy scent upstairs, this room was permeated with a strange oily smell.

Sophie walked into the middle of the room. She spread her arms out wide and turned around slowly. "This room is going to be the first thing people see when they come in. This is going to be the whole front of the store." She pointed to an empty space on the right. "I want to have a case of breads over there—whole wheat, rye—and English muffins, and cranberry-nut, blueberry-lemon, and white chocolate raspberry muffins over there. I want a table in the middle filled with nothing but cookies—the dark-chocolate-walnut-toffee ones, coconut macaroons, peanut butter drops with the little Hershey's Kisses in the middle, and sugar cookies. And then on the left, I'm thinking pies: apple, peach, and cherry daily, and maybe chocolate cream espresso for special occasions. Plus, I want to have a wall for all different kinds of specials. Maybe a certain bread—like Irish soda bread for St. Patrick's Day, fruit-cake for Christmas, or challah bread for Passover—whatever." She looked at me, her face shiny with perspiration. "What do you think?"

I shrugged. "Good."

"But?"

"But it sounds like a lot." I shoved my hands deep into my pockets. "It sounds like a whole lot. Can you do all that?"

"I can try." She studied me for a few seconds without saying anything.

"What?" I asked finally.

"You know this is my dream, right, to have my own place, my own bakery? To create amazing things for people to eat?"

I bit the inside of my cheek. "Yeah. I mean, I guess I do now."

"Well, when something's your dream, you do whatever it takes to make it happen." She shrugged. "Even if it seems like too much."

I waited, hoping she wasn't going to start in again on her "you gotta have fun" speech.

"You have a dream, don't you?" she asked instead.

I looked away uncomfortably. "Well, yeah. Of course."

"What is it?" Sophie asked. "What's your dream, Jules?"

"Didn't we already talk about this?" I could feel my defenses starting to rise. "In my room, right after my graduation? You know I want to be an attorney and get on the whole legal fast track."

Sophie nodded slowly. "I know that's going to be your job," she said. "But is that your dream?"

I crossed my arms. "Yes. Now can we drop it?"

Sophie nodded. "Come on," she said. "I want to show you the kitchen."

"Actually, I think I need some air," I said. "The smell in here... Can we go for a walk or something?"

"Yeah," Sophie said. "Definitely. I should've given you a mask to put over your face before we came into this room. I've been using turpentine on the walls and the fumes are really strong. Come on."

Outside, the day was warming up fast. More people had appeared on Main Street, walking dogs or just hurrying down the sidewalk. A man in biker shorts and bright red clogs was sweeping the sidewalk in front of the Brown Bag Delicatessen, and a herd of men holding coffee cups had gathered in front of a little convenience store called Stewart's. They were laughing and talking, lifting their caps to scratch their heads and then placing them back on again.

"Let's head this way." Sophie pointed in the direction of the high school. "It leads right into East Poultney, where there's an adorable little mom-and-pop store and a real gorge with a waterfall. We can get some drinks at the store and then sit for a while by the waterfall. I always go down there when I need to think. It's great."

I fell into step next to her, wondering when the topic of Maggie was going to come up. Should I say something now? Or wait until later, when we were alone in the house? I needed to do something. There really wasn't much time.

We made our way down the neat little street, past the library and a bookstore with two white cats sitting in the front window, past the church with its pale front doors and a Dunkin' Donuts— all without talking. Finally, as we crested a small hill next to the high school, Sophie turned to look at me. "Feeling any better?"

I nodded. "Yeah, much."

"Good. Fresh air is always the best thing when you feel light-headed."

We walked a bit more.

"It really is a cute little town," I said. "I like it."

"Me too." Sophie sighed softly. "You know, I'd never even heard of Poultney until I saw the ad in the paper for the house. But when I came down to see the place, I just fell in love with the house and the town. I'm so glad I bought it." She kicked a stone in her way, watching as it bounced and skidded along the road. "So how're Mom and Dad?"

I shrugged. "Call them. Ask them yourself."

She looked at me out of the corner of her eye. "Oh, we have this thing, the three of us, where we don't talk for a while after a good fight." Her tone sounded easy, bored even, but I could hear fragments of something else around the edges. "It always happens like this. We just have to let enough time pass until we forget what it was we were even fighting about, and then someone—usually Mom—calls again, and everything is forgotten and forgiven—even if it's never mentioned again." She lifted her arms straight above her and stretched. "I think the longest we ever went without talking was about eight months. It was right after Goober was born. I think I called Dad an asshole. Maybe even a fucking asshole." She sighed. "It took him a while to get over that one. It just takes time, whatever it is. Always, always time."

"Don't you think that's kind of stupid?" I asked. "I mean, no offense, but why didn't you just call and apologize to Dad for saying that, instead of wasting all that time not talking?"

"Who said it was wasted time?" Sophie asked. "I don't consider not speaking to them for eight months wasted time. It was actually a pretty good time, now that I think about it."

I shook my head, pushing down the angry annoyance inside me. It was a little after nine in the morning, but I could already feel the heat beginning to prickle the tiny hairs on my arms. The trees on either side of the street were a deep jeweled green. Small clusters of cornflowers and stalks of Queen Anne's lace dotted the sides of the road, and the drone of summer insects murmured around us.

"Listen," I said, taking a deep breath. "I have to talk to you about something."

"Ahhh…" Sophie reached into her pocket and withdrew her cigarettes. "So there *was* another purpose to the trip."

"Sophie." I said her name gingerly, as if it might break. "I know about...Maggie." It felt strange to say the name, stranger still to imagine all over again that it had once been attached to a real person. A sister of mine. And hers.

Sophie's lips pinched the cigarette in her mouth. It was still unlit. She withdrew it carefully, staring at it between her thumb and forefinger for a moment, and then reinserted it once more. Cupping her hands carefully around it, she snapped open her lighter, held the flame to the tip, then placed the lighter back inside her pocket. A deep hit from the cigarette produced a yarn of smoke from her lips. Finally, she nodded. "Okay. Then they finally told you." She studied something in the distance. "When?"

"A day or two ago." I tried to think back. "The night of my graduation. You'd already left."

Sophie nodded, inhaling deeply again on her cigarette.

I waited, but she didn't say any more. "Sophie, why didn't *you* ever tell me about her? Mom and Dad said they were trying to protect me, but what about you? How could you keep something like that a secret all these years? Didn't you think I had a right to know?"

Sophie turned her head, looking out across the enormous field to our right. Whip-slender stalks of grass fretted to and fro in the breeze, and a weeping willow, large as a locomotive, clouded the air with blooms. "They told me not to," she said slowly.

"Who did? Mom and Dad?"

"Yes. They told me never to talk about it. And I didn't." Her voice had taken on a numb-sounding quality. She turned her head again so she was looking directly at me. "But it was eating me alive, Julia. That was the whole reason why I came down for your graduation. So that the four of us could start talking about it. Or try to, anyway."

"Seventeen years later? You finally thought it was time to start talking about it *seventeen* years after she dropped dead from an asthma attack?"

"Asthma attack?" Sophie looked startled.

"Yeah. That's what Mom and Dad told me. That Maggie had terrible asthma. They said that's what she died from. She got all worked up and started crying really bad, and..." Sophie's face paled. She had dropped her cigarette. "That's what they said, Sophie." I took a step toward her. "When she was four. What's the matter? Why do you look like that?"

"What else did they tell you?"

"Not much, really." My voice shook. "Sophie. What's wrong? Isn't that what happened?"

Instead of answering, Sophie turned around and began walking back toward town. "Sophie?" She kept moving, faster and faster. Little clouds of dust kicked up around the backs of her boots and the cuffs of her overall pants drooped against the sidewalk. "Great! You're just gonna turn around and leave? Without answering me?" She moved farther ahead, creating more distance with every step. I lifted my hands and then let them fall against the sides of my legs helplessly. "Fine! Go ahead and leave then! It's the only thing you ever do when things get hard!"

She stopped. Her hands clenched into fists as she whirled around and marched back in my direction. Pieces of her hair had come loose from underneath the bandanna. She was breathing hard. "That is *not* what happened to Maggie." Her words came out with great effort, as if part of her was trying to old them back. "They did not tell you the truth."

"Then what is the truth?" I whispered.

She stared at me, her eyes as big as the cornflowers on the road. "You know what?" she said. "I don't even fucking know anymore."

"What do you mean, you don't *know?* Of course you know! Dad said you were there! He said you saw everything!"

"Dad said that?" Sophie's voice was hoarse. "That's what he said?"

"Sophie." I put my hands on her shoulders. My fingers were trembling. "Sophie, just tell me about Maggie. That's why I came up this weekend, okay? I wanted—I felt like I needed—to get your side of the story. That's all. It's not a big deal, Sophie. Whatever it is. Just tell me, okay? Tell me what happened."

———

Later, it seemed that the whole world fell away from us in that moment. The wind stopped blowing. The insects ceased their humming. Even the trees and the flowers shrank into the distance, fading against the tall grass, disappearing into the green.

It was just Sophie and me on that road, under the hot sun, looking at each other for the very first time.

"I can't," Sophie said, shrugging my hands off. "I thought I could, but I can't. I just can't."

And then she turned and walked away from me again. This time I let her go.

chapter
19

A huge part of me wanted to run after her, to yank her by the arm, spin her around, and scream, "What do you mean you can't? This is our family we're talking about! You can and you will!"

But I didn't. Those kinds of words might have worked on me, but Sophie was someone else entirely. I was afraid to keep pushing, afraid of what it might do to Sophie, afraid of what Sophie might do to me.

Instead, I watched as she raced back into town, her legs making long, determined strides over the sidewalk, her spine tall and rigid. She had shoved her pack of cigarettes into her back pocket, hitched up the waist of her overalls, and her arms swung by her sides. Only her chin, which was lowered slightly, gave the slightest indication that anything was wrong. When I couldn't see her anymore, when she made the turn into the driveway of her little ramshackle house, I turned around and started walking in the opposite direction.

I didn't have the slightest idea where I was headed. From what Sophie had said earlier, if I kept going straight I would either end up at some mom-and-pop store in East Poultney or at the bottom of a gorge. I didn't even know what a mom-and-pop store was, and I sure as heck wasn't interested in hanging out in the bottom of a gorge. I made a sharp right instead, and walked swiftly down a shaded dirt road behind the high school.

It felt good to move again after so much time in the car, even if my legs did feel like tree trunks and there was a sour taste in the back of my mouth. What was I supposed to do now? There was no study guide in the world that would show me the steps to follow after a family secret had been exposed. Another one of Dad's attorney mantras drifted through my brain: *"Well, what are your options?"* My options? I didn't *have* options. I was here in Vermont for thirty or so more hours and then I had to go home. I had to start an internship at the courthouse, get ready for college, finish registering for fall classes at the University of Pittsburgh.

Didn't I?

There were a lot more trees on this road, and a lot fewer houses. A thick canopy of green blocked out the sun, scattering the road with pale, leafy shadows. I kept going, slowing only when I heard a whirring sound ahead, followed by two emphatic grunts. White and purple irises swayed beneath the front windows of a yellow house, while the lawn (woefully in need of a good cut) stretched out before it like a hairy carpet. Pieces of shale formed a kind of haphazard path through the grass, and the front door was dressed with an enormous wreath made entirely of what appeared to be little white rocks. At the top of the house, a thin line of smoke curled out from inside a brick chimney.

It was like looking at a painting, or turning the page in one of the fairy tale books Mom had read to me as a little girl and seeing this house—this very house, in all its perfect imperfections—spread out before me.

"That's where I want to be," I thought.

Right there.

Right now.

Inside that house.

Nowhere else.

Another grunt—louder this time—followed by a slapping sound, made me jump. I tiptoed forward a little bit, keeping close to the thicket of bushes on my right. Someone was pacing back and forth across a brick patio in the backyard, muttering under his breath. His baggy pants hung low over his hips, while the sleeves of a cotton shirt were pushed up to the elbow. A black hat, soft and droopy, sat atop brown shoulder-length hair, and his hands and arms were covered with dried mud all the way up to his elbows.

He paused from his pacing suddenly, to stare down at a strange looking contraption on the left-hand side of the patio. It had a backless chair, three legs, a broad, flat surface with a wheel in the middle, and another smaller ledge above it. Without warning, the man reached back and kicked the whole thing to the ground. One of the legs broke off instantly, sailing through the air like a miniature baseball bat, while the rest of it slumped against the patio. I gasped instinctively and took a few steps backward.

The man looked up, his dark eyes narrowing as he spotted me. "Hey!" He strode across the grassy lawn, his muddy hands clenched into fists. "Who are you? What're you doing back here? This is private property!"

I turned, ready to bolt, when I realized that he didn't look that much older than me. Plus, he was kind of cute. His face was smooth, with just a shadow of a beard around the edges, and the outer edge of his left ear was pierced with tiny silver hoops. He was wearing black Converse sneakers, and a wide silver ring on one of his thumbs. "I'm sorry," I said, taking a few steps back just to be safe. "I'm not from here. I was just taking a walk, looking around."

He was in front of me now, hands on his hips, breathing with a slight effort. Up close I could make out a tiny white anchor that had been sewn onto the front of his hat, and the color of his eyes, a light green with an amber starburst pattern around the iris. "Do I know you?" he asked.

"No." I took another couple of steps. "I'm leaving. Sorry."

"Where're you from?"

"Me?"

"Yeah." He nodded. "You."

"Silver Springs."

He blinked.

"In Ohio," I added quickly.

"Ohio?" he repeated.

"Yeah." I felt a twinge of defensiveness. "Why? Is there something wrong with Ohio?"

"Nothing's wrong with Ohio. It's just . . . far."

"It's not that far." I shrugged, as if the trip had been the easiest thing in the world. "I made good time."

"So what're you doing in Poultney?"

"Visiting my sister. She lives here."

"Who's your sister?" he asked, crossing his arms over his chest. "I know everyone in this town."

"Sophie. Sophie Anderson?"

His forehead lined into a frown and then relaxed again. "Oh wait, is she the one who's renovating the house on Main Street?"

"Yeah. That's her."

"It's gonna be a deli or something, isn't it?" He uncrossed his arms and held one out straight in front of him. With the fingers of the other hand, he began scraping off chunks of mud.

"A bakery, actually."

"You here to help her out or something, then?"

"Oh no. I'm just here for the weekend. Just today, really. I'm leaving tomorrow."

"Not that close, huh?"

"Excuse me?"

"Your sister and you. You're not that close, are you?"

I bristled. "What makes you say that?"

"Well, you live in Ohio, and she lives here in Vermont, and you've come all this way for a visit, but you're only staying for a day..."

"Because I have to get back," I said indignantly. "Besides, just because I don't get to see her much doesn't mean we're not close. People can be close without seeing each other."

He nodded, still immersed in the task of cleaning his arms. "True."

"Why're you covered with mud?" I asked, emboldened by the personal nature of his last question.

He looked up at me and grinned. He had a beautiful smile that spread across his whole face, and small chiseled teeth. His nose had an odd sort of flatness to it—just at the tip—as if someone had leaned in and pressed it against the palm of his hand, but it only added to his good looks. "This isn't mud," he said. "It's clay." He jerked his head toward the back of the house. "I'm a potter."

He was a potter? He didn't look much older than Milo. "How old are you?" I asked.

He laughed a little. "What's that got to do with anything?"

If Mom had told me once she'd told me a hundred times never to ask people their age. It was horrible manners. I dropped my eyes and kicked a little at the dirt around my foot. "No reason. You just ... look kind of young, I guess. To be a potter, I mean."

"I'm twenty-four," he said. "And I wasn't aware that there was an age limit for potters. How old are *you*?"

"Seventeen," I answered. "Almost eighteen."

"You gonna be a senior this year?"

"Actually, I just graduated. I'm going to college in the fall."

"Oh. Cool. I'm going to Seattle in the fall."

"Seattle?" I repeated. "To do what?"

"Set up a pottery studio. Do my own thing."

I looked up, studying him for a moment. "What kind of pottery do you make?"

He went back to picking the dried clay off his arms. "Stonewear, mostly. Vases, mixing bowls, mugs. I just finished a big pitcher that..."

His voice trailed off. "Well, actually, the pitcher didn't turn out that great."

"Was that what you were kicking around up there?"

He snorted. "Among other things."

"Rough day?"

"You have no idea."

"I'm having one of those days myself," I said.

He stopped picking. "Your sister?"

I didn't answer. It was Sophie, sure. But it was so much else too. Even if I couldn't put it into words yet.

He looked back down when I didn't respond. Shrugged a little. "Whatever. It's none of my business." He stuck out his hand suddenly. "Aiden," he said.

"Julia." I took his hand in mine. It was warm and rough. "Nice to meet you."

"And you."

"Well, I have to get back." I didn't have to get anywhere, really. It just seemed like the thing to say. "Good luck on your pottery." I paused. "Or should I say, cleaning up your pottery."

Aiden raised only his left eyebrow. "Thanks."

I started walking down the road again as he moved back up the lawn. But I paused again as the stone wreath on the front door caught my eye. "Hey, Aiden!" I yelled.

He turned. "Yeah?"

"Did you make that wreath on the door?"

He shook his head. "That's my dad's!" He cupped his hands around his mouth. "He's into making weird stuff like that. It amuses him."

I smiled and waved. "Tell him I like it!"

Aiden lifted his arm. "Will do. Later!"

"Later?" I thought to myself, walking down the remaining length of road.

Later when?

My head began to pound along the inside of my temples as I crossed Main Street. Sophie's house was less than half a block away. I stopped when I glimpsed her blond hair in the distance. She was sitting on the railing of the front porch, her hands braced on either side of her. Her back was to me, and her feet swung in front of her.

What if I didn't leave tomorrow? What if I stayed? What would happen if I gave Sophie the time she obviously needed to talk about Maggie? The sudden thought sent prickles along the tops of my arms. Mom. Dad. The internship at the courthouse. Mom. Dad.

Jesus. I would have to call Mom and Dad. They would say I wasn't staying on course. Which I wasn't. Suddenly, inexplicably, I was thinking of veering off in my own direction. And the worst part about it was that I wasn't even sure if it was the right thing to do. What if I was making a huge mistake? What if, by staying here for however long it was going to take, I was screwing up everything they had worked so hard to lay down for me, brick by brick, year after year?

I squeezed and unsqueezed my hands as I watched Sophie light a cigarette and exhale the smoke toward the porch ceiling. A chip of paint, large as a lemon, fluttered down and landed lightly on top of her head. Sophie reached up with one hand and pulled it out of her hair. She looked at it a moment, and then threw it—hard—across the porch. Her shoulders slumped as she steadied herself along the railing again, and her head hung low between them.

"Okay," I whispered to myself as I resumed walking again. "Okay, Sophie. All right."

chapter
20

"Hey," Sophie said as I came into view. She put out her cigarette against the porch railing and stuck the butt into her pocket. Even when she was younger, Sophie had always been big about not littering. "I was just starting to wonder if you were going to come back. Where'd you go?"

"Just for a walk." I sat down at the top of the steps, resting my forearms against my knees, and looked out across the street. The maroon awning over Perry's front window cast a strange rectangular shadow on the sidewalk.

"Yeah?" Sophie hopped off the railing and came over to sit by me. "Where to?"

"Just around."

She nodded. The unsaid thing about Maggie hovered heavily between us, a dark invisible shape. I could almost feel her approaching it and then pulling back. Tiptoeing up only to turn and run away again.

"So listen," I heard myself say, even before I had a chance to think about saying it. "I've decided I'm gonna stay."

"What?" Sophie asked.

"I'm gonna stay. Here." I patted the boards of the porch next to me. "With you. I thought… you know, that you might want some help with the bakery and stuff, and that I would hang around for a while. For however long it takes."

Sophie didn't say anything. But she wasn't really breathing either. "Really?" she said finally.

"Really."

A little whimpering sound came out of her mouth, and she blocked it with both hands. "I just… God, Julia, I don't know what to say. I've never actually talked about it. Maggie, I mean. I guess I need some time."

"I know. That's why I'm staying." Holy shit. I had actually said it. Twice, even! The magnitude of my decision loomed suddenly before me. I pressed my lips together but the sob coming up from the back of my throat was too big. It pushed its way out like a fist, exploding into the air before me in a loud puff of sound.

"Julia!" Sophie moved in close to me, the side of her leg pressed up against mine. "Julia, it's okay! Really, it's okay. You don't have to stay." She said the words over and over again, while circling her hand on the small of my back. "Listen to me. I'll be fine. We can work this out some other time. Really. It's not a big deal."

My crying slowed when she said that. "No, it *is* a big deal." The words hurt as they emerged from my clenched throat, but I said them again anyway. "It is a big deal. It's our lives, okay? It's…" I let my forehead sink against the heels of my hands as fresh tears sprung to the corners all right my eyes. "It's… everything, okay? And I'm staying for you, Sophie, but I think I might be staying for me too. I don't know. I just . . . I want to stay."

Sophie didn't say anything, but her hand kept up its steady circling along my back. Her face was close to mine. A cigarette smell drifted out from her hair.

"Okay." I lifted my head finally, tried to shrug her hand off. "I'm okay."

"Chill," she said.

"I'm still staying," I said softly. "Don't think I'm not still staying just because I broke down and cried a little. I can't help it. Things overwhelm me sometimes, that's all."

Sophie guffawed softly. "Join the fucking club."

We sat there for a few moments, just breathing. The air seemed heavy suddenly, but light too, full with the sensation of new possibilities.

After a while, Sophie cleared her throat. "Jules?"

"Yeah?"

"I just want you to know that this is probably the nicest thing anyone's ever done for me." She paused. "Ever."

I sidled an inch closer. Slipped my arm through the crook of hers. Rested my head on the curve of her shoulder.

We stayed that way for a long while—not saying anything—as people continued to fill and then empty Perry's restaurant across the street.

chapter
21

Sophie convinced me to lie down for a while, and I did not object. I was still exhausted from my all-night trip, and the emotional toll from my decision had given my limbs a Gumby sort of quality. Still, I unpacked my clothes from my suitcase, refolding them neatly and sliding them into the dresser drawers. The room I was staying in looked and felt a little like an empty barn. The least I could do was keep it neat. The sound of scraping drifted up from outside as Sophie got back to work, but I rolled over to one side and stared at the almond-colored walls until my eyes grew heavy and finally closed.

A thrumming noise from the corner of the room woke me. It was coming from the top of Sophie's dresser. I stood up unsteadily. My phone, which was next to a small ceramic dish filled with dried lavender and a picture of Goober as a baby, was vibrating violently.

My heart lurched as I peeked at the front of it.

"Hello?"

"Jules?" I closed my eyes at the sound of Milo's voice. No one said my name like he did. No one in the world.

"Yeah?" I paused, and then said, "How'd you get my number?"

"I asked Zoe for it." I could hear the sound of a Certs clicking against his teeth. "You don't mind, do you?"

He asked Zoe for my number? "No, it's fine. It's just...you've never called me before."

"I know. Actually, I've been trying to call you for the last three days. Do you usually not answer your phone?"

Three days? He'd been trying to call me for three whole days? Was he serious? "Oh, I turned it off. I've been sort of busy."

I stretched out on the bed again and pressed my fingers against my rib cage. Beneath it, my heart was bouncing around like a tennis ball.

"Oh." He coughed. "So listen, I hope this doesn't sound too weird or anything, but I was wondering if maybe you would meet me somewhere. Like at Mo's downtown? We could get some coffee and...I mean, there are some things I want to tell you. Things I should've said the other night at Melissa's party."

I almost laughed then, realizing that he had no idea where I was, and wiped my eyes with the back of my hands. "No, actually I can't."

"Yeah," he said, a little too quickly. "You're still mad then, huh?"

"No, I'm not mad. I'm in Vermont."

"Vermont?"

"Yeah, you know that little New England state that makes really good maple syrup and has all the different-colored leaves?"

"Did you go visit your sister?"

"Yeah, I did."

"Oh," Milo said. "Well, that's cool. When're you coming back?"

I paused. "Well, I was going to stay just for the weekend. But then I changed my mind. Just this morning, actually."

"Oh." There was a trace of anxiety in Milo's voice. "So how long will you be up there then? Zoe said you had an internship. You'll be back for that, right?"

At the mention of my internship, my throat got tight. I got up from the bed and walked over to the window. There was a tiny Laundromat across the street, right next to the House of Pizza. Rows of washers and dryers lined the opposite walls. I wondered if Sophie did her laundry there.

"I don't really know how long I'm going to be here yet," I replied. "Sophie and I... we're kinda going through some stuff, that's all. And we need time to figure it all out. The internship... well, I can't worry about that right now."

"Wow." Milo's voice was soft. Maybe even a little impressed. "Okay. Well, have you told your parents?"

"Not yet."

"What do you think they'll say?"

"I can't even imagine." I tried to laugh, but it didn't come out.

"You think they'll be okay with it?"

"No."

"Yeah," Milo said softly. "I don't either." He paused. "You're okay, though. Right?"

"Yeah. I think I am."

"Well, that's what counts then."

I could hear him grunting softly as if he was shifting his pillows behind him. "Are you sitting in that little window seat upstairs?" I asked suddenly.

"Yeah." He sounded surprised. "How'd you know that?"

"Just a guess," I said.

Neither of us said anything for a moment. If he were here in front of me right now, I thought, I would take him over to Perry's and watch him eat breakfast. Maybe he would order the special, those horrible-sounding creamed chipped grits or whatever they were. Or maybe he wouldn't order anything. Maybe we would just sit at the table by the front window and look at each other over the steam of our coffee cups.

"Listen, will you tell Zoe that I'm here?" I asked. "I haven't called her yet and I don't want her to . . . you know, worry."

"Sure," Milo said.

I could hear the sound of charged air in the phone between us. More than anything at that moment, I wished I could reach through it and touch his face. Even if he pulled away again.

There was a long silence.

"Listen, about the other night," Milo said finally. "When I told you I . . ."

"Can you not?" I interrupted. "Not now, I mean." I took a deep breath. "I don't mean to be rude. It's just that with all the stuff going on here I really can't take one more thing on my plate right now."

"Okay," Milo said. "But . . . is anything wrong?"

My eyes filled with tears. "No."

"All right. Well, will you at least let me know when you're back in town and everything? I'd really like to...get together. Just for coffee or whatever. No big deal."

"I'll call you," I promised.

chapter
22

I waited until Sunday to call home. After everything that had tran-
spired the day before, the thought of any more excitement gave me
a headache. I slept restlessly for most of the night, but when the
first slivers of light peeked over the edge of the bedroom window, I
slipped out of bed and headed outside. Poultney was still as a post-
card. Not a car or a person in sight. Even the air was motionless, as
if holding its breath until the sun finally made its decision to appear.
I snapped open my phone, and held my breath as it rang.

"Hey." Zoe's voice was thick with sleep.

"Hi," I said. "I just wanted to call and tell you myself that
I'm going to stay in Vermont for ... a little while. Maybe even a few
weeks—I'm not sure yet. My sister and I are going through some
stuff, and ..."

"Thanks for the update," Zoe said. The hurt in her voice was
palpable. "Milo filled me in yesterday."

"Zoe ..." I bit my lip. "About what I said in the park the other
day ..."

"Yeah, no, it's cool. Actually, you know what? It's fine."

I closed my eyes.

"You have fun," Zoe said. "Eat a lot of maple syrup. And you know, call me when you get back. If you feel like it."

I opened my eyes again as the dial tone sounded.

Her words felt like a slap in the face.

But maybe I deserved it.

I walked a long time before calling home. And when I finally did, I sat down, as if the weight of what was coming might be too heavy to withstand. An empty field loomed before me, wide and green as an ocean, edged on one side by a small tangle of wild rose bushes. Behind them, the sun continued its slow ascent, washing the sky in gold.

Mom answered, as I knew she would. Her voice was bright and crisp, devoid of sleep. She'd been up for hours. "Hi, Mom."

"Hello, sweetheart. I was hoping that was you. Are you on the road yet?"

"Not yet. Listen, can you ask Dad to get on the other line? I need to talk to both of you."

There was a pause. "Is everything okay?"

"Yeah." I tried to make my voice sound casual. "Everything's fine."

"All right. Hold on." There was the bustle of movement, Mom's hushed, firm voice waking Dad, and then the jangling of the phone as Dad lifted it to his ear. "Okay, honey," Mom said. She sounded slightly more far away. "We're both on."

"Morning, Julia," Dad said. "Everything okay? You need something?"

I cleared my throat. "No. I mean, yeah, everything's okay. But I need to tell you something. Both of you."

"All right." Dad's voice was louder now, with forced expectancy.

"Well." I cleared my throat again. "I, I'm going to stay here. In Vermont. For a little while longer."

"Oh." Mom's monosyllabic answer was barely a whimper, which I might have missed if I hadn't been listening for it.

"Okay," Dad paused.

"Sophie and I . . . we need to work some things out. Between us. And it might take some time."

The silence on the other end of the phone was deafening. I fixed my gaze on several dandelion seeds as they danced along in the wind, scattering like a handful of rice. "Hello?" I said into the phone. "Are you there?"

"Are you sure, Julia? Is this something you really want to do? Right now, I mean?" Mom was pleading. Before I could answer, Dad jumped in.

"Your mom's right. You and Sophie should definitely get together and discuss whatever things are bothering you, but now is not the time. I worked very hard to secure that internship for you at the courthouse, and there is no guarantee—none at all—that I will be able to get the same thing for you next summer."

"But . . ."

"Actual courthouse experience is invaluable, Julia. Especially for a prelaw major. You will be able to include it on your resume.

Before college. If you stay in Vermont, honey, that opportunity will be gone."

"Yeah, I know." I could feel myself starting to deflate, the surety I had felt just moments before floating off into the wind along with the dandelion seeds.

"You've worked so hard to get to this point, Julia." Mom's voice was unsteady. "You don't want to mess things up now."

"How would it be messing things up?" I asked. "It's not like I'm telling you I'm not going to go to college. It's just an internship I'd be backing out of."

"It is not just an internship," Dad said firmly. "It's the establishment of real, viable contacts in a court of law. Where, if you work hard enough, you will be practicing your own cases someday."

"God, Dad. I don't know."

"You don't know what, honey?"

I don't know anything right now. Not like I thought I did. "I'm just trying to figure a lot of things out," I said instead.

"What things?" Dad asked. "About Sophie? Maggie?"

"Yes." I bit my lip, realizing something for the first time. "And me too, Dad. Stuff about me."

"What are you trying to figure out about yourself, Julia? College? Are you worried about going away?"

"No," I said. "Going away isn't the problem."

"Then what is?"

"I'm just trying to figure out what's best for me."

"Oh, sweetheart," Mom said. "Just come home. We just don't want to see you throw away any opportunities that might open future doors. You have to trust us on this one."

My phone beeped.

"Can you hold on one second?" I asked. "Someone's on the other line." Before they had a chance to answer, I switched over.

"Dude, it's me," Zoe said.

"Hey."

"Have you talked to your parents yet?"

"I'm talking to them right now. They're on the other line."

Zoe made a snorting sound. "How's it going?"

"How do you think it's going? I gotta go. They're waiting."

"Wait! Wait!"

"What?"

"So listen, I was still kind of pissed before, when you called," Zoe said. "About the argument we had and everything. I've been lying here, though, thinking about all of it." I held my breath. "You know I love you more than anything, Jules, but I don't want to see your face anywhere near Silver Springs for the rest of the summer."

I exhaled. "Gee, thanks."

"You need to stay there, Julia. You really do."

"Why?" I lowered my voice to a whisper, as if Mom and Dad might somehow be able to hear me through the other line. "Why do you think that?"

"It's just a feeling I have." Zoe paused. "A gut feeling that tells me you'll regret it for the rest of your life if you don't."

"Really?"

"Yeah," Zoe said. "I don't know what the details are, or what's going on between you guys, but I'm pretty sure your sister needs you right now, Jules. *You*. Not your parents. Not a therapist. Just you." She took a deep breath. "After everything you told me about her and the whole deal with Milford…that's just how I feel. Plus, it's not gonna hurt anyone if you get a little time to yourself to figure some stuff out. You deserve it. Anyway, that's my speech. That's what I should've said the first time you called. You do what you want, obviously. I gotta go get a Dr Pepper. I'm dying of thirst."

"It's seven in the morning, Zoe."

"Exactly. I'm usually on my second one by now."

"Thanks, Zoe," I said.

I held my breath as I clicked back over to Mom and Dad. "Hey," I said. "You guys still there?"

"We're here," Dad said.

"So…I'm gonna stay." I said the words carefully. "I've decided that's what I want to do right now. I don't know how long it's going to take, but I'll keep in touch."

Dad cleared his throat roughly. "Have you heard anything we just talked about, Julia?"

"Yeah," I said. "I heard you. I heard every word. I love you guys. I'll talk to you later." I let my hand drop slowly to my side, still holding the phone, but I did not hang up.

"Julia?" Mom's voice, tinny sounding and far away, came through the receiver. "Julia? Are you still there? Honey?"

More dandelion seeds scuttled in front of me, their feathery shapes silhouetted against the morning light.

"Julia!" Dad demanded. "Julia Anderson!"

I reached down with my thumb and closed the phone.

chapter
23

Sophie was outside, scraping paint off the side of the house, when I got back from making my phone calls. The muscles in her tattooed arms, bared beneath a sleeveless T-shirt and denim overalls, strained like smooth extension cords under her skin. Two braids, which hung down on either side of her face, had been tied back neatly with her red bandanna. She stopped when she saw me and put down her scraper. "You're an early riser too, huh?"

"Not really. I couldn't sleep much."

She frowned. "You okay? You look like you just ate a plate of worms or something."

I laughed lightly. "Actually, I just got off the phone with Mom and Dad."

"Oh, yeah? You tell them you were staying?" Sophie picked up her scraper again, looking at me out of the corner of her eye.

"Of course I did. Why else would I call them?"

"What'd they say?"

I leaned against the side of the house. "Oh, they were thrilled.

They told me it was about time I did something like this and that I should stay as long as I could."

Sophie grinned. "That's the kind of modern, progressive people they are." She stopped for a minute, and let her hand fall down against her leg. "Seriously, though. You okay?"

I shrugged. "Yeah, I'm okay."

"Good." She pointed to another scraper sitting on top of a pile of rags. "That one's for you. Watch me first." She slid the little metal tool across a length of curling paint. Brown flakes dropped like a cascade of dirty snow against her boots, landing in a neat pile on the grass next to them. "Not so hard, right?"

"I guess not."

She stepped back, making a space for me. "Go ahead. You try it."

I picked up the scraper and then slid it across a new strip of paint. Halfway through, it caught and stuck, bending the tool backward and spewing minuscule spatters of paint up toward my face. "Ugh!"

"Don't worry," Sophie said, brushing at my cheeks with her fingers. "It just takes some practice. You'll be okay." She reached into her pocket and pulled out a blue bandanna. "Tie this over your hair. Otherwise, you'll get little flakes of paint in it. They're impossible to get out." She nodded at my khaki pants and T-shirt. "You got any crappier clothes than that?"

I shook my head.

"Upstairs," she said. "Second drawer in my dresser is where I keep all my work clothes. Take whatever you need."

I plodded upstairs slowly, placing my phone down next to the baby picture of Goober, and got out the clothes. It was weird that I fit into Sophie's overalls. For the first time I realized that I wasn't smaller than her anymore. I walked into my room to change and saw a notebook on the dresser. It wasn't just a regular notebook. It was a sketch notebook, with a charcoal hand and pen drawn on the front. The pages were heavy, like thin cardboard, and there were at least two hundred of them.

"Sophie?" I came back outside again, holding the notebook up questioningly.

Sophie grinned. "You like it?"

"What's it for?"

"What do you mean, what's it for? It's for you, dork. So you can draw. I'm good company, but I'm not gonna be able to entertain you 24-7." She shrugged. "Not that you need entertaining, but I thought you might want to doodle a little during some of your down time."

I put a hand on my hip, ready to tell her I didn't draw or doodle, that she shouldn't have gone out and bought me something just because she was glad that I was staying. But none of it came out. Instead, I just stood there looking at her, a vague gratefulness rising inside of me.

"It's not a *pony*, Julia." Sophie shrugged. "It's just a sketch pad. Use it if you feel like it, or leave it in your room. It's not a deal breaker, okay?"

"All right." I put the pad down gently and picked up the scraper. "You want me to work right here next to you?"

"Nope." Sophie shook her head. "Other side." She grunted as her scraper got caught behind a chunk of paint. "Let's get started. I work on the outside of the house in the mornings, when it's still cool out. In the afternoon, we'll move inside. It's still early. We can work for a few hours and then break for breakfast."

It didn't take long to get the general hang of the scraping. But it was just about the most boring thing I'd ever done. And I wasn't very good at it. It was a messy job, which, with my lack of expertise, I only made messier. In a matter of minutes, my hands and wrists were covered with so much flaked paint that I looked like a giraffe. So were my overalls, my sneakers, and my T-shirt. We were working at eye level now, scraping the sides of the house we could reach easily. It was going to be impossible, I thought, once we got to the lower—or upper—sides of the house. And how long would it take? Weeks? Months? The whole summer?

Across the street, the lights had been turned on inside Perry's. A few men idled again in front of Stewart's, coffee cups in hand. The sky was full of light now, waiting for the day—and the rest of Poultney—to awake. I lowered my head and kept scraping.

Sophie meandered over to my side of the building about ninety minutes later. She stood back a few feet behind me, crossed her arms, and surveyed my progress. "Not bad, Jules. You skipped a few spots here"—she reached over and pointed—"and here, but that's okay. You can get them later." I bit my tongue. Signing up to help out around the house for a while was one thing. Getting criticized for how I did it was a whole other deal. "Why don't you put your stuff down and go wash up," she said. "We can go across the street for breakfast."

I was ravenous. But my arms were so sore I wasn't sure if I was going to be able to hold a fork properly. I held them under the stream of water, letting the liquid run through my sore fingers. A large blister, smooth and white as a mushroom cap, was beginning to form at the base of my middle one. I rummaged through Sophie's medicine chest in her bathroom until I found a box of Band-Aids and stuck one over the blister.

Sophie was waiting for me on the front porch. "There you are!" she said. "Hungry?"

I nodded eagerly. "What about Goober?" I asked, falling into step next to her as she crossed the street. "It's Sunday. She should be coming back today, right? From camping with Greg?"

Sophie lifted her chin a little and then scratched under it. "They actually called last night while you were asleep. Goober begged me to let her stay with Greg for the rest of the week. They're having a blast." She shrugged. "What could I say? It's the summer, right?" I nodded, trying not to let my disappointment show. At this rate, I'd never get a chance to see my niece.

The warm, salty smell inside Perry's made my stomach rumble. It was only nine o'clock, but the little restaurant was already full. Walt and Lloyd lifted their arms simultaneously as Sophie came into view. Jimmy stared out the window.

"Working hard out there!" Walt said approvingly.

"Looking good!" Lloyd echoed.

Sophie clapped her hand over the top of my shoulder as she paused next to their table. "She's gonna stay, boys! My baby sister's gonna stay and help me fix up the house!"

Walt raised his eyebrows. "Hey, that's great!"

"Sure," Lloyd said. "I see how it is. You tell us to back off, but your sister comes to town and she gets free rein of the place." He grinned and sucker punched Sophie lightly in the arm. "How long are you staying?" he asked, looking at me.

I squirmed uncomfortably and picked at the Band-Aid on my hand. "I don't know yet." I glanced over at Sophie, who nodded and grinned.

"Long as it takes, boys. She's gonna stay as long as it takes."

"Well, let me help you out today." Lloyd nodded in my direction. "She ain't gonna make very much progress if she keeps using that scraper the way she is. All she's doin' is prettyin' up the grass."

I frowned. People sure were generous with criticism around here. And I wasn't too happy about them sitting in here watching me through the front window while I worked. Even if these guys were supposed to know everything. Honestly, it creeped me out a little.

Lloyd ran a thick finger over the space between his nose and upper lip. "You're going up, down, over, across, backways, and sideways, Julia. You ain't gettin' nowhere that way. You gotta keep that scraper going straight. In the same direction." He mimed the correct way to use the scraper, holding both hands up near his face and then pushing them forward in a straight line. "Nice and straight. Over and over. The whole time."

Sophie put her hand over my shoulder again. "Go easy on her, Lloyd. She's just starting out."

"Oh, come on, now!" Lloyd said. "Startin' out's the easy part. You don't go easy on someone when they're just startin' out. You go easy on someone when they've got blisters on top of blisters and they're about ready to throw a hammer at someone." He grinned. A large silver tooth flashed on the side like a nickel.

Sophie slapped Lloyd gently on the shoulder and winked at me. "We'll remember that, Lloyd. Thanks." She gave a wave to the other men. "We're gonna go eat. See you a little later."

"Get the special," Walt said.

"What is it?"

"Ham and gravy with biscuits. It'll knock your socks off."

chapter
24

Neither of us got the special. I ordered the pancakes again, with a side of scrambled eggs, two pieces of bacon, and a large orange juice. Sophie decided on two eggs over easy, a homemade buttermilk biscuit, and three sausage links.

"Can I ask you something?" Sophie asked, after we had settled back against our chairs. Her stubby fingers, tipped with blunt, dirty fingernails, were threaded through the handle of her mug.

"Sure," I said.

"What's it feel like to be a valedictorian?"

I shrugged and looked down at my placemat. "You have to come first in your class if you want to stand out."

"Huh," Sophie said. "I thought you might've given me something a little bit more interesting than that, Julia."

I began to fold the edge of my napkin back origami style. "Like what?"

"I don't know. Awesome? Incredible? Everything you always dreamed of?"

"Maybe it wasn't my dream," I said, folding my napkin more tightly. "Maybe it was someone else's dream for me."

Sophie paused, her toast halfway to her mouth.

"My turn," I said quickly. "I have a question."

Sophie blinked. Then she picked up her fork and stabbed at the yolk of her egg. Yellow goo bled out slowly. "Go ahead," she said softly.

"It's about Maggie," I said.

Sophie stopped chewing.

"I just want to know what she looked like, Sophie." I spoke quickly, as if my words might stop her from getting up and running out of the restaurant. "That's all. Can you just tell me what she looked like?"

Sophie's jaws resumed working again. She rubbed a piece of toast in the middle of the yolk, and put it in her mouth. "You mean when she was four or when she was a baby, or what?"

"Either, I guess…" I let the words trail off. I hadn't really thought about it.

Sophie shrugged. "Well, which one? She was around for four years. Do you want to know what she looked like when she was born, when she was one, two, three…"

"Stop it!" The words came out louder than I expected. Walt and Lloyd turned in their seats. I pushed my napkin over my mouth, and lowered my eyes. "Stop it, okay? You're being a jerk, and you know it."

Sophie inhaled deeply and then set her fork down. "Listen," she said. "I'm not trying to be a jerk. If you want to know the truth, I was up all night trying to figure out how to tell you everything, and I still don't know where to start."

"You don't have to start anywhere," I said miserably. "I know this is going to take time. And I'm staying because I want to give you that. It's just...it's hard not knowing."

"I know." Sophie put her hand over mine. "And I want to tell you how it happened, you know? The right way. In order, I mean. First this, then this, then that." She raked her fingers over the top of her bandanna. "I just want to make sure I get it all, okay? There's so much, Jules. Every time I think I'm ready to start telling you something, I think of something else that I forgot, and then I get so worried about not telling you everything that I just shut down completely."

For a moment, just for a moment, I tried to imagine what it was that Sophie was going to eventually get around to telling me. Maybe if I were in her shoes, I'd need her to go a little easier on me.

"How about this?" I suggested. "How about if and when a thought comes to you—any thought, it doesn't have to be in order or from the beginning or whatever—and you feel like talking about it, you just say it. Right then. No matter how weird it sounds or how out of place it might seem. Is that something you think you could do?"

All the air seemed to go out of Sophie, as if someone had pulled a cork out of the top of her head. "Yeah," she said. "Okay. That might work."

A few minutes of silence passed. Sophie sipped her coffee, but she didn't eat any more of her breakfast. I finished my pancakes and eggs and pushed my mug forward when Miriam came back around.

"She was beautiful," Sophie said after Miriam had left again. I looked up, startled. "She looked a lot like you when she was a baby. Except instead of brown hair, she had this big, thick tuft of black hair. It was like a mohawk or something. It ran the length of her head, from her forehead all the way to the back of her neck, and just stuck straight up. It was the weirdest, cutest thing I'd ever seen. And she had huge eyes. Wide, wide blue eyes, just like yours. Dad used to call them ocean eyes."

"My eyes are green," I pointed out.

"They didn't used to be," Sophie answered. "When you were a baby, they were blue. They changed to green later."

I sat back, slightly amazed by this tiny fact.

"I loved that head of hair of hers," Sophie continued. "I was only four, you know? Little kids get a kick of out of stupid stuff like that. And I was just fascinated with it. I was always trying to brush it, or clip on those little plastic barrettes when she was sleeping." She shrugged. "It never really worked, though. Maggie had a hard time during her first year. She cried constantly. It was this weird little cry—really soft and sad, almost like she was whimpering. It would've been all right, I guess, if it didn't go on and on and on. It drove me crazy."

Sophie began to trace the rim of her coffee cup with the pad of her middle finger.

"Dad was really good with her then. I don't know how he stood all the noise, but he did. He'd stay up all night with her sometimes, just rocking her and singing to her until she fell asleep. He had a terrible voice, but he'd sing to her for hours. 'Row, Row, Row Your Boat.' 'Rock-a-Bye Baby.' 'Somewhere Over the Rainbow.' Even when she got older, Maggie could never go to sleep unless Dad sang to her first."

I barely breathed as Sophie continued to talk, afraid that if I did, I might miss a single spoken—or unspoken—word.

"Mom and Dad thought all the crying was because she had colic. You know that thing that some babies get where they're just born fussy? They had all these tests done on her, and took her to different doctors, and nobody could find anything, until finally, when she was about six months, I guess, one of the doctors said that he was pretty sure she had asthma. He gave Mom and Dad this tiny little face mask, which they would put over Maggie's face every night. Her medicine, which was being pushed out by an inhaler connected to the mask, would mist over her nose and mouth, so that she could breathe it in. They did that twice a day, every day, until…"

Sophie's face darkened. She rolled her bottom lip over her teeth, and then pulled her package of cigarettes out of her pocket.

"You're not allowed to smoke in here," I said gently.

"I know." She withdrew a cigarette and held it between her fingers.

"Anyway, even with the treatment, Maggie still cried. I didn't understand that it was because she couldn't breathe right, you know? That she couldn't catch her breath. All I could see was this new little person who wouldn't let me touch her hair, who hogged all of Mom and Dad's time and left me out in the cold." Sophie ducked her head, scratched the side of her chin, and then winced. "Once, when it seemed like the crying would never stop, I ran into her room and shook the sides of her crib and screamed at her to shut up." She glanced up at me quickly, trying to gauge my reaction. "And that wasn't all of it. I told her that I hated her and that I wished she'd never been born."

"You were four," I said softly. "You were jealous."

"I know," Sophie said in a way that sounded as if someone else had already told her that—and she didn't believe them, either. "Dad came running into her room that night, pulling at me, dragging me away from Maggie's crib. He had me by the wrist—hard—and he marched me down to my room and shut the door and told me to stay in there for the rest of the night." Sophie's eyes looked through me. "A long time later, after I stopped crying, I crept out into the hallway and sat there and listened to him sing Maggie to sleep. I closed my eyes and pretended that I was in bed, with my purple comforter pulled up to my chin, and that he was really singing to me."

She looked down at the cigarette, which she had begun to clench, and then snapped it in half. Letting the broken pieces fall to the side, she chewed the inside of her mouth and looked up at me. When she spoke again, her whole voice was different, as if she had flipped a switch inside. "Listen, I don't want to demonize anyone by telling you all of this. Especially Mom or Dad, okay? Things happened the way they happened and that's sort of the end of it. I don't want you to think that I'm blaming anyone. I was always sort

"You stink?" Sophie grinned.

"A little."

"That's nothing," she said. "Wait'll I get you up on that roof. Then you'll know what it feels like to sweat."

I smiled, groaning inwardly. This was by far the most laborious physical activity I had ever done in my life. How much harder was it going to get?

Sophie swatted me on the side of the arm. "I don't want to burn you out, though. You've done enough for today. Go upstairs, take a shower, and lie down for a while. Relax. I was thinking we could order some Chinese food for dinner. They've got a great place just a few miles away. You like Chinese food?"

"Love it."

"Chicken and broccoli?" she asked, pointing her scraper at me.

"Shrimp and snow peas," I said. "Extra spicy."

"You got it," Sophie said. "Go get clean."

———

The shower felt good against my hot skin, almost like a salve. I stood under it for a good while, letting the water run over the planes of my face and down my hipbones. I had two more blisters on my fingers, and my shoulder blades hurt when I tried to rotate them, but when I got out of the shower I felt strangely refreshed. The scent of Sophie's mint and grapefruit body wash lingered on my skin, and my hair smelled like apricots. I fastened my hair back with a rubber band and pulled on a pair of clean jeans, a T-shirt, and shoes. Then I headed downstairs.

Sophie was sitting on the side porch, smoking a cigarette and talking on her cell phone. "Yes, I *know*, Greg," she said. "You've told me that at least a million times. Hold on, okay?" She pressed the phone flat against her shoulder. "What's up? You're not going to lie down?"

I shook my head and pointed to the phone. "Is everything okay?"

Sophie dismissed the question with a wave of her hand. "Oh, yeah."

"Is Goober there?" I asked. "Can I say hi?"

"She's napping," Sophie said. "We'll call her tonight."

"Okay," I said. "I'm gonna walk around then. I'll see you in a little while."

"Go down to East Poultney!" Sophie said as I headed down the driveway. "I'm telling you, you'll love the gorge! It's beautiful!"

chapter
26

I told myself I was going to keep walking in the direction of East Poultney. I'd read about gorges. And now that I thought about it, there had actually been a question about a gorge on my SATs. But I'd never seen a real gorge before. It would be interesting. Something different. An adventure.

Except that when I came to the fork in the road behind the high school again, my feet had other plans. In ten minutes I found myself at the foot of the little yellow house again, studying the flagstone path that zigzagged through the grass and the strange stone wreath on the door. There was something about this house, I thought. Something that made me want to stay, to go inside and take off my shoes and sit down in one of the kitchen chairs. It would smell like cedar and apples and the wooden table in the center of the kitchen would have an enormous jelly jar in the middle of it, filled with wildflowers. Along the windowsills would be a line of the same small stones that were in the wreath, set up like so many round dominoes. The only sound in the house would be my breathing, or maybe the soft footfalls of a cat slinking in and around my chair. Nothing else. No one else.

A faint whirring sound from the back of the house made my heart beat a little faster. I moved up the lawn cautiously, wondering if Aiden would come charging down again like he had the last time and order me off. The whirring sound got louder as I reached the top. I flattened myself against the side of the house and then rolled my eyes. What was I doing, sneaking around some strange house like this? This was so stupid. Practically stalkerlike, if you really thought about it. Which was not me.

I turned around quickly and headed back down the expanse of lawn.

"Hey!" I froze as Aiden's voice charged out at me. "Julia?"

He had the same black hat on his head, and the same black Converse sneakers. Only his T-shirt—red, with a print of Pink Floyd on the front—was different. I thought fast. "Oh, hey, Aiden. Hi. Um… sorry to bother you. I was just looking for something. From the other day, I mean. I think I might've dropped it around here." I scanned the grass around my feet helplessly. "On the lawn, I mean."

He strode down toward me, his lanky frame tilted back slightly from the pull of the hill. "What'd you lose? I'll help you look for it."

"Oh, it's nothing." I took a few steps backward, desperate to get out of the lie. I hated lying. Plus, I wasn't good at it. "Seriously. Go back to work. It's nothing."

"No, really." He was in front of me now. "I was gonna take a break anyway. What'd you lose? I'm good at finding things."

Damn. "I, um, I think I lost an earring. But seriously, it's not a big deal. I can totally get another pair."

But Aiden was already hunched over, peering through the grass. "Tell me what it looked like," he said. "Gold? Silver?"

I closed my eyes, scurried a few feet away from him, and then quickly, furtively, withdrew one of the small rectangular amber studs that Mom and Dad had given me last year for my birthday. "Um...they were amber," I said. "And sort of...rectangular shaped." I gasped and made a show of reaching down into the grass. "I found it! Here it is. Oh my God, I can't believe I found it!"

Aiden came over toward me. "Cool." He watched intently as I reinserted the earring. "Amber's a great stone. I don't blame you for wanting to find it."

I nodded, relieved the scene had ended.

"Did you just get in?" Aiden asked.

"In?" I repeated, before I realized what he meant. "Oh no. Actually, I never left. I've been here. In Poultney. All week."

"Oh yeah?" Aiden shoved his hands into the pockets of his jeans. "What happened?"

"Nothing, really. My sister and I just decided that I would stay a little longer. We wanted to, you know, extend our visit."

Aiden raised one eyebrow.

"What?"

He shrugged. "Nothing."

I could tell he didn't believe me. So what? What did I care if he knew what was going on with Sophie and me? In the first place, it was none of his business. And in the second place, well, it was none of his business.

He motioned briefly with his arm. "Come on up," he said. "Now that you're staying a while, I can show you the stuff that I do." I didn't move. "If you want to, I mean." He shrugged. "You did seem interested before."

I watched the soles of his Converse sneakers as I followed him up the hill. The laces, tied carelessly in a single knot, drooped on either side in wide loops. It reminded me of the time Dad tried to teach me how to tie my shoes: "*bunny ear, bunny ear, criss-cross, loop*." For as intelligent as I was—even back then, at four years old—this simple task had eluded me. I simply could not, no matter how many times I tried, get the bunny ears to cooperate. Finally, I had kicked off my shoe, hurling it across the room in exasperation. Dad had been shocked by my outburst. Speechless even, for a moment. "That's something I would expect Sophie to do," he said finally. "Not you, Julia." The disappointment in his voice—as well as the comparison to Sophie—was something I never forgot. Ever.

"Holy cow," I said now, surveying the patio, which seemed more or less to have been transformed into a pottery studio. There was even a partial roof over half of it, shadowing the bricks underneath. A brick wall, no higher than my knees, was flanked at either end with flat, raised pedestals. On top of each pedestal was a design made out of little white stones.

"Did your dad make these too?" I stared down at one. It was a starfish. Tiny stones, no larger than ladybugs, had been arranged into what looked like swaying pieces of seaweed on either side.

"Yeah." Aiden stood next to me, regarding the starfish. "That was the first one he ever did. It took him about a year. The other one"— he stopped and pointed at the other end of the wall—"only took him about six months. He's gotten pretty good at it now." I walked down to examine the other design. It was a tree with bare branches. No leaves at all. Just stark limbs, stretching out in all directions, like spindly fingers.

"They're so beautiful," I said, running the pads of my fingers along the pebbly surface. "And so sad."

"Sad?" Aiden raised his left eyebrow again. "How do you get sad out of a stone tree? Or a starfish?"

I shrugged, embarrassed suddenly, and walked over to the large contraption I'd seen the day before. The broken leg had been reattached with duct tape. Several magazines had been wedged under it for leverage, but it still sat at a slight angle. In the middle was a large mound of pale brown clay. "Tell me about this thing. What is it?"

"This," Aiden said, squatting down to examine the taped leg, "is my Laguna Pacifica Glyde Torc 400." He looked up at me. "Or your basic pottery wheel. I was right in the middle of centering a new piece when you came by."

"Centering?"

"Yeah," Aiden said. "After you prepare the clay, you've got to center it on the wheel. It's actually pretty hard to do. Sometimes it takes me four or five times to get it just right."

"Can you show me?"

"Now?" Aiden asked.

"Well, yeah. I mean, if you want to."

Aiden hesitated, but only for a moment. "Okay." He straddled the little chair attached to the far end of the wheel and yanked off the mound of clay in the middle. "Centering is pretty much just what it sounds like," he said. "You've got to make sure your clay is directly in the middle of the wheel. Otherwise, you'll just fight the clay the whole time you're trying to shape it." He turned the mound over, looked at it, and then plopped it firmly on the wheel. "Doesn't look too hard, does it?"

"Not really."

"Okay, now comes the hard part." He looked up at me expectantly. "You ready?"

"Yes."

Aiden pressed a pedal beneath the wheel with his foot. It began to turn, slowly at first, and then more rapidly. I sat down along the edge of the wall, watching as his hands pressed and pulled and shoved the clay between them. His whole body tilted as he leaned into the wheel, almost as if he was forcing the clay in a direction it didn't want to go. Suddenly, like a tree trunk growing at superspeed, a column of clay began to rise up from between his fingers. And then in the next moment, even under his flat, steadying palms, it flopped over and sank down into a heap. It looked like a crushed baby elephant's trunk.

Aiden sat back. "And that is what happens when your clay has not been centered properly." He began scraping the mound off the wheel again. "You know, all the glory around this process goes to the shaping and the decorating and even the firing of the clay, but centering is really the most important thing of all. None of your pieces will ever work unless the middle is strong enough."

He started again, putting the clay down and kneading it back and forth as the wheel began to turn. Small grunts came out of his mouth as he worked. Overhead, a few yellow leaves from a birch tree fluttered lightly, and somewhere in the distance I could hear a dog barking.

"I think it's . . . ," Aiden said. "Come on, come on!" All at once he sat back, his hunched shoulders releasing themselves, and exhaled. "There she is!" he said. The wheel was still turning and the clay had not been shaped into anything worth mentioning. But it was centered. And even as it sat there, pale and bloblike, I thought it looked almost strong. Maybe proud, even. And ready.

chapter
27

I could smell the Chinese food as soon as I walked into the house. My stomach growled. I'd been so immersed in Aiden's pottery lesson that I hadn't even realized how hungry I was—or how long I'd been gone. By the time I walked back, the sun was low in the sky. Not quite dusk, but still. I'd been gone for hours.

"Jules?" Sophie's voice came out from one side of the house.

"Yeah, it's me. Where are you?"

"Living room," she said.

The living room was completely empty, except for the red and white checked tablecloth Sophie had spread out on the floor. Two stubby-looking candles, their flames soft and flickering, anchored opposite corners, and white cartons of food—some with chopsticks sticking out of the middle—had been placed in the middle.

"Oh, it's so nice!" I squatted down, crossing my legs in front of me, and reached for a carton. It was filled to the brim with shrimp, snow peas, slivered carrots, and water chestnuts. I pulled a large pink shrimp out with my fingers and stuffed it into my mouth. "Mmmm. Spicy shrimp is my favorite. Thanks!"

"I never knew you liked Chinese food." Sophie picked up a carton of brown rice and began eating it with chopsticks. "You should've said something. Mom and Dad and I would've taken you out to a Chinese place for your graduation."

I shook my head, trying to form words around the wad of food in my mouth. "Mom's allergic to MSG."

"She is?" Sophie's chopsticks paused by her lips. "Since when?"

I shrugged. "Since forever, I guess. I don't know. We've never eaten Chinese at home."

"Where do you eat it then?"

"Zoe and I get it a lot."

Sophie sighed softly. "Thank God for Zoe."

I stopped chewing. "What's that supposed to mean?"

"I'm just glad you have a friend like that," Sophie said.

"Like what?"

"Like..." I could tell Sophie was backtracking, choosing her words carefully. It made me even angrier.

"Like what?" I said again.

"Why are you getting all bent out of shape here?" Sophie put her chopsticks down. "What'd I say?"

"Nothing. But I can just tell you're going to say some judgmental thing about how Zoe brings me out of my shell or how pitiful I would be without her."

"Pitiful?" Sophie repeated. "Julia, the last word I would ever use with you is pitiful. Pitiful is some helpless little thing. An injured rabbit, maybe. Or a bird with a broken wing. Not you. Ever."

I inhaled tightly through my nostrils. The spiciness of the shrimp had cleared them considerably. "Okay then, what were you going to say?"

"All I meant," Sophie said, "is that I'm glad you have someone who exposes you to different things." She leaned forward a little, put her hand on my knee. "I mean, you have to know by now that Mom and Dad have kind of raised you in a bubble all these years. They've protected you from a lot of different things." She shrugged. "I'm just glad Zoe's there to remind you that life isn't a bubble. That's all."

I plopped the shrimp carton down. "Just because I didn't know about Maggie doesn't mean I was raised in a bubble, Sophie. I've had a totally normal childhood, just like every other kid out there."

Sophie cocked her head. "I'm not saying your childhood wasn't normal. I'm just saying it was the one Mom and Dad planned out for you."

"Of course they planned it out for me! All parents plan their kids' lives." But even as I said it, I could feel something sinking inside.

"Up to a point," Sophie finished. "You're eighteen now, Julia. Or you will be, at the end of the summer. And you're still going along, step by step, exactly by the rule book Mom and Dad made up for you the day you were born. The one that said we couldn't talk about Maggie. The one that said I was too messed up to fix. The one that said you—under no uncertain terms—had to be perfect."

I stared at her, realizing suddenly that I was crying, which made me more furious. I brushed my tears away impatiently. "They never said that. They never once used the word 'perfect' when it came to me, Sophie. Never."

Sophie looked at me. Shadows from the candles flickered across her face, illuminating her right eye. It was a light green color, made even paler by the light. "Jules," she said softly. "After everything that happened with Maggie, and then how screwed up I got..." She shook her head. "I'm not saying it was their fault. But you were all they had left. And they wanted to make damn sure that after the mess with the first two kids, their last kid came out great. Perfect, even."

"Why do you keep talking about yourself like you're some kind of freak?" I was pleading with her now, begging her to take it back. Didn't she know what it did to me that she saw herself as just a screwup? We came from the same parents, had the same blood. If she was a screwup, then what did that make me? "You're not screwed up. You're not too messed up to fix."

Sophie shrugged. "I know what I am," she said. "And I'm working on it. You, though, you need to figure out who you are. For yourself."

I shook my head to block out the sound of her voice. This was way too much for me. Figure out who I am? What did that even mean? Was that just some statement to make me feel better? To sidestep the real issues—whatever they were? I couldn't be sure anymore. I wiped my hands on a napkin and stood up. "You know what? I can't do this any more. I'm going to bed."

Sophie stood up too. "Jules, come on. Don't."

"You need time for your stuff." I gritted my teeth. "And I need time for mine. So back off, okay?"

She dropped her eyes.

I left her there, the candles still burning in the empty room, and went upstairs.

I lay in bed for a long time, listening to Sophie move around downstairs, trying not to revisit the things she had said to me. But they were there, rolling around inside my head, hitting and clicking off each other like so many marbles in a game. It was like I could actually feel my life, a large, perfectly stitched leather bag, splitting apart at the seams. Rip. Rip. Rip. Any minute now, everything inside was going to come spilling out until it all lay in a pile at my feet. Then what would I do?

chapter
28

Once, when I was ten, I'd come home from fifth grade with all A's.
The only blip on the screen was a B in gym, which I'd gotten because
I couldn't climb the long, dangling rope hanging from the ceiling.
Mom's face lit up when she saw my report card and then dimmed
again as she spied the B. "What happened in gym?" she asked. I told
her about the rope. Two days later, Dad installed a thick length of
rope from the garage ceiling. Every night after dinner he took me out
to the garage and helped me work on my climbing skills. He even
started me on a push-up and pull-up routine to improve my upper-
body strength.

I rolled over impatiently in bed. Lots of parents did stuff like
that, didn't they?

There was another incident—this one outside of school. I was
in eighth grade and had been invited to the movies by a girl named
Rachel Terwilliger. She was shy and quiet like me and I was thrilled
that she had asked me to go. Mom insisted on picking up Rachel
so that she could meet her mother, and then drove us to the movies.

We had explicit instructions to call her as soon as the credits started rolling so she could come back for us.

But when the movie was over, Rachel wanted to walk home. I hesitated. I wasn't allowed to walk anywhere alone after eight p.m. I wouldn't be alone, Rachel argued. And it was only seven thirty. I gave in quickly, afraid that if I didn't she would never ask me to hang out again. We laughed and talked all the way back. Rachel's house came first and I waved good-bye and set off for home. Mom cut me off at the end of our street, swerving the car into the curb so sharply I thought she was going to hit it.

"Get in this car!" she said. "Right now!"

The lecture I received when I got home has yet to be matched, both in intensity and length. Mom and Dad were beside themselves. Didn't I know, Dad asked over and over again, the things that could happen to me? Out there? Alone? It went on and on. I wasn't allowed to speak to Rachel and I was grounded for three weeks. They needn't have bothered. I never walked anywhere alone again—not that year, or all the ones after. Especially after dark.

Parents did that sort of thing too, I thought, shifting again in the bed. Besides, even if they didn't, Mom and Dad deserved a break. They'd lost one daughter and had all but waved good-bye to Sophie. Of course they would be overly protective with me.

I got up out of bed and walked over to the window. Through the sheer curtain I could make out the lights across the street at Stewart's. There were still a few trucks parked in front; someone was pumping gas into the back of a pickup. Down a little ways, a boy and girl about my age were sitting on the small stoop in front of Perry's.

This wasn't about Mom and Dad, I realized suddenly.

It was about me.

What kind of person had I become after all these years of coddling and sheltering?

And more important, what kind of person might I have become without it?

I walked over to the dresser and took out my phone. My fingers quivered a little as I dialed Milo's number.

He picked up on the third ring. "Julia?"

"Hi."

"Are you back?"

"No. That's why I'm calling, actually. I just wanted to let you know that I'll probably be here for a while. Maybe even the rest of the summer."

"Oh." The disappointment in his voice was palpable. "Wow. I didn't think you'd really stay that long."

"I didn't either," I said. "I mean, that wasn't the plan. Everything just sort of changed though, after I got up here. It's weird, you know?"

"Yeah."

"Milo? Can I ask you a question?"

"Sure."

"If you didn't take me to the prom as a favor, then why did you ask me? I mean, was it just because you and Cheryl broke up and you needed someone to go with?"

Milo cleared his throat. "Sort of."

I bit my lip. "You could've gone with anyone. Melissa Binsko, or Carrie James, or even Samantha Evans. Any of them would've gone with you."

"They're all idiots," Milo said. "I wouldn't have had any fun with them."

"Did you have fun with me?"

"Well, yeah!" He paused. "Did you have fun with me?"

"Yes," I said softly. "Until . . . well, you know, the ride home."

There was a brief silence. "I guess it didn't ruin everything," Milo said finally. "I mean, we're still talking."

I smiled. "Still?"

Milo laughed softly. "Okay, so maybe we've just started talking."

"I'm glad we've started talking," I said. "It's kind of funny, really."

"What is?"

"I mean, you and I have exchanged all of about ten words since you moved here. Most of the time I wasn't even sure you knew who I was."

"What are you talking about?" Milo sounded insulted. "I asked you to the prom!"

"I know. But that doesn't mean you know me."

Milo paused. "No," he said slowly. "I guess not. Jules? Will you call me again? Soon?"

"Yes," I said. "I will."

chapter
29

Although one of the bedrooms upstairs still needed work, Sophie was intent on getting the front room on the first floor in shape first. It had a rectangular front window and wooden floors. A large chandelier, delicate as a jellyfish, hung suspended from the ceiling. Sophie and Lloyd had already prepped the floors and sanded the walls. She still needed to apply primer and a fresh coat of paint, build and install shelves, and put down some kind of new flooring.

"Here," she said the next morning, sticking a paint roller in my hand as we walked back from Perry's. "The primer's over there. You start on the back wall, and I'll work on the front." Breakfast had been a somber event; neither of us had said much or even made eye contact, and Sophie joked around with the weirdos from the Table of Knowledge, which annoyed me and made me feel left out at the same time.

Working inside the house, though, was definitely an improvement from working outside. Not only were we out of the sun's glare, but a roller proved to be a much easier tool to wield than a scraper. Sophie set up a radio, propping it on four old milk crates in the corner, and cranked the volume.

I made a face as a strange-sounding country song came on, but Sophie started slapping the sides of her legs and singing along.

"I shot a man in Reno,
Just to watch him die . . ."

"Who *is* that?" I asked.

Sophie stopped swinging her hips from side to side. "Who is that?" she repeated. "You've never heard of Johnny Cash?"

"No."

In response, Sophie walked over to the radio and turned it up even louder. The man's throaty voice surged within the four walls.

I moved my arm all the way up and then all the way back down again, just like Sophie had showed me. Straight, clean lines. No back and forth. No shortcuts. Lloyd and Walt were probably peering through binoculars over at Perry's, just so they could tell me tomorrow what I was doing wrong. I wouldn't put it past them.

Sophie sang every word of the song right to the end, and then turned the radio back down.

"I can't believe you've never heard of Johnny Cash," she said again, picking up her paintbrush. "The man is a legend. Plus, Dad listens to him all the time."

"I've never heard him in my life," I said.

Sophie stopped painting. "What're you talk . . . ?" Her voice drifted off. "Wow, I guess that was back in Milford. He used to listen to country music all the time. Constantly, almost. That's how I got into it. He played Johnny Cash so much I memorized the whole album." She scratched her head. "Yeah, now that I think about it, I don't remember him listening to it at all once we moved to Silver Springs. Not even once."

I kept painting. More before-and-after information that still didn't add up.

"So what kind of music do you listen to?" Sophie asked.

I shrugged. "Just stuff on the radio."

"Like what? Pop? Rock? Classic rock? What?"

"I don't know. All of it, I guess. Whatever's playing. I don't really have a genre of music I listen to."

There was a pause. Then, "Did you just say *genre* of music?" Sophie had stopped painting and was looking at me from across the room.

"Yeah, so?"

She blinked a few times and then turned back to her wall. "Nothing, I guess. Never mind."

Now I stopped painting. "No, what is it?"

Sophie shrugged but didn't turn around. "Sometimes I forget how smart you are."

"Because I used the word 'genre'?" I paused. "Don't you know what that word means?"

Sophie turned around slowly. "Yes, I know what it means. It means a type of something. A specific subset or genus, if you will."

I was confused. "Well, if you know what it means, then why does my saying it make me the smart one?"

"Because I don't use that word in everyday conversation," Sophie said. "You do."

"Whatever." I turned back around. "You're weird."

"Yeah," Sophie said. "I am definitely a specific genre of weird." She laughed. It was the first time I had heard her laugh since I'd arrived. It was a nice sound.

I kept my face to the wall so she didn't see me smile.

We worked in silence for a while, the only sound the slurp of the rollers against the walls.

"Okay, I have something," Sophie said quietly about ten minutes later. "About Maggie. You said to just say things when they come, so here it is."

"Okay." I could feel my breath catching in the back of my throat. "Go ahead."

Sophie was still facing her wall, painting with wide, steady strokes. "I don't know if Dad still does this or not, but back then, he used to go into the office on Saturday mornings."

"He still does," I said. "He likes to practice his closing arguments when there's no one around."

"Yeah, right," Sophie said. "Exactly. Okay, so it was a Saturday. Mom wasn't feeling well or something, and he wanted to let her sleep in. But he had to go into the office. So he bundled Maggie and me up and took us with him." She turned around finally, gesturing with the paintbrush as she talked. "He got us all set up with paper and pens, and even let me sit at his secretary's desk so I could play with the phone and pretend I was grown up. I was thrilled. More than thrilled. I just remember being so happy that Dad had given me something that didn't include Maggie. Something for me. Even if it was just pretend." She paused, and settled her hand against her hip. "Maggie, though—she was about three at the time—caught on pretty fast that I'd gotten the better end of the deal. She ditched the pen and paper Dad had given her and started bugging me. She was hanging on my legs and whining to get up in the chair and play with the phone." Sophie shook her head. "I remember being so aggravated. God, she just friggin' annoyed the hell out of me. Always whining and needing and crying and begging." She paused. "Fuck."

I had stopped painting, turning away from the wall to listen. Sophie's head was low between her shoulders. "You were just a kid," I offered. "Kids get aggravated by stuff like that."

"Yeah, but I smacked her." Sophie said. "*Hard.*" Her voice shook. "Right across the face. Right against her little cheek." Her lips trembled, and she bit the bottom one with her teeth. "I'll never forget the look on her face. It was just a split second, right before she started screaming, but it was like everything inside of her sort of crumpled. Like I'd stepped on her or something. Crushed her." Sophie looked down at the floor. "It was the first time I realized that she really loved me. I mean, to make her crumble like that."

I didn't like what Sophie was saying. I listened with one ear as she described Dad charging out of his office, demanding to know what the fighting was all about, and then sequestering both girls on opposite sides of the room. For the first time, I wondered if I really wanted to know what had happened to Maggie all those years ago.

"Were you ever mean to her like that again?" I asked.

"I never hit her again," Sophie said slowly. "But I could've been a lot nicer to her too. There were other times…" She stopped, her voice drifting off. "More times, I mean, when I just acted like a jerk. You know, not playing with her, ignoring her when she tried to get my attention." She winced, remembering. "God, she was always trying to get my attention. Sophie! Sophie! Sophie!" She turned around suddenly, ashamed, and dipped her brush back into the can of paint.

I watched her arm move up and down the wall with a new kind of force, the muscles in her shoulders straining as she applied another coat of paint to an already finished section.

I turned around then, and did the same thing.

chapter
30

I was in seventh grade when the call came about Goober's birth. Sophie had been out of the house for almost five years by then, and her visits home—which were already occurring less and less—had dissolved into long, drawn-out screaming matches, mostly with Dad. I remember how long it took to get to the hospital. And how silent it was in the car.

Sophie seemed startlingly skinny when we saw her, especially since she'd just had a baby. Her bare arms looked bony sticking out of the blue hospital gown, and when she got up at one point to shuffle to the bathroom, I could not make out even the smallest curve of a belly. Her face was unnaturally pale too, as if the blood had drained out of it, and her lips were dry and cracked. She was happy to see us, though, and cried a little when Mom hugged her.

The nurse brought the baby out of the nursery, wheeling her into the room in a big plastic bassinet that had been set atop a metal cart. I remember thinking she was not very cute. In fact, she was kind of squished looking. Still, I cooed along with Mom and

Dad as they bent over her, trying to wiggle their index fingers into her tightly closed fists. Sophie leaned her head against the pillow and watched them tiredly.

After an hour or so, Mom and Dad left to get some lunch. I stayed with Sophie, not ready to leave her just yet. She patted the side of her bed and I scooted up next to her. "I'm glad you're here, Julia."

"Me too."

"How's school?"

"Pretty good."

"What about your classes? How're they going?"

I had all As, but I didn't say that. "They're all right. I like my math teacher. He's cute."

Sophie grinned. "I had a cute math teacher once. In tenth grade." She leaned her head back against her pillow. I could see the veins beneath the skin of her neck. "God, that seems like so long ago."

"It was a long time ago."

She lifted her head. "Yeah, I guess it was." There was a pause as she looked over at Goober sleeping soundly in her bassinet. "Can you believe I'm a mother?"

I shrugged. "I guess I'll get used to it." I started to ask about Goober's father, but something inside told me not to.

"Do you think I'll be a good one?" Sophie asked.

"A good what?"

"Mother," she said. "A good mother."

"Well, yeah. Sure. You'll be great." I reached out and pulled the bassinet a little closer to the bed. "Besides," I lied, "she's so cute." I looked back over at Sophie, and was startled to see her eyes pooled with tears. "What's wrong?"

She shook her head. "I don't *feel* anything," she whispered. A single tear rolled down her face as she spoke. "Nothing." I was too afraid to ask her what she meant. Sophie kept talking, her eyes wide and unblinking, as the tears leaked out. "You know that rush of love you're supposed to feel when you look at your baby for the first time?" I nodded dumbly, although I had no idea what she was talking about. "I haven't felt it, Julia. Not once. Not when they gave her to me to hold after she first came out, and not after they cleaned her all up and gave her back to me." She stared vacantly into the basket. "What's wrong with me?" she whispered.

"Nothing." I could think of nothing else to say. "Nothing's wrong with you."

Suddenly, as if someone had shaken her, she blinked, and then pressed the heels of her hands against her eyes. "Oh my God," she said. "I'm sorry. I can't believe I just said all that. I'm so sorry. I have all these hormones swimming around inside of me right now and ..." The color had come back into her cheeks, a deep flush of pink that started at the bottom of her throat and made its way up. She flattened her hands against the sides of them, as if to stop the heat from rising. "Agh!" She uttered a funny little scream. "I'm sorry, Jules. Really. I didn't mean to scare you."

"It's okay." I turned back toward the bassinet, because her apologies made me feel embarrassed. There was no need for them, but she did not understand that.

"You want to hold her?" Sophie asked behind me.

"Can I?"

"Of course you can." Sophie pulled the bassinet over until it was even with her side of the bed. She lifted Goober carefully with two hands and then placed them in the cradle of mine. I couldn't believe how light she was. It was like holding a loaf of bread. Goober stirred a little as the transition was made, and scrunched up her nose, but then she settled back down again and the wrinkles disappeared from her face. Her skin was as smooth as a petal and deep pink. Tiny eyelashes stuck out like the edges of a feather, and her lips were shaped like a heart.

"Wow," I whispered, looking back over at Sophie. "She really is adorable."

But Sophie was looking past me, out the window, at something I could not see.

chapter
31

Sophie got a phone call around four o'clock that afternoon that made her face go pale. "What is it?" I asked. We were still painting and I had paint everywhere—in my hair, on my arms, even on my face.

She snapped her phone shut and shook her head. "Oh, nothing. Just some stupid stuff with the bank. I still have a bunch of papers to sign for the house." Her eyes swept the room as if looking for something. "Listen, let's stop for today, okay? I'm gonna have to go up to Rutland for a little bit. It's only about twenty minutes away, and it shouldn't take long. Will you be all right here without me?"

"Well, yeah. Of course. Are you sure everything's okay?"

She shook her head again. "It's nothing. Seriously. Don't worry about it." She glanced out the window. "I've been using Jimmy's truck when I need to go places, but it'd be great if I could just take the Bug now. You mind?"

"The keys are in my suitcase," I said.

She roared out of the driveway, spewing dust and pebbles

beneath her tires. I watched until the green car made a left at the light, and then I went back inside the house. I pulled off my dirty clothes and got into the shower. Sophie's shampoo did nothing to erase the paint spatters from my hair. I leaned forward, examining the sullied strands in the mirror. It looked like I had a really terrible case of dandruff. Ugh. And my eyebrows were a mess, thick and stiff as barbed wire. I opened the mirror, poking around for a pair of tweezers. There was a tall bottle of pink Barbie shampoo, several packets of matches, a tube of toothpaste, and some dental floss. That was it. I shut the mirror. Of course Sophie didn't pluck her eyebrows. She probably didn't even own a tube of lipstick.

I leaned closer to the mirror again, examining the rest of my face. My skin looked a little more tan. My cheeks were fuller too, probably from all the pancakes I'd been eating at Perry's. There were dark circles under my eyes—most likely from my lack of sleep the night before—and a few blackheads on my nose. Still, not terrible. Even with the barbed-wire eyebrows and paint-speckled hair.

I got into clean clothes and brushed my hair. A tiny pot of blackberry lip gloss was in the bottom of my suitcase. I slicked it over my lips and rubbed them together.

Good enough.

I headed out the door.

Everything seemed to slow down inside as I stood in front of the yellow house again—my heartbeat, the chattering inside my head, even the pulse in my wrists. My breathing became more measured, my anxiety a non-issue. The name of this street was Furnace Road, which puzzled me. If I'd had anything to say about it, I would have called it Shady Tree Lane. Or maybe Maple Leaf Drive. Something pretty and delicate. Something alive and beating.

Aiden was working behind his wheel when I walked up the lawn. His hat was down low over his eyes, and one Converse sneaker tapped out a beat as he swayed slightly with the spinning clay. He stopped when he saw me, and turned off the motor.

"Hey," he said. "You're becoming a regular."

I winced, taking a step backward. "I shouldn't...I mean..."

"Hey, relax," Aiden said. "I was just making an observation. I didn't mean anything by it." He reached out suddenly and, with a swipe of his hand, crushed the small clay shape in front of him.

I gasped. "What did you do that for?"

"It's no good," Aiden said. "I didn't get it centered right."

I held out my hand. "Can I try?" Aiden looked up in surprise. "I mean, if it's okay with you."

"Have you ever worked on a pottery wheel before?" he asked. "No."

Aiden hesitated and then got up from his seat. "Okay." He scraped the mound of clay off the wheel and kneaded it for a few minutes, then handed it to me. I held it in my hands, trying to get used to the feel of it against my skin. It was surprisingly dry—and heavy. Not very pliable either. I could feel the muscles in my fore-arms flexing as I squeezed it, the tips of my fingers pressing until they turned white. "That's it," Aiden said as I worked it back eventually into a mound. "Now put it on the wheel and see if you can get it centered."

I nervously glanced at him out of the corner of my eye and sat down on the little stool. My feet touched a corner of the magazine pile and the wheel was at chest height, directly in front of me. I reached out and pressed the clay down on the wheel.

"Okay, wait," Aiden said. "You can't just set it down all dainty like that. It's got to be attached to the wheel. Really stuck on. Pick it up and try again. And this time, bring your arms up and really fling it down. Use your whole body."

"Fling it down?" I repeated. "Won't I break the wheel?"

He shook his head. "Nope. It's built for that."

I tried to remember the last time I had flung anything anywhere. Maybe a sneaker when I was learning to tie my shoes? The action was so foreign to me that just thinking about slamming the clay down on the wheel made me giggle.

"Come on!" Aiden said. "You can do it! Throw it!"

I lifted my hands tentatively. Bit my lip. Stared at the black marker in the middle of the wheel. And then I let my arms fall, hard. The clay hit the wheel with a dull thudding sound—and then stayed there.

"Awesome!" Aiden said. "Perfect. Now step on the pedal, get her started."

The wheel moved much faster than I expected it to, and I shrieked as the clay began to wobble back and forth. "Lighten up on the pedal," Aiden encouraged me. "And lean in with your whole body so you can get that clay in the middle of the wheel. There's nothing pretty about this process, so don't worry about looking all graceful or anything. Lean in. Give it your whole weight."

He let me go through the process three times. Three times I flung the clay on the wheel and bent over it, trying desperately to push—and then keep—the clay into the center. Three times I failed.

But as I walked back to Sophie's place a little later, I couldn't help but smile.

The clay had a mind of its own. I could respect that.

chapter
32

It was early the next week by the time we finished priming the walls inside, and we were halfway through scraping paint on the outside. We worked until early evening on Tuesday, sanding and cleaning the floor. Walt had loaned Sophie his electric sander, which cut most of the work in half, but Sophie insisted that I do the corners with a small piece of regular old sandpaper. By the time the shadows outside had begun to lengthen and the sun had fallen behind the trees, my fingers were so sore I wondered if they would remain attached if I used them to do anything else.

"Why did you ask those Table of Knowledge guys to stop helping you again?" I asked, struggling to my feet.

"Because I want to do this on my own," Sophie answered. "I like doing things on my own. Come on, let's get something to eat and hit the hay. We've done a lot today. You tired?"

"Tired?" I repeated. "Try exhausted."

She punched me lightly in the arm. "You'll be okay after a good night's sleep. Let's find some grub."

In my opinion, Sophie's kitchen was the best thing about the whole house. With three brick walls—one of which framed a floor-to-ceiling window—real marble countertops (which Jimmy had found in a quarry), upper and lower cupboards, and a wooden pot rack dangling from a length of chain from the ceiling, there was not much else that needed changing. Sophie said she and Jimmy were still thinking about tearing out most of the cupboards to make room for another oven, but that was still up for debate. Now, she opened and shut the cupboard doors, looking for something to eat. "What do you feel like? I can make some pasta, some macaroni and cheese..."

I dropped down heavily on top of a stepladder that was propped against one of the brick walls, and leaned my head back. "Anything's fine. I don't know if I even have the strength to chew."

"I wish I knew how to cook better." Sophie scanned the contents of another cupboard and then shut the door. "I can bake you into the grave, but ask me to put together a chicken dinner, and I wouldn't know where to start."

"Then just bake something. We don't have to have a dinner-dinner. I'll eat anything." I watched through the window as a baby squirrel made its way up the trunk of a large oak tree next to the house.

"Yeah?" Sophie put her hands on her hips. "Okay, then. You feel like some biscuits?" I didn't have to answer. She had already rolled up the sleeves of her shirt and was grabbing flour, baking powder, and salt out of the cupboard. She measured them into a bowl, reached for a pinch of salt and tossed it in. Next, she cut up a stick of cold butter into neat little cubes, poured in a measuring cup of milk, and mashed the whole thing in between her fingers, pressing and turning it inside the bowl. After a few minutes, she dropped a small, round mass of dough onto the flour-sprinkled marble countertop and began pushing it with the heels of her hands.

"What are you doing?" I asked.

"Kneading," Sophie said. She lifted one shoulder, brushing a piece of hair out of her face. "You have to do this to make it soft and pliable. Otherwise the biscuits come out sort of dumpy."

"Dumpy?" I repeated.

"Yeah, like big hunks of Play-Doh." She rolled her hands against the now baby-smooth mound, pulling it back with her fingers. "You gotta give it some love, you know? Get all the rough edges out by pulling it a little this way, and then pulling it a little that way. You'll see."

My exhaustion faded as I watched my sister work. It was exactly the way I remembered, when I used to sit on the step outside the kitchen at home. Sophie's fingers flew over and under and then on top of the dough. Finished with the kneading, she pulled and stretched it into a circle, and then started rolling it with a pin. When she got it to a thickness that she seemed to like, she dipped the rim of a water glass into some flour, then pressed it down into the dough, forming small, perfect circles. She brushed each biscuit with a coat of melted butter, and finished with a sprinkling of sugar, then placed the tray in the oven. Her confidence and the way she knew her way around her ingredients filled me with awe all over again.

"I bet you could bake anything," I said finally, as she set the timer.

"I'll try anything when it comes to baking." Sophie nodded toward the oven. "I've made those biscuits so many times over the years I don't even need a recipe. The trick is the butter. It's gotta be cold."

"You really do like baking, don't you?" I said stupidly.

"I don't think there's anything else in the world I'd rather do," Sophie said. She had started washing at the sink; clouds of soap suds encircled her wrists. A soft, floury scent had already begun to fill the room. "I love everything about baking."

I felt a twinge of jealousy. "I remember one time you told me that your favorite thing about baking was being in the kitchen with a head full of ideas."

Sophie laughed. "That sounds pretty accurate."

"What else do you like about it?"

She shook the soap suds from her hands and then leaned against the sink. For a moment she stared out at the fading light through the window, then she turned back around. "I think the preciseness of it. Baking demands an exactness that I love. It calms me down for some reason. Centers me." She shrugged. "It probably sounds really weird, but I like the fact that when you bake, you have to follow a specific set of rules in order to get the right result." She wiped her hands on the edge of her jeans. "A lot of people like to cook for the exact opposite reason—if they add too much of this or don't have enough of that, they don't have to worry; they can just substitute something else. Not knowing how or what they're going to end up with is exciting, I guess." She shook her head. "Not me. I'd rather know right from the beginning what I'm going to get."

She pulled a dishcloth from her shoulder and began wiping it over the countertop. "Besides, I never feel this way anywhere else."

"What way?"

"Happy," she said simply. "I'm happier in a kitchen than anywhere else."

chapter
33

We had three biscuits apiece, warm and slathered with real butter, along with several hunks of cheddar cheese and cold slices of apple. It was, I thought as I lay in bed later, one of the most perfect meals I could remember having. The biscuits were ridiculously good, pillows of lightness that melted on my tongue, and the apple and cheese were crisp and flavorful. Sophie was still working downstairs, applying a second coat of primer to the front room. She never stopped. I felt guilty going to bed, but she had insisted and I hadn't objected.

Now, after lying there, listening to her muted movements beneath the floor, I got up and padded across the room to the dresser. The sketch book Sophie had gotten me was in the bottom drawer, and I took it out. A soft laugh came from somewhere in the back of my throat as I opened it up and stared at the blank page. God. I couldn't really draw. Drawing was just…something to pass the time. Something that broke up the monotony of studying and thinking and worrying all the time. Though I didn't have to bury it completely. A lawyer was allowed to sketch, wasn't she?

I dragged one of the milk crates over to the window and pushed back the curtains. For a moment I just looked out at the street. Ten feet ahead of me, one of the street lamps threw a small pool of light onto the sidewalk below. Beyond that, the Laundromat, the pizza place, and Perry's sat in the dark.

Suddenly, beneath the street lamp, the squirrel I had seen earlier appeared. It paused for a moment, then sat up on its haunches, nibbling something in its tiny paws. Without thinking, I picked up my pencil and began to draw. First the tiny head and ears. A slightly bulbous stomach, and a thin, bottlebrush tail.

Would I ever be as good a trial lawyer as Dad? Dad had an assertiveness, an arrogant confidence about him that I did not. He'd always said you needed to have self-reliance to stand up in front of a jury. The words you chose could determine the outcome of the entire trial, so *how* you spoke was critical. You had to be staunch. Committed. Fierce. Things that—at least right now—I was not sure I was. Could those qualities be learned? Or did you just have to have it in you, the way Dad did?

The squirrel scampered on, but I kept drawing. The stretch of buildings across the street: the Laundromat, Poultney Pizza, and Perry's, each one aglow under the street lights. I'd never sketched anything in the dark before. It was thrilling in a way, trying to capture the absence of light.

An hour came and went as I moved the pencil across the page. What if Dad had been a banker? Would working with money have appealed to me the same way the law did? What if he were an electrician? Or a cook? Was it possible that I would have latched on to whatever he did? It was hard to know. God, it was hard to know anything these days.

I held my breath as I heard Sophie coming up the stairs. She paused just outside my door..I sat motionless, wondering if she had heard me. But then she moved on, going into the room next to mine and shutting the door.

I kept my lights off and continued drawing.

———

Later, I woke to a strange sound. For about ten seconds, I couldn't remember where I was. My eyes roved frantically around the darkened room, taking in the unfamiliar window and the enormous oak tree, like a peeping Tom, behind the glass. Then my eyes fell on the tiny neon sign blinking in Perry's window across the street and I remembered. But the sound—what was that? I crept out of bed and tiptoed down the hall to investigate.

The door to the next bedroom was open just a crack. A tiny circle of light from a lamp on the floor revealed Sophie propped up on her elbows on top of a bright blue sleeping bag. There was nothing else in the room except for a wadded up drop cloth in the corner. The single window was bare, its edges chipped with old paint. Behind it, the thinnest sliver of a moon illuminated a circle of coal black sky.

Sophie was still in her T-shirt and overalls, but her shoes were paired neatly against the far wall, and she had taken the bandanna off her head. Her braids had been loosened and her hair hung in smooth, yellow waves alongside her face. She was looking down at something small and flat in between her arms—a book? a photograph? a card?—and weeping uncontrollably.

Suddenly, she picked up the object, pressed it to her chest, and rolled over on her side, away from me. She groaned, as if the movement had caused her physical pain, and brought her knees up against her chest.

I thought of going to her. It was probably something to do with Maggie, something she alone had to come to terms with. Over the last few nights, I'd found myself wishing that I had laid down better ground rules when we made the agreement about talking about Maggie. Something more definite than the "whenever she felt like talking about it" arrangement. It gave Sophie too much leeway.

But maybe leeway was what she needed. Maybe I was the one who needed to be more patient. I stood silently, rooted to the spot for a long time without moving, until the soft cries coming out of Sophie turned into slow, hiccupy breathing. Then I turned around and went back to bed.

chapter
34

The next day, on my usual walk down Furnace Road, the growl of a motor sounded behind me. I turned around and leaped to the side of the road as Aiden came hurtling toward me on an orange moped with black flames painted on the sides. Dust flew out from under its wheels, and the handlebars were as thick as arms. He came to a sudden stop, turning the handles sharply so the back wheels spun and growled. "Hey!" he grinned. "I was hoping I'd run into you today. You wanna go for a ride?"

I looked at the ever-present soft black hat on top of his head. "Where's your helmet?"

"No helmet," he said. "We don't have to wear them up here."

"Up here?" I repeated. "You mean you can't get head injuries in Vermont?"

"Something like that." Aiden grinned again. "Come on. This is just a quad. It's not like we're on a motorcycle. And I won't take you out on the road. We'll just stick to the dirt trails in the back." He held out his hand.

I looked down at my shoes.

"Come on," Aiden said. "I'll go real slow."

I looked up.

"Promise." He held up a palm. "Scout's honor."

I took a step forward and swung my leg over the back part of the seat behind him.

"Hold on around my waist," Aiden said, turning slightly to talk to me. His breath smelled like warm coffee. I put my hands tentatively on the sides of his jeans. "Tighter," Aiden said. "Come on, hold on."

"I thought you said we weren't gonna go fast," I said.

"We're not. But you still have to hold on. Otherwise you'll go flying backward." My nervousness evaporated when he said that, and I adjusted my hands, threading three fingers on each through his belt loops. "Atta girl," he said. "Okay, here we go."

Aiden veered off Furnace Road almost immediately, hurtling through brush and leaves until we reached a dirt trail. After the initial heart-stopping sensation of moving forward and my fear of being thrown off the vehicle whenever he turned the wheel disappeared, I sat back as we sped along and actually looked around. We were riding through an entire forest house, it seemed, with walls made only of trees, and a carpet of dirt and pine needles. Up ahead, there were more trees, their leaves green as jade, with pockets of blue sky peeking through, and then more trees after that. The smell out here—mowed grass and sun-drenched hay—was new to me. Aiden's back curved slightly over the handlebars, but I could feel the heat of his skin next to my arms. I closed my eyes, feeling the sun on my face, and wished for a moment that we could just keep going.

We didn't, of course. The quad emerged suddenly from inside the forest house, spinning into an enormous yellow field. Tightly rolled haystacks, thick as tractor tires, dotted the field in a haphazard checkerboard pattern, and overhead the sky was as blue as a marble.

"Want to sit for a while?" Aiden asked, getting off the bike without waiting for an answer. I followed him as he walked over to a patch of grass and sat down. "I love it out here," he said. "Sometimes I run out and leapfrog over all of those haystacks. Just for the hell of it, you know?" He raised his eyebrows. "It's harder than you think."

I smiled. "It's pretty out here. So quiet."

"And the light," Aiden said, stretching out his hand. "Look. It's perfect. Right now, especially, when the sun's low like this."

I'd never really looked at light before. But now, as I watched a few insects swoop lazily through the air, I realized that Aiden was exactly right. There was a clear, amber sort of hue to it, like looking at honey through the bottom of a glass. "I can tell you're an artist," I said.

Aiden looked at me. "How so?"

"The light and everything. You noticing it like that. Regular people don't notice the way light looks."

Aiden stared back out at the field. "You gotta pay attention," he said softly. "To all of it. Otherwise, you might miss something. Anything can change your life. You never know. You just have to be patient. And watch."

We sat there for a few minutes without saying anything.

"I think I'm waiting for my life to change," I said suddenly. What? Where did that come from? "I mean, kind of," I finished.

"Oh, you don't want to do that," Aiden said.

"Do what?" I felt a surge of impatience. He always seemed so sure of himself. It was borderline cocky. Not to mention annoying.

"You don't want to wait for your life to change," Aiden said. "That's a huge mistake."

"You just said..."

"No." Aiden cut me off with a raised index finger. "I did not say to *wait* for your life to change. I said to pay attention for something that *could* change your life. There's a huge difference. If you want to change your life, do it. But don't wait for it to change or you'll be waiting around forever."

I bristled for a moment. The only thing worse than annoying, cocky people was when they were right. "You know a lot for only being twenty-four," I said finally.

Aiden pulled his hat down low over his ears. "I've lived a lot for being twenty-four," he said. "You pick up some things along the way."

"How've you lived a lot?" I asked.

He raised his eyebrows. "Wouldn't you like to know."

I blushed. "Well, it seems like whatever you picked up has worked."

"Maybe," Aiden said. He grinned. "You ever leapfrog over a haystack roll before?"

"I've never even seen a haystack roll before," I said, gazing out at the field. "Those things look like gigantic cinnamon buns."

Aiden was already a quarter of the way across the field by the time I caught up to him. His slender legs cut through the tall grass, and I watched in amazement as he jumped up and straddled a haystack. He cleared it with ease, landing neatly on the other side, and then cupped his hands around his mouth. "Your turn!" he shouted. "Give it a big running start!"

I'm about as athletic as a chess player. And those haystacks were a lot bigger up close than they had appeared from a distance. Still, I ran like hell. And when I soared over the top of that haystack, flying through the air like a sack of arms and elbows, and made it to the other side, I couldn't help it—I screamed like I had won some kind of Olympic medal.

"You okay?" Aiden said, standing over me.

I was flat on the ground, trying to catch my breath. "Yes!" I said, letting him pull me to my feet. "I want to do it again!"

chapter
35

Sophie was upstairs folding laundry when I got back. "Hey!" she said. "How do you feel about a movie?"

"Sure." I leaned against the doorway, watching as she rolled up a pair of jeans and then threw them into her drawer. She did the same thing with her shirts and her overalls, even her underwear. Mom would have a heart attack if she saw how Sophie kept her clothes. She'd spent a good deal of time showing us both how to match up our seams and fold things in thirds.

Sophie pulled a sweatshirt over her head. "We have to drive to Rutland; Poultney doesn't have a theater. It'll only take about twenty minutes." She looked at me strangely. "Were you rolling around in a haystack or something?"

I brushed off a few loose pieces of hay. I hadn't told Sophie about Aiden, and for some reason, I didn't want to yet. "No, I tripped and there was a pile of grass and stuff."

Sophie threw me a sweatshirt. "You'll need one of these. It gets cold here at night. Even in the summer."

I drove. It was the first time I'd been back in the Bug since arriving in Poultney. It felt weird. It felt stranger still to have Sophie next to me in the passenger seat.

"You eat yet?" Sophie asked as we made the turn at Castleton Corners. A sign for Rutland indicated that it was only ten more miles down the road.

"No. Did you?"

She shook her head. "Nope. We can stock up on popcorn and candy, though. Eat till we're sick."

"What kind of candy do you like?"

"Oh, I have a very deliberate strategy when it comes to movie food," Sophie said. "I never deviate it from it, either. Large popcorn with extra butter and a box of peanut M&M's, which I sprinkle..."

"On top of the popcorn?" I finished. "Me too!"

Sophie looked at me and grinned. "You're kidding! I've never met anyone else who did that."

"Oh, it's so good! All that sugar and salt combined?" I grinned, watching a pair of red taillights in front of me. "Hey, did you talk to Goober? She's coming home soon, right?"

Sophie sighed. I felt myself tense, waiting for bad news. "She wants to stay another week, Julia," she said. "I'm sorry."

I wrinkled my forehead. "Did you tell her I'm here? I mean, does she know I'm in Poultney, staying in her room?"

Sophie nodded. "She knows."

"Well…" I struggled for words, at a loss. "I mean, can we go up there? To Greg's? We can…"

"She's not there." Sophie's voice was sharp. "I told you, Jules. They're camping."

"They're still camping?"

"Yes!" Sophie nodded her head. "They're still camping. This is what they do. It's their thing. Especially in the summer, all right? Jesus."

"Okay." My hands were gripping the steering wheel. "God, you don't have to bite my head off."

"I didn't mean to." Sophie leaned her head back against the seat rest and she closed her eyes. "I'm sorry. I'm just tired."

I glanced over at her. She did look paler than usual. The veins in her neck stood out like thin cords, and her eyelids were the color of a faint bruise. Even her hair looked limp and exhausted. "You're working too hard," I said. "You need to take a break, Sophie. Seriously."

"Mmmm…" She did not open her eyes. "That's why we're going to the movies."

"No, a real break," I said. "Like, a few days off from working so you can sleep and do nothing kind of a break."

"Oh God." Sophie opened her eyes. "I don't have a few days. I've got to get this house in shape and the bakery opened before the summer's over. I have to start making some money."

"Well, you're not going to get anything up and running if you're falling down from exhaustion," I argued. "Why don't you at least sleep in tomorrow? You don't have to get up at five every morning.

Seriously. You'll work better and more efficiently if you're well rested."

Sophie was looking at me out of the corner of her eye. "You sound like Dad sometimes. You know that?"

"Dad?" A green Rutland sign came into view. "Do I turn here?"

"Yeah," Sophie said. "The movie theater's right down the block." She paused. "Sounding like Dad isn't a bad thing. It was just an observation."

I snorted. "Any observation you make about Dad tends to be a bad thing."

Sophie sat up straighter. "That's not true."

"It is true. You never have anything nice to say about him. Mom either, for that matter."

Sophie's face creased in the dark. She looked at me for a moment, as if to say something, and then sat back again. "Well, it's hard. We have a lot of... history, the three of us."

"I know, I know." I pulled the car impatiently into the parking lot and turned off the engine. A group of kids were outside the theater, huddled in small groups, punching each other and laughing. "Come on," I said. "Let's get in there before they do."

Sophie was looking at me.

"What?" I asked.

She blinked. "Just... don't make light of it, okay? Don't say things like 'I know, I know,' when I tell you we have a history. It makes it hard for me to say anything when I hear that kind of impatience in your voice."

"All right." I nodded, feeling my face get hot. "I won't."

She stared straight ahead, watching the teenagers. A few of the boys were wearing hoodies, and the girls, in thin T-shirts and jeans, were underdressed for the cool night. Their teeth chattered as they laughed, and they hugged their arms tightly around themselves.

Sophie's teeth worked the inside of her lip, and her eyes squinted against the parking lot lights. Suddenly, she put her hand on the door. "Okay, let's go. I need to pig out and turn my brain off for the next two hours. None of this heavy shit tonight. You ready?"

"Ready," I said, getting out on my side of the car.

We were settled in our seats with extra-large buckets of popcorn, peanut M&M's, and a liter of soda when I leaned over in Sophie's direction. "I'm sorry," I whispered in her ear. "About sounding impatient."

She turned and kissed me on the nose.

chapter
36

The movie was full of inane, disgusting bathroom humor that for some reason struck me as horribly funny. I couldn't remember the last time I had laughed like that. At anything. Sophie laughed too, although she was much more vocal about it, throwing her head back at certain points and whooping. We giggled violently all the way back to Poultney, reliving the funniest parts over and over again. By the time we pulled into Sophie's driveway, the muscles under my ribs ached and I had a stitch in my side. Laughing like that had done something else to me too; I felt lighter somehow, as if something had emptied itself.

"Whew!" I wiped my eyes. "God, I feel like I'm going to puke."

Sophie laughed and got out of the car. "It's still early. You want to go over to Perry's for a cup of coffee or something?"

"Sure."

Perry's was empty except for Miriam, who was reading the newspaper horoscopes behind the counter, and the Table of Knowledge. The three men looked over as we walked in, their meaty faces breaking into grins. Even Jimmy smiled and nodded.

"Well, whaddya know," Lloyd said. "You girls here for a nightcap?"

Sophie made a *pshaw* sound. "We're just here for coffee, Lloyd. Unless you've got anything we can put in it?"

Lloyd laughed and patted his breast pocket. "Nothing that won't burn the lining off your delicate little stomachs."

Sophie raised an eyebrow. "Try me someday."

Walt tapped the space next to him with three fingers. "Pull up a chair, girls. We got the whole joint to ourselves."

Sophie and I exchanged a look. I shrugged. "Okay," Sophie said. She pulled out a chair for me and placed it between Lloyd and Walt. I sat down tentatively, arranging my hands beneath my legs. Sophie pulled up another chair next to Jimmy, turned it around, and straddled the front of it. "We just got back from the movies," she said. "Best thing I've seen in years. I almost wet my pants laughing so hard." She nodded across the table at me. "Even Julia laughed."

The men turned to look at me. "Julia laughed?" Walt repeated. "Well, I'll be."

"Yes, I *laugh*," I said. "I laugh at a lot of things."

"Well, that's good to know," Walt said.

"I've never heard you laugh," Lloyd said. "Hell, I'm not sure I've even seen you smile!"

I grinned hugely, then relaxed my face again.

Lloyd nodded approvingly and eyed his tablemates. "Very nice," he said. "You have good teeth too. You should do that more often."

Just then, Miriam came over with coffee cups and saucers. She set them down in front of Sophie and me and filled our cups. "Anything to eat, girls?"

"Try the lemon meringue pie," Walt said. "Jimmy and I just had a piece. It'll knock you out."

Sophie looked over at Jimmy. He nodded. "Okay," Sophie said. "I'll have a piece of the lemon pie, Miriam. Jules, you want anything?"

"They have strawberry shortcake," Walt said. "With real biscuits. Miriam'll heat it for you too, if you want. I don't know about you, but I gotta have my biscuit warmed all the way through when I have shortcake."

"For crying out loud, Walt." Miriam put a hand on her hip. "Why don't you just rewrite the menu?"

I ordered the shortcake. Miriam brought it over a few minutes later, along with Sophie's pie and fresh coffee. Walt was right. It was delicious. I dug in, spooning up mouthful after mouthful of strawberries, whipped cream, and biscuit until my plate was clean.

"You thought at all about what color you're gonna paint that kitchen?" Lloyd asked. "Or you just gonna leave it bare?"

Sophie licked the back of her fork and then set it down against her empty pie plate. "Funny you should ask. I was actually hoping we could talk about it together. I'd like to paint three of the walls a very light yellow. And I was hoping that Julia would do something to the last one."

I looked up from my plate. "Do something?" I repeated.

Sophie grinned. "Yeah. Draw something. It doesn't have to be anything fancy. You know, maybe a little mural. Of anything."

"You an artist, Julia?" Lloyd asked. Next to him, Walt stuck his thumbs behind his suspenders and looked at me.

I sighed. "Sophie likes to think I can draw because I used to doodle when I was younger."

Sophie sat forward eagerly. "Oh, you should have seen the little pictures she created. Miniature fruit and vegetable people with tiny hats and striped legs." She stopped talking, her eyes getting wide. "Oh my God! That's what I want you to draw! On the wall in the kitchen. You can do a whole scene with the fruit and vegetable people." She bounced up and down a little in her seat. "Will you do it, Jules? Will you, will you, will you?"

"You want fruit and vegetable people on your kitchen wall?" Lloyd asked. "You sure about that, Sophie?"

I stared at my sister, not sure if what I was feeling was embarrassment, anxiety, or pride. She nodded her head eagerly at Lloyd, still looking at me. "I'm one hundred percent sure," she said. "I'd love it. I would totally, totally love it."

The men turned in my direction now. Sophie was still staring expectantly at me, eyebrows high on her forehead, lower lip caught between her teeth.

"Okay," I said. "If you want me to."

Sophie's face split open into an enormous grin. "Fantastic! Thank you."

"A produce-people mural," Walt mused, draining his cup of coffee. "Now *this* I gotta see."

chapter
37

Alone in my room afterward, I withdrew my phone from under my pillow and dialed Milo. The sound of his voice in my ear made me warm all over.

"How are you?" I asked.

"Good. Bored. There's not much to do around this crappy little town, in case you forgot. I got a summer job at the Pantry Quik, though. Night shift. I'm actually leaving in about five minutes."

"The night shift?" I repeated. "Why'd you take those hours?"

"Didn't have a choice," Milo said. "It was that or nothing."

"You reading anything good?" I tucked the phone between my shoulder and chin and reached for my sketch pad.

"*The Tommyknockers*," Milo said. "It's actually better than I thought it would be."

"Is that another Steven King?"

"Yeah. He's a suspense genius."

"Is he another scary truth teller?" I started with his hair, sketching pieces of it this time in a thatched pattern to bring out the thickness of it, ending with a slight curl where the ear would be.

"A what?" Milo sounded startled. "Um…maybe. I never really thought about it that way. Stephen King, a scary truth teller. I guess he could be, if you can tell the truth while you're writing fiction. I don't know." He paused. "Wow. I can't believe you remembered that."

Of course I remembered that. I remember everything about him. "I'm a nerd," I said. "I remember everything, remember? It's my job."

He laughed. "So what're you and Sophie doing? Just hanging out?"

"Hanging out? Are you kidding? We're working our butts off. Sophie's opening a bakery in her house. We're redoing the whole thing. Top to bottom."

"You're redoing the house?" Milo repeated. "Wow. Is it in bad shape?"

I laughed softly. "Yeah, you could say that." I shaded his eyebrows, unruly in the middle where they were the thickest. "But it's coming along. It really is. We've been doing a ton of work."

"I did construction one summer back in Portland," Milo said. "I liked it."

"What kind of construction?"

"Just the roof of a house, really. It wasn't too hard. But I liked being up there, in the bones of it, you know? Seeing everything all laid out like that. And whaling away with my hammer was pretty cool too."

"We have these older guys helping out." I told him about the Table of Knowledge. "But Sophie doesn't use them very often. She's kind of stubborn about it, really, insisting on doing it herself. I think she's trying to prove something."

"Well, maybe you should let her," Milo said. "Maybe she does have something to prove."

I stopped sketching, looking down at the face before me. Milo was right. Maybe Sophie did need to show herself that she could do this. Who was I to stand in her way?

"You doing anything for fun?" Milo asked. "Or just working all the time?"

"Well, I take long walks in the afternoon. And I met a really nice guy on one of them. He's a potter. His name is Aiden. He lives right around..."

"A guy?" Milo repeated.

"Yeah." I felt a twinge. Was that jealousy I heard in his voice? "He's been teaching me how to make things. Out of clay. I told you, he's a potter."

"What's he like, really old?" Milo asked.

"No. He's twenty-four."

Milo didn't say anything.

"What's wrong?"

"Nothing." There was a pause and then, "Aren't you coming home at all? Even just to visit? I mean, your parents must be going crazy."

"No, no visits," I said softly. "I need to be here. I'm staying here until I don't have to anymore. Then I'll come back."

"Yeah. Okay." I could hear Milo getting up and walking around the room. "I kind of miss seeing you in your window," he said. "That's all."

My heart began to pound. "What window?"

"Your window. In your bedroom. The one you sit in every afternoon after school, doing your homework."

Oh, Milo.

"Listen," he said. "I have to go. My boss at the Pantry Quik docks my pay if I'm even two minutes late." He paused, hesitating. "Will you call me again, though? Soon?"

"Okay," I said. "I'll call you this weekend."

"Great," Milo said. "And Julia? If you need anything, anything at all, I'm here. All you have to do is ask."

I put my pad and pencil down and stared out the window for a while after he hung up. Why did there have to be so many layers to everything, so many unseen—and unsaid—parts? Why couldn't everything just be spread out, flat and even, so you could just see it for what it was? It could be like an enormous table, full of food. Over there, next to the mashed potatoes, would be the way Milo felt about me. And on the left, beside the broccoli, would be the way I felt about him. The truth about Maggie would be right in the middle, alongside the centerpiece, and all the reasons for Sophie's anger would be sitting on the plates, ready and waiting. We could come to the table, all of us, and see what it was we wanted, what we felt hungry for. And because we could see it—and even taste it—we could decide if we wanted to take it or leave it.

Did anyone ever do that?

Was there anyone who even knew how?

chapter
38

Two days later, when Aiden offered me another afternoon ride on his quad, I hopped on. We sped through the forest once more, zig-zagging through a maze of tree trunks and pine needles until finally bursting out onto a road.

I gripped the sides of his jacket. "I don't want to go on the road without a helmet," I said. "Seriously. Can we go back?"

"We won't drive on the road," Aiden said. "I just want to show you something." He turned off the motor and beckoned me toward a stone bridge a few feet away. I leaned over the side next to him. Beneath us was a waterfall, set between two sloped—and very rocky—banks. A stream, thin as a snake, wound its way out from under the falls and then disappeared under the bridge. "Pretty," I said.

"This is the East Poultney gorge," Aiden said. "It is pretty. But it's dangerous too. Those rocks are a lot trickier to navigate then you might think." He took off his hat. "I come down here all the time, just to sit and hang out. It's where I get a lot of ideas for my pottery designs."

"You've learned how to navigate over the rocks, I assume." I glanced in Aiden's direction.

"Oh, yeah. I've been climbing around this place for years. It's the people who don't know what they're doing that get in trouble." He pointed toward the rushing column of water. The sound it made, gushing over the boulders, reminded me of a teeming rainstorm—steady, rapid, and forcefully liquid. "Sometimes, when the light is weird and milky, like right before a storm, that waterfall can look almost gray," Aiden said. "Like slate or even smoke. It... I don't know, I love to look at it like that. It's cool."

I stared at the water, trying to imagine it looking like smoke. "I think Sophie comes down here too."

"Sophie?" There was a thin film of dust all over Aiden's face from the ride. It made his features look slightly blurry. "Really? I've never seen her."

I shrugged. "She's been bugging me to come down here ever since I got here. She said I'd love it."

"It's a cool place," Aiden said. "I'm going to miss it."

We stared down into the gorge for a few moments without saying anything. A loneliness swept over me then, as I tried to imagine being in Poultney without being able to pop in and visit Aiden whenever I wanted. I liked his company—and not just because he was cute. "When are you leaving?" I asked.

"Two weeks," Aiden said.

I looked at him in surprise. "Two weeks! I thought you said the end of the summer! Why so soon?"

"I found a studio the day before yesterday. And a roommate too. No use putting off what I can start now."

I gazed back out at the water. "What are you starting now?"

Aiden looked at me. "The rest of my life," he said. "Just like you."

I came into the kitchen the next night to find Sophie beating egg whites in a bright copper bowl. Her hair had been pulled back into a ponytail, and her cheeks were pink from exertion. I leaned against the butcher block. "What's that?"

"Oh, I'm just making a lemon meringue pie for the Table of Knowledge boys. It's been a while and they all love it." Sophie lowered the whisk for a moment and took a deep breath. "This whipping by hand is killing me, though. I gotta start doing some push-ups again— get some more upper-body strength."

"Why don't you use the mixer?"

"Oh no," Sophie said. "I always use my copper bowls when I do egg whites. It's the only way."

"What's so special about a copper bowl?"

"Well," said Sophie, "there are actually ions in copper that mix with the egg white and make them very stiff. Egg whites made in a copper bowl will never fall over or deflate." She glanced up at the rack of pots hanging above her. "All of my pots are copper too. Did you ever notice?"

I stared up at the gleaming pots for a moment. They were a beautiful color, like a burnished pink, and so shiny I could see my reflection in them. "Wow. I actually didn't notice. Who would've thought baking had so much science involved?"

Sophie raised her eyebrows. "Cool, huh?" She picked up the whisk again and tapped it on the side of the bowl. "So. You given any thought to your mural yet?"

I walked over to the wall slowly. It was about the size of the chalkboards we'd had in school—pretty tall and wide. It was going to take a lot of fruit and vegetable people to fill it up. "Actually, I kind of have."

Sophie started beating the lemon filling. "And? What'd you come up with?"

I turned around. "I don't think I want to do it."

Sophie stopped beating. "Why?"

"I mean the fruit people. I don't want to draw the fruit people. I know you think they're cute, but..." I walked over to the butcher block and leaned my elbows on the smooth wood surface. "I've sort of moved on from that kind of stuff, Sophie. There are other things I can draw now, other things I've been drawing. I'd just... I'd like to do something else. If that's all right."

"Of course that's all right!" The words came out of Sophie in one big exhale. Her eyes were wide. "That's more than all right. What were you thinking?"

"Well, I've been fooling around with that sketch pad you got me..."

"Eh? Does big sister know, or does big sister know?"

I smiled. "And I've sort of been sketching... well, the street I guess. From my window at least. With the Laundromat and the pizza place and Perry's..."

Sophie had put the whisk down again. "Oh, Julia." She was

shaking her head. "Main Street? On the wall of my kitchen? It'll be beautiful. It'll be gorgeous. Please do it. Please. I would love it."

"What if it's not good enough?" I asked. "What if you hate it?"

"That's impossible," Sophie said. "I would never hate it."

"How do you know? You've never seen my sketches."

"How could I?" Sophie cocked her head. "Up until this point, you've more or less denied the fact that you even draw."

I looked down at the table. "I don't know. It's just... God, I don't even know if it *is* drawing. It's probably still just doodling. Just goofing around."

"Can I see the picture you did in your sketch pad?"

I could feel my face flush. "Right now?"

"Yeah. Right now."

I shook my head. "I don't know."

Sophie came around from her side of the table and put her hand on top of mine. "Listen to me," she said. "For a long time, I thought that I should try to be somebody worthwhile, like a doctor or a nurse or a teacher. You know, to make my mark on the world. And then after I did that, I could screw around with flour and butter and eggs. Maybe on weekends, when I had extra time. Like baking wasn't a good enough profession. And so I held back from really doing it, from going all the way with it. I told myself I wasn't good enough, that I could never make bread because I was too impatient to let dough rise, and I should *never* try cheesecake because I burned everything made with dairy. But that wasn't really true, Julia."

She took a deep breath.

"You know, people make mistakes doing what they love. That's human nature. What I bake won't be great every single time. What you draw will probably never be perfect. But the biggest mistake people make isn't how well they draw this line or crimp that crust. The biggest mistake people make is never finding or doing what they love at all."

A few silent seconds passed. Outside, I could hear the dull footsteps of someone walking along the sidewalk, the muted roll of tires against the street.

"You found it," I said finally. "What you love."

"I did." Sophie nodded. "And now it's your turn."

chapter
39

Over the next few days, I spent most of the morning in front of the wide kitchen wall, laying out a rough copy of the drawing I had done in my notebook. Sophie and I had gone out and bought me real sketching pencils with soft lead. The difference was astounding, both in texture and smoothness. Plus, the new pencils erased much more easily. Which was a good thing. A really good thing, since I erased more than I drew.

My anxiety mounted every time I took a step back and looked at the wall. What was I thinking? Did that look like a tree or a dying plant? But the quiet thrill that jolted through me each time I stepped back up to it with a new eye, a clearer idea, was unlike anything else I'd felt before.

I kept going.

Drawing.

Erasing.

Drawing some more.

"Can I ask you a personal question?" I bit my lip, waiting for Aiden to answer. Sophie had gone somewhere with Lloyd to pick out more tile for the roof, which meant I had a free afternoon. Aiden had fashioned a rough sort of seat for me out of an upside-down milk crate and a throw pillow so I could sit and watch him work. Just now, he had successfully centered a piece of clay and was beginning the process of forming it.

He nodded, not taking his eyes off his hands. "Go ahead."

"If it's too personal—I mean, if it upsets you or anything, just…"

"Don't worry about it." He cut me off, squinting at the flat clay rim. "Just ask."

"Are your mom and dad…I mean, are they divorced? You said you lived here with your dad, but you've never mentioned your mom."

"My mother died a few years ago." Aiden volunteered this bit of information with such aplomb that I almost gasped.

"Oh my God, I'm so sorry," I said.

"Thanks," Aiden said. "Dad and I have pretty much come to grips with it now, but it was awful for a while. It was sudden—a car accident right outside of Manchester. Middle of the night. Real dark. Rainy. Route 30 is super narrow. No lights. They said she was killed on impact. I doubt the truck even saw her coming."

"God," I whispered.

Aiden rested his hands on his lap and looked at me. "You ever know someone who died?"

I hesitated for a split second, and then shook my head. "No."

"It's so weird," he said. "For the longest time—months!—I thought I was stuck in some kind of bad dream. Like I was asleep and I couldn't wake up. Have you ever had that kind of sensation?"

I nodded. Some days, like the one on Main Street, when Sophie had been so close to telling me, had felt like that. It was hard to shake. Harder still to forget.

"The call came in the middle of the night," Aiden went on, "and I remember Dad waking me up so we could go to the hospital, but none of it felt real. Even when the sun came up the next day and then the day after that, it still didn't feel real. It just felt like... I don't know. Impossible. It didn't... fit, like someone was trying to ram a puzzle piece into our life that didn't fit. And even though it was too big, too wide, too friggin' ridiculous, it still kept trying to push its way in."

He shook his head.

"Did it ever fit?" I asked softly. "I mean, did it ever start to become real?"

Aiden nodded slowly. "I went down to the gorge and camped out by myself for a week. I had to get away from Dad. He was a mess. He'd come home with his pockets filled with all those rocks, you know? He wasn't making anything out of them then; just collecting them. He'd come home and empty hundreds of them out of his pockets onto the dining room table and then sit there with his head in his hands for the rest of the night. It was making me crazy. So one day I just packed up my shit and went down to the gorge."

"And being there, down by the water, made it real for you?"

"Not right away," Aiden said. "It was October, so for the first three or four days I just sat in front of the fire, freezing my ass off and telling myself that I was cool with everything." He paused, starting the wheel a little, cupping his hands protectively around the little piece of clay. "And then on the last night, I was lying in my sleeping bag, looking up at the stars, which was something my mom and I used to do all the time. Except that I couldn't see any stars. Not a single one. It was cloudy, so they must've all been hidden." He shook his head. "It was just so *dark*. Like all the lights in the whole world had gone out. I have never in my life felt so alone. And right then I felt my mother's absence for the first time. I knew that night that she was gone. For real."

"Oh, Aiden." I put my hand on his arm.

"No, it was good," he said. "It was what I needed. Before, I was walking around in a kind of cloud. Not really seeing or feeling or hearing anything. None of it was real. When I felt that... thing rip through me like that, I knew I was going to be okay again. Because I could feel it. Even though it hurt, I could feel it. And that was so much better than not feeling anything at all." He laughed. "I went a little wacky after that, too, running under the waterfall, howling up at the moon like a wolf, screaming and yelling like a banshee." He winced a little. "I don't know. Realizing she was gone hurt more than anything in the world, but it felt good to get myself back too."

A silence settled in between us then; the only sound was the soft whir of the pottery wheel.

"How is your dad with it now?" I asked finally. "I mean, was he able to come to grips with it too? Like you?"

"He's...better." Aiden frowned, thinking. "I think the stone things he makes helps him. My mom used to collect little things like that, especially when we went to the beach. She'd take these long walks and come back with the front of her shirt filled with pieces of beach glass and shells and things." He shrugged. Something passed over his face and then disappeared again. "We haven't been back to the beach since she died," he said. "But I think it helps Dad to keep collecting things for her."

I had to restrain myself from reaching out and hugging him.

Instead, I picked at the skin along the edge of my thumb and didn't say anything more. Neither did Aiden.

The late afternoon light waned along the horizon, a pale curtain settling over the curve of blue. And when the shadows lengthened across the road and the church bell sounded its evening knell, I said good-bye and walked back to Sophie's.

chapter
40

I took a long bath that night, soaking in Sophie's claw-foot tub with the raised sides and curled edges. It wasn't very clean, and the metal soap dish was rusted on the bottom, but the water was warm and sudsy and smelled good, like coconut cream. My mind drifted back to Aiden, and the conversation we'd had earlier. "*It felt good to get myself back too.*" What a concept, getting yourself back. What did that even mean? And why, if I didn't understand it, did it keep resonating so deeply with me?

I slid under a pile of suds as a faint knock sounded on the door. "Julia?"

"I'm in the tub!"

"I know you're in the tub," Sophie said. "I heard you running the water. Can I come in?"

I leaned forward, scooping more suds over the exposed parts of my body, and then sat back again. "Okay."

Sophie walked in. She was holding a plate of something that looked like pale brownies in one hand. "I just made a batch of blondies. I want to sell them in the store, but I need you to tell me what you think first. I'm not sure I added enough chocolate."

I took a small bite of one as Sophie settled herself into a corner and set the plate down next to her. "Ooh, I love them!" I took another bite. "Why do you call them blondies?"

Sophie pulled out her cigarettes. "They're the same idea as a brownie, except reversed. Less chocolate. More cake."

"Well, I want another one. And if you had these in the store, I would buy at least two dozen."

"Awesome." Sophie grinned and offered the plate to me again. I took two this time.

"Aren't you going to have one?" I asked.

"I already did," she said, lighting a cigarette. "I'm blondied out."

I chewed thoughtfully, watching her smoke. "Do you smoke in front of Goober?"

"Absolutely not." Sophie peeled a bit of tobacco off the tip of her tongue. "Never have, never will."

I settled my head back against the tub. A faint water stain, like a splash of old coffee, shaded the far corner in the ceiling. "Well, I'm glad. She doesn't need to see you doing that."

Across the room, my sister's voice bristled. "I agree," she said. "That's why I don't."

An uncomfortable moment passed between us. Then I sat up and looked directly at her. Tiny wisps of hair stuck out from behind her ears. "Have you ever been in love?" I said finally. "I mean *really* in love?"

Sophie's fingers, which were just poised to take the cigarette out of her mouth, froze for a second. Then she smiled. "Yes."

"With who?"

"Eddie Waters," Sophie said.

"Eddie?" I stared at her wide eyed. "From high school? Really?"

Sophie tilted her head back against the wall. "Oh God, I adored Eddie. Every single thing about him, right down to the last black curly hair on his stomach. I would have gone to the ends of the earth and back for that boy."

"But...but you treated him like garbage!" I spluttered. "I was there! I remember. You were so mean to him all the time!"

Sophie looked down at the floor. The bib of her denim overalls was freckled with flour. "I know. I was. I was horrible to him. But I loved him. God, I loved him with my whole heart. I don't think I've ever loved anybody else like that since."

"Why were you so mean to him if you loved him?" I was genuinely flabbergasted. "I mean, it must have ended because of all the things you did to him, right? All those things you said, how you acted. He couldn't take it any—"

"I know," Sophie interrupted. "Don't you think I know, Julia?"

I settled back a little. "I just...I don't understand."

Sophie shrugged. She took a long drag of her cigarette and then tilted her head back, letting it stream out again from between her lips. "I don't know why I acted like that either. Eddie treated me like a princess. And I just..." She paused as a shiver ran across her shoulders. "I don't know. I couldn't stand it. It didn't feel right, being treated well like that. I didn't deserve it."

"Why?" I was incredulous. "What did you ever do to not deserve being loved?"

Sophie looked over at me all of a sudden. Her eyes were shiny, the bottoms rimmed with tears. She took another brusque drag of her cigarette and then brushed off the front of her overalls. "Who knows?" Her voice had changed completely. It was callous now, annoyed. "I mean, who knows why people do anything they do, right?"

You do, I wanted to say.

You know why, Sophie.

"Was it because of what happened?" I asked. "With Maggie?"

Sophie shrugged. "Oh God. You can blame everything on your childhood these days, can't you? I mean, I don't know. Maybe a little. Mostly I think I was just an angry, unhappy person about everything back then. And I took it out on everyone else because I didn't know what to do with it. Poor Eddie got the worst of it."

"We did too," I said softly. "It wasn't just Eddie you were mean to. It was all of us. At home."

Sophie stared at me for a few weighted seconds. Then she blinked. She stood up, took one last drag of her cigarette and threw it in the toilet. I looked straight ahead as she walked out, listened as the heavy thump of her boots against the floor got fainter and fainter down the hallway. Had I actually thought my sister was going to apologize for her behavior back then? Did I want her to? Would it change anything?

I slid all the way underwater then, staring up at the ceiling through the sheet of warm liquid until I had to come back up for air. I did it once more. And then again. The fourth time I went under, I opened my mouth and let out a yell. Just a little one. Enough so that bubbles came out of my mouth and I could hear the warped sound reverberating in my ears. I came up for air, gasping. And then I took a deep breath and went under once more. This time, I blocked my ears, squeezed my eyes shut, and screamed until I ran out of air.

chapter
41

"What was your mom like?" I was over at Aiden's again. It was a quiet afternoon, the air cool and windy. He was working on a new piece, something small, almost fully formed.

Next to Aiden's eye, a tiny muscle moved. "Well," he said after a moment. "She was an artist."

"Really? A potter, like you?"

He shook his head. "No, she painted. Watercolors, mostly. Some oils. She had a studio down in Manchester where she sold a lot of her work. We have a few framed ones in the house still. Dad put them up after she died. She'd never let us hang any of her stuff when she was around. She hated looking at her work."

"Why?"

Aiden shrugged. He was up on his feet now, one hand submerged into the cavity of the clay, the other guiding it from the outside. The inside was getting wider and wider by the second. It looked like a vase, but I knew that with just a slight shift of his hand, it could turn into anything.

"I think a lot of artists are like that," he said. "My mom had a friend who was an author. Hell of a good writer. I read all his stuff, and I'm not even a reader. Anyway, we had him over for dinner one night and he told us that he's never read one of his books all the way through. Not one. When I asked him why, he said he just couldn't bring himself to do it; that he knew he'd find a million spots in the book where he should've done this or should've said that. It'd drive him crazy to see all the mistakes he'd made, mistakes that he couldn't do anything about anymore." He shrugged. "I think Mom was the same way."

"Wow," I said softly. "If I was that good at something, I can't imagine never wanting to look at it again."

"Well, that's what happens when you're a perfectionist, I guess," Aiden said. "Nothing's ever really good enough. And if nothing's ever good enough, then what's the point of looking at it, right?"

I kept my eyes on the vase—or pot, or whatever it was. The piece was much bigger than I originally thought it would be. Aiden had started off with a lump of clay the size of a fist, but it had transformed into nearly double its size. "She was really fun too," he said suddenly. "She had this weird kind of laugh—sort of like a giggle that would go up real high and then come back down again. It made you laugh, just hearing it."

"Did you guys do things together? Just you and her?"

He nodded. "She loved the quad. When I was little, she took me all over the place on it. Then when I learned how to drive it, I'd take her. She'd put her arms around me and hold on real tight and say, 'Take us to the moon, Aiden. Go on, take us to the moon.' "

"The moon?"

He smiled. "It was just her way of telling me to go wherever I wanted. As far as I wanted."

"Did you ever get lost?"

He nodded. "God, lots of times. That was the best part."

"Why?"

He sat back down slowly, still angling his fingers along the inside of the piece. "Who wants to know where they're going all the time? That's boring. When you get lost, you see things you never knew were there in the first place."

The wheel was slowing down. Aiden's fingers slowed with it, tapping the sides gently until it came to a complete stop. My eyes widened as I stared at the perfect little bowl—no bigger around than an orange. "It's so cute!" I said. "But what're you going to eat out of that? It's so small!"

"It's not for eating," Aiden said. "It's a different kind of bowl. For something else."

"Like what?"

"You'll see." He looked at it for a moment, and then leaned in and touched the rim again, very lightly, with the pad of his index finger. "There," he said. "Perfect."

Aiden put the tiny bowl on a shelf next to another bowl and a small vase. "This is where I leave everything to dry," he explained. "It takes a few days." He walked over to what looked like a large black canister in the corner of the patio and checked a tiny thermometer attached to one side. "This is the kiln. There's a vase in there I'm firing." He picked up a small bowl and dipped his fingers into it. "And now that it's reached 1660 degrees, I can salt glaze it."

"What's that?"

Aiden held up the bowl. "Watch." He pinched a small amount of salt between his fingers and deposited it through a hole at the top of the kiln. There were actually many holes along the rim, tiny rectangular openings, and Aiden moved from one to the next, sprinkling fingerfuls of salt through them. "Salt does amazing things to clay," he said. "The crystals actually explode when they hit the heat, and then turn into a vapor. It's the vapor that transforms the look of the clay."

"How?" I asked. "What's it do?"

"It makes the clay glossy, and the surface gets this sort of orange-peel texture. But the really cool thing about salt glazing is that no two pieces ever look the same. Each one is completely unique, depending on how much or how little salt you use."

"Who taught you how to do all this?" I asked.

Aiden shrugged. "My mom got me lessons when I was about twelve. That was where I learned all the basics."

"So..." I paused. "I mean, did they tell you you should be a potter?"

Aiden looked at me curiously. "Tell me to be a potter?"

I shifted uncomfortably. "Yeah, did they see that you were good at it and tell you that that's what you should do?"

Aiden's face took on a blank quality. "They encouraged me to do it. But they didn't tell me that I should be a potter." He laughed.

"Actually, though, I made it easy for them. After I found pottery, I didn't want to do anything else."

"Really?"

"Yeah."

"Did you ever try anything else?"

"You mean like accounting?" Aiden grinned.

I shrugged. "Anything."

"No," he said. "But I didn't have to. Pottery's my thing. It's always been my thing." He paused. "How about you? You have a thing?"

School. Being smart. Grades. Or maybe—possibly—drawing.

"I don't know," I said. "Maybe."

"Maybe?" he repeated. "It ain't your thing if you say maybe."

How were you supposed to know? Apparently I didn't possess that gut-feeling thing that Zoe did. So how did it work? Was someone going to show up eventually and tell me? "Julia Anderson, your thing is law." Or, "Julia Anderson, your thing is sketching."

"Okay," Aiden said. "I'll bite. What is it?"

I stared at the orangish blue flames behind the tiny peepholes of the kiln. "Well, I'm majoring in prelaw. In college, I mean."

"So law's your thing, then?"

"Yeah." And then, "I mean no. No. It's not."

Aiden looked over at me.

"No." My voice was firmer. "No. It's definitely not."

"So you're doing it because . . ." Aiden gestured with his hand, indicating that I should go on.

I looked over Aiden's head at the trees, raised like a green arch behind him. A large shadow on the right obscured most of the leaves, but on the left, where the sun was bright, I could see them perfectly. Some hung limp and flat; others were curled over slightly, just at the tips, like shy little girls.

"Julia?" Aiden's voice was soft.

"I don't know." I lowered my eyes so I was looking at Aiden again. "I honestly don't know anymore."

chapter
42

It rained the next two days—a steady, heavy rain that turned most of Main Street into one giant puddle, and saturated the rest of the ground into a muddy, squishy layer. With her repeated trips to the Rutland bank—which took a good amount of time—along with her trip to get roofing tile, and now the rain forcing us to work inside, Sophie was hell-bent on picking up the lag.

We concentrated on the front room, which was by far the most time-consuming. Most mornings were spent on our hands and knees, sanding ourselves into oblivion. In the afternoons, we spread drop cloths over the floor and got to work painting. Sophie had chosen a pomegranate red for the walls, with cream trim around the edges. The color looked putrid in the can, but as we began to spread swaths of it over the walls, I stood back, surprised. It was gorgeous.

I was about two-thirds of the way done with my wall when Sophie leaned over and turned down the radio. She had splotches of red paint on her nose and a hole in the knee of her overalls. "I just thought of something," she said.

"What?"

"About Maggie. Well, about Dad, really. Back in Milford. Before you came along."

I could feel my shoulders tense slightly as I dipped my brush back into the vat of paint. "Okay."

Sophie coated the wall in front of her for a few seconds and then reloaded the roller, working the excess off along the ridges of the paint tray.

"His practice was struggling," she said. "And I guess to cope with that, he started drinking. A lot. Beer mostly. He might've drunk other stuff, but I don't know. And it wasn't a regular thing. The refrigerator might just be a refrigerator for weeks at a time, which meant that things were okay. And then other days when I'd open it, looking for a piece of string cheese or an orange, I'd see the stacks of blue and white cans lined up on the left side, neat as could be. It was always a Friday night when the cans appeared, and they were always, *always* gone by Monday morning." She wrinkled her forehead, remembering. "One time, I counted the whole mess of 'em. There were thirty-six." She shook her head, as if the number still amazed her. "He would drink thirty-six cans in a single weekend. That's a case and a half of beer."

The only cans I had ever seen in the refrigerator growing up were Diet Coke and the occasional Slim-Fast, when Mom was trying to lose a few pounds. There were never any surprises when I opened the refrigerator; the shelves were always filled with hamburger and green grapes, bottled water, eggs, salad greens, and orange juice. Sometimes, if Mom had cooked the night before, there would be leftovers, carefully wrapped in foil, stacked like little pyramids on one side. No blue and white cans. Ever.

"What was he like when he drank?" I asked.

"What was he like?" Sophie repeated my question carefully, as if she had to reach back and retrieve the memory from an old, dusty place without disturbing anything else around it. "Drunk, obviously. But not always the same kind of drunk. Sometimes he'd just sleep. Other times he'd sit on the sofa for the whole weekend, without moving, and just stare at the television. He wouldn't even get dressed. He was there physically, but the rest of him was gone. Completely gone."

I'd never once seen Dad inactive. If he wasn't at work, he was out in the yard or hammering something in the upstairs bathroom or installing a new light fixture above the kitchen sink. He'd built the deck that led out into our backyard one summer, and he had transformed the basement into a finished room, complete with carpeting, new wallpaper, and furniture. At night, if he felt restless, he took a walk. And not just around the block. Sometimes he would be gone for hours, walking for miles, returning only when the sky had darkened and the moon had settled itself in for the night.

"Mom made herself scarce whenever he got like that," Sophie continued, "and she'd take Maggie and me with her. We'd go to the mall or the movies, eat lunch at some dumpy restaurant, and then go shopping some more. We'd sometimes be gone the whole day. At night, we'd tiptoe back inside the house as quietly as we could. Mom always slept with me on those nights. Always. I figured things out eventually, but before I did, whenever I'd ask her what was wrong with Dad, she'd just say something like 'He's not feeling well. We just need to leave him alone right now.'"

Sophie turned around again and began to drag the paintbrush over the wall.

"Sometimes, though, we didn't leave. Sometimes we stayed home, and the two of them would argue. It's funny. I never heard or saw them argue about anything else, ever. It was only when the blue cans came into the house." She paused, leaning back to examine her work. "You know, he hurt her once. During one of those arguments."

I lay the paintbrush down on the drop cloth next to my shoe. Tiny pinpoints of heat bloomed along my neck. My hands, which continued to quiver, had turned icy cold. Muscles I did not know I had—in my shoulders, my stomach, my throat—constricted themselves into tiny, tight knots.

"Hurt her?" I repeated.

"It was before Maggie came," Sophie said. "I saw the whole thing, because I used to hide behind the couch when they fought. Part of me really believed that I could jump out and make them stop whenever I wanted to. And another part of me was just scared. They were so fucking *loud* and they said such horrible things to each other—words I'd never heard of, but could just tell, by the way their faces looked, that they were mean, you know? Hateful."

I'd witnessed a few of Mom and Dad's arguments growing up, but they were so infrequent that I could barely remember them. Once or twice they had bickered at the dinner table, but neither of them had raised their voice, and no one had uttered a curse word. In fact, the only times I'd ever heard them really disagree with one another was when I was in bed and they were in their bedroom—and even then, they made it a point to keep their voices hushed. Strained, but hushed.

"Anyway," Sophie continued, "they were in the living room and Mom was following Dad around, bugging him about the blue cans. She kept poking him in the back for some reason, because he wouldn't turn around, he wouldn't acknowledge her. And all of a sudden he just turned and shoved her. With both hands. Right in the middle of her chest. Mom flew back—I remember she was actually airborne for a second or two—and then she hit the corner of the coffee table in the middle of the room." Sophie reached up with her fingers and pressed them against her left ear. "She hit the side of her head, right here..."

I stood up quickly, and then steadied myself as the room began to sway around me. "Jules?" Sophie asked. Her voice was far away.

"I need some air." I forced my legs to walk out of the room and concentrated on steadying my hand so I could turn the doorknob. The rain was coming down in sheets, but I stepped out anyway, shutting my eyes against the torrent, taking short, shaky breaths. A loud buzzing noise sounded somewhere inside my head. The cold drops pelting my eyelids and my cheeks stung like pieces of ice, but I lifted my face up and did not turn away.

Once, in tenth grade, I had come back from studying at the library and heard Mom and Dad talking upstairs. They weren't yelling, but their voices were loud enough that I stopped in my tracks, listening.

"If I could take it back, I would, Arlene. You know I would."

"I don't want you to take it back." Mom was crying. "I want you to make it right!"

"How am I supposed to do that?" Dad's voice was pleading. "What do you want me to do?"

Mom cried harder. "I don't know."

I could hear Sophie behind me, somewhere in the roar of the rain. "Jules?" Her arm encircled my shoulders. "Jules? Come back inside. It's okay. We'll take a break. Get you dried—"

"That's why she wears the hearing aid, isn't it?"

Sophie's arm went limp. "Yes," she whispered.

I began to walk. My legs moved heavily inside my soaking pants, and water streamed down the length of my hair.

"Jules!" Sophie called behind me. "Where are you going?"

I moved forward, walking faster and faster, propelled by a sudden and unknown urgency.

"Jules! Come back!"

But I did not go back.

I did not look back.

I just kept going, moving toward something in the distance that I could not see.

chapter
43

Main Street was a wet blur of colors. I could barely make out the orange lettering of the Stewart's sign across the street. The tiny green lawns that fronted the other buildings had all but drowned in brown puddles, and the Dunkin' Donuts sign bled electric waves of orange and pink. A lone car drifted by, parting the water in the middle of the street like the Red Sea. I didn't bother to step aside; by now, it was impossible to get any wetter.

The rain itself did not particularly bother me, and I had never been inside a church, so there was no reason for me to stop suddenly when I reached the front of St. Raphael's, with its wide white doors. Maybe it was because it was at the end of the street. Or maybe I was intrigued by the fact that one of the doors was open a little, held in place by a small red brick. Whatever the reason, I climbed the steps, pulled open the door, and stepped inside.

Shivering overtook me almost immediately, a violent trembling that made my teeth chatter like castanets. My overalls were so heavy that moving forward out of the tiny vestibule I had just entered took effort. I swung open another door and stared. Rows of empty pews lined the huge room, and the vacant altar at the front was a lonely compilation of wood and marble statues. The stained glass windows were as dark and melancholy as winter. In one corner, a marble woman, all in white, stared out at me with empty eyes. Long robes clustered around the bottom of her bare feet, and a mantle covered her head. One of her arms was holding something, while the other remained empty and outstretched.

This place looked even emptier than I felt. I turned to leave and glimpsed a shadow in the far left corner. Blinking remnants of moisture from my eyelashes, I squinted through the shadows. An old man was sitting in the very front row, staring straight ahead. The collar of his tan windbreaker was rumpled and wet, and white tufts of hair curled along the back of his neck.

What was he staring at so intently, I wondered. And why was he in here all alone? Still shivering, I slid into the very last pew and hugged my arms against my chest. For a while, I just stared at the back of the man's collar, at the streaks the rain had made along the slippery material. Anything to block out the impossible fact that twenty years ago my father had deafened my mother. Anything to prevent the impossible task of trying to understand how, even as a little girl, I had never completely believed her explanation about why she wore a hearing aid. Trying to comprehend all of it was like being in the middle of some vast vortex.

The man in the front row stood up. Walking slowly toward the marble woman, he pulled something from the pocket of his coat, placed it carefully on the flat pedestal where she stood, and then turned back around. Pulling a Red Sox baseball cap from his jacket, he adjusted it on top of his head, moved slowly toward a side door near the front, and disappeared.

When I was sure he was gone, I walked slowly toward the marble statue. My pants were as heavy as plaster, but it was the shivering that made it difficult to walk. Up close, I could see that the woman was holding a little boy. His feet were also bare and his tiny marble curls clustered gently around his face. I looked down at the base of the statue.

There, in a neat row, was a single line of perfectly white stones. Hundreds of them.

chapter
44

Sophie draped another warm towel over my head and rubbed. I closed my eyes, inhaling the blended scent of lemony fabric softener and paint primer, which seemed to infuse everything now. It was a strange combination—sweet and acrid at the same time. Sophie's fingers gripped my head and rubbed down, over and over again, until finally I pulled away.

"What?" she asked. "Too hard?"

"I can do it myself," I answered, grabbing the towel from her hands. "I'm not a baby, you know."

Sophie plopped down on the other side of the bed. "I'm sorry," she said miserably. "I can't do anything right today, can I?"

She was still in her own wet clothes, despite insisting, when I finally returned, that I get into a hot shower. I hadn't realized how cold I actually was until I stood naked under the hot water. My fingers were blue. The tips of my ears were so cold, the water felt as if it was scalding them. Now, I sat on the edge of her bed, wrapped in her big green bathrobe. My feet were encased in a pair of red and blue knitted slipper socks that came up to my knees. A cup of chamomile tea was resting on top of her dresser, which, for some reason, looked oddly bare, as if something was missing.

Sophie watched me rub my hair for a moment more without saying anything. Then she brought her fingers to her forehead, kneading the skin gently. The sleeves of her thin T-shirt clung to the sides of her arms and the knotted ends of her red bandanna dripped against the top of her overalls. "God," she said again. "I knew I shouldn't have…"

I stopped drying my hair. "Shouldn't have what? Told me about Dad? Told me the truth?" Sophie looked at me quizzically, as if trying to understand my tone of voice. "Because at the very least, Sophie, that is what you should have done. A long time ago. What you shouldn't have done—for the last twenty years—was keep it a secret." I let the towel fall into my lap. "I mean, I can almost—*almost*—understand the whole code of silence about Maggie, since I never even met her. But Mom? *Mom*, Sophie? I would have never kept something like that from you!"

"How do you know?" Sophie's eyes flashed. "You've never been in the same situation—not even remotely. In all the years you've grown up with Mom and Dad, I bet you've never heard them say one negative thing to each other, let alone witnessed a scene like that. So don't tell me what you would or wouldn't have done. You don't have the faintest fucking idea what you would have done!"

"Yes, I do!" I yelled. "I know exactly what I would have done! And you know why? Because I know what the word loyal means. And I know that there is nothing more important in the world than being loyal to your family—no matter what!"

Sophie's lower lip trembled as she stared at me for a long

moment. "Oh, Jules," she said, sinking down against the bed. She buried her face in her hands, rocking back and forth slowly. Then she lifted her head. "He used to say the exact same thing to me."

I stared at her. "What're you talking about? Who did?"

"Dad," she said sadly. "He used to give me the whole loyalty routine too. 'Nothing is more important than being loyal to the family.'" She stood up and began to pace around the room. "That's how he convinced me never to talk about Maggie. Or Mom. Or even me." She looked at me. "Do you know where I went that summer after I graduated from high school?"

My brain started to race. That was the summer I won the Acahela Summer Camp Spelling Bee and Sophie had freaked out, throwing my trophy down the hall. A few days later, she had moved to Portland, where she was going to start classes at the University of Maine that fall.

"You went to Maine," I said. "For school."

"I didn't go to Maine!" Sophie's eyes were huge. "I went to a fucking psychiatric hospital in New Jersey, Julia! For four weeks!"

My face flushed hot. "What are you talking about? Mom and Dad never said anything about you—"

"Mom and Dad have never said anything about anyone!" Sophie said. "Think about it. They've never said anything about Maggie, they've never said anything about me, they've never even hinted at the reason for Mom's hearing aid. I had to go live in a mental ward for four weeks because I was losing my mind living like that! Do you know what's it like to live your whole life with horrible secrets inside you, screaming to be let out? Do you know what that does to you?" Her face was pink with rage; spit flew out from between her teeth. "It makes you crazy," she said, shaking her head. "It makes you completely and certifiably crazy." She shrugged, defeated. "Dad said everything had to be kept in the family. Taking it outside of that was breaking the family circle."

"But *I'm* family!" The sides of my head throbbed with the force of my words. "I'm not some outsider, hanging around the circle, Sophie! I'm your sister! I'm part of you. I'm part of all of you. I'm family!" Something broke inside of me when I said those words, a sheet of glass splintering into a thousand pieces. "What was so wrong with me that none of you would talk to me? What did I do to deserve being shut out? Did I not fill Maggie's shoes well enough? Were Mom and Dad's expectations of me too high? Did I..."

Sobs overtook me then, blocking the words in my throat, and I cried with abandon, like a baby left behind in a darkened room.

"Oh, Julia." Sophie encircled me with her arms. "It's not you. It was never you. Ever."

"Then what was it?"

"It was them," Sophie said helplessly. "They were afraid, I guess."

"Of what?"

"Are you kidding?"

I shook my head. "No. I'm not."

"Of being found out," Sophie said. She began to rub her hand in small circles along my back. "Of getting called out on the fact that Attorney Anderson and his beautiful wife, Arlene, weren't actually perfect."

"But all families have problems," I said, thinking of Milo and Zoe's parents. And Aiden's too.

Sophie shrugged. "I don't know. Maybe they thought if other people saw us as perfect, they could stop worrying so much about the fact that they weren't. Or maybe it kept their minds off the things that really needed to be addressed—and never were."

"Like Dad's drinking."

Sophie nodded. "And Maggie's death."

My brow furrowed. "But Maggie's death was an accident. I would think it would make people feel sympathetic toward them."

The little circles on my back slowed and then stopped completely. "Not when the death is their other child's fault," Sophie said.

I turned around slowly. "What do you mean, your fault? It wasn't your fault." My heart lurched. "It was asthma...wasn't it?"

"The asthma was part of it," Sophie said. "But it wasn't the cause of death."

"What was?" The question felt like a needle going through my ears.

"Drowning," Sophie answered. The stare she gave me was both venomous and frightened. "She drowned, Julia. And it was my fault."

chapter
45

Sophie got up then and walked out of the room.

But I just sat there, too stunned to move.

Had I heard her correctly? Drowned?

Where? How?

Sophie's fault? It had to be a mistake. I looked around. Where had she gone? She couldn't drop a two-ton word like that and then leave.

I bolted off the bed. "Sophie!" It was empty downstairs; the lights were off. "Sophie!" I screamed again. "Where are you?"

No answer. She'd only walked out fifteen seconds ago. Where could she possibly have gone? I flung open the front door. The rain had slowed to a light drizzle and the light, pale and watery, had already started to change. I ran out on the front porch, side-stepping the hole in the middle, and leaned against the rickety banister. Main Street was still empty, save for a string of cars parked outside of Perry's. Perry's front window was streaked with rain, making it impossible to tell who was inside. Still, I knew she was in there, probably spilling everything to the Table of Knowledge guys. God forbid she tell me the whole story. I was just her sister. Better to tell three old yahoos-or-whoever-the-hell-they-were from Small-town, USA, so they could cluck their tongues and give her "advice." Unbelievable.

I ran inside and pulled on a pair of clean jeans, a T-shirt, and one of Sophie's sweatshirts. It was impossible to avoid puddles as I raced across the street, so I sloshed deliberately through them, drenching myself again. I didn't care.

Walt, Lloyd, and Jimmy looked up as I walked into Perry's. They were eating pieces of cream pie. Lloyd was licking his fork. A big blob of whipped cream sat like a cotton ball on the collar of his shirt. An older woman with beautiful white hair and blue rain boots on her feet was sipping from a cup in a nearby booth. Miriam was behind the counter, wiping it down with a dishcloth.

"Hey, Julia." Walt said. "How're you—"

"Where's Sophie? Did she come over here?"

Walt put his fork down slowly. "Sophie's not here. Why? She's not over at her place?"

"Obviously not. Or I wouldn't be looking for her here, would I?"

"What's wrong?" Lloyd asked. He had finished eating and had inserted a toothpick in between his bottom teeth. "You two have a fight?"

"It's none of your business." I turned to leave, and then thought better of it. "Actually, you know what? Maybe some of it is your business. I want to know what she's been telling you. About my family." I yanked a chair out from underneath a table nearby and set it down hard between Jimmy and Walt. "I know you guys have all your 'knowledge' talks over here. I've seen her come and talk to you when she's bummed out, and I've seen the way you pat her on the back and shake your heads and talk to her until she feels better. So I want to know what she's been talking to you about that she doesn't say to me?"

The three men stared at me. Even Jimmy, who had been stirring his coffee with a straw, stopped and looked at me.

"She's never talked to us about your family," Walt said finally. He leaned back and hooked his thumbs behind his suspenders. "Not ever."

"She told you about me." I glared at Lloyd. "You knew I was valedictorian of my class."

Lloyd dismissed me with a shrug. "She talks a lot about people she's proud of. You getting all hot under the collar 'cause she's proud of you?"

I ran my palms against the flat of my legs. "Fine. What does she talk to you about then? The weather?"

Walt nodded his head slowly and leaned back on his chair. "Well, yeah. Sometimes she talks about the weather. Sometimes she talks about what needs to be done in the house. Sometimes she talks about what she's planning on making when she opens the bakery." He shrugged. "Sophie talks about all sorts of things."

I stared steadily at him. "You're lying."

Walt let his chair down with a thud and raised an eyebrow. "Is that so? And what am I lying to you about?"

"Sophie said you give her advice. About important things. She said that's why you're called the Table of Knowledge." I stared at the three of them. "You must think I'm an idiot if you think you can sit there and tell me that you're giving her advice about how many inches of snow you're going to get this winter."

Lloyd laughed and took the toothpick out of his mouth. "That about sums it up, darlin'. Studying the Farmers' Almanac gives us lots of credibility in this town!"

Walt, who had been watching me with a look of increasing concern, took his spoon out of his coffee. "What's going on, Julia? What're you so upset about?"

I shook my head. If they didn't know anything, I certainly was not going to be the one to tell them.

"You two have an argument?" Lloyd asked again.

"Yeah." Struggling to hide my embarrassment, I turned to go.

"Julia!"

I turned as Walt called my name. "Best thing to do when you're angry is to sit a while." He nodded. "Just sit. Don't do anything crazy."

"Crazy?" I thought. "You want to see crazy? Let me tell you about the time my big sister got locked up in a loony bin—then you can talk to me about crazy."

I pushed open the door and walked back into the rain.

chapter
46

I decided to go back to the house and wait for Sophie, afraid that if I started traipsing through town looking for her, she'd come back, find me gone, and leave again. I stayed in the kitchen for a long time, rummaging aimlessly through her cupboards, opening and shutting her refrigerator door. What was I looking for? Did I expect the answer to the terrible question I had in the back of my head to just come falling out of a cabinet?

How had Maggie drowned?

Had it been an accident?

Sophie had been seven. Maybe she and Maggie had been swimming at a pool together. Mom would've been sitting in a fold-up chair off to the side, reading a magazine, watching them with one eye. Maybe Maggie had slipped and gone under. Would Sophie have held her under? It couldn't be. It was impossible. Sophie wasn't capable of something like that.

Was she?

I thought about the explosive scenes between her and Mom

and Dad over the years, how she screamed and cursed at them, clenching her fists as if trying to restrain the violence inside them. Or the hatred in her eyes the day she had ripped that spelling trophy out of my hand and flung it down the hall. She'd even told me about the time she'd slapped Maggie across the face. Could the jealousy she felt toward her little sister have propelled such rage? Was something like that in her?

I stared at the front of the refrigerator. A picture of a caterpillar Goober had drawn was tacked to the front with little strawberry magnets. Next to it was a torn-off piece of paper with the name *Greg* and a phone number written beneath it.

I went back upstairs, walking around restlessly. It was still gray outside. The empty bedrooms felt darker and more ominous somehow, and when a car backfired outside, I screamed. Shaken, I went from room to room, turning on all the lights, and then came back and sat on Sophie's bed. My eyes roved around the room like an afterthought: walls, floor, dresser, bed...

Wait.

I stood up slowly. There *was* something different about the dresser, something I had glimpsed before, but not registered. I walked over, trying to place what it was.

And then, like a cold hand settling on my shoulder, it came to me.

On wooden legs, I walked out of Sophie's bedroom and into the spare one across the hall. Sophie's empty sleeping bag was still flung on the floor next to the lamp. The drop cloth was still bunched in the corner, and the windows were streaked with rain. The only things missing were Sophie's shoes.

I squatted down slowly next to the sleeping bag, and felt around until my fingers came into contact with something hard and sharp. Drawing the picture frame out, I stared down at Goober's face, and then clutched it against my chest.

"Oh my God," I whispered. "Goober. Where are you, baby?"

chapter
47

"Where's Goober?" I demanded, looking around at the three men inside Perry's. It was dusk. Most of the tables inside the little restaurant were filled now. Miriam was racing around the room, serving plates of their famous chicken stew and biscuits. The white-haired woman was still there, reading the newspaper now, in between bites of chicken stew and a small bowl of peas. I leaned on the back of an empty chair next to Jimmy and glared at them one by one.

"Goober?" Walt said. "Who's Goober?"

I pointed at Jimmy shakily. "Sophie...she said you talked to her all the time." I struggled to keep my voice steady. "That's what she said. She told me you only talked to people you felt like talking to, and that Goober was one of them." I was pleading now, begging Jimmy for information.

He did not look up from his coffee cup.

"Who is Goober?" Walt said again.

I collapsed into the empty chair so that I would not fall to the floor. "Sophie's daughter. She's four. Her name is Grace, but we've all called her Goober since she was born."

Lloyd raised an eyebrow. "Oh, Gracie!" he said. "Yeah, yeah, we know Gracie. You call her Goober? I quiz her on the state capitals all the time. She already knows about ten of them." Lloyd nodded at me. "She probably got your brains. She's a smart little thing, I'm telling you."

Walt was studying me carefully. "Why're you panicking about Gracie? She's probably up at her father's place. In Rutland."

I shook my head. "Greg gets her every other weekend. That's it. Goober's been gone for almost three whole weeks now. And every time I ask her where she is, Sophie makes up some excuse about them going camping." I slammed my hand on the table. "Who camps for three whole weeks with a four-year-old?"

Patrons looked up, alarmed at the sound of my voice, and then kept eating. Miriam glanced over at Lloyd and raised an eyebrow.

I struggled to lower my voice, turning to Jimmy. "Listen to me. I know something's wrong. I can feel it. Please, please tell me what's going on. Please just tell me what you know."

Jimmy looked up. He touched the brim of his Red Sox hat lightly and then cleared his throat. "Sophie come back yet?"

"No." I planted my hands flat on the table in front of me. "She hasn't. We were . . . having a . . . a discussion . . . and she got upset and left. She walked right out of the house. I didn't see where she went and I don't know when she'll be back." I leaned forward. "Where's Goober, Jimmy? Do you know?"

Jimmy gazed at me. His eyes, a slate blue color, were grave. "You need to find Sophie first."

"Oh my God, are you kidding me? I told you I don't know where she went!"

"She'll be back," Jimmy said calmly.

I paused, clenching my fists in frustration. "What are you hiding? What do you know about Goober that you aren't telling me?"

Miriam came over then, and set her coffee pot deliberately on the table. "Would someone like to tell me what's going on here?" Her eyes scanned Walt, Lloyd, and Jimmy, before settling finally on me. "Is there any reason you're giving my dinner crowd a collective heart attack?"

I shook my head and buried my face in my hands. I was spent.

Walt reached out and put a hand on my arm. "Easy there. Just take it easy."

"Next outburst, you're going to have to take a walk." Miriam picked up her coffee pot. "I'm sorry, but I mean it. I can't have this kind of drama in here. People are trying to eat their dinner."

"Okay." I nodded behind my hands.

Next to me, Walt sighed. "Anyone ever tell you that you jump to conclusions before you know all the facts?"

"You think so well on your feet, Julia, which is exactly the kind of trait you need to become a good lawyer."

I sat back slowly. Blinked. How was it that nothing—not one single thing—made sense anymore? When had everything I knew, or everything that I thought I knew, been turned upside down, shaken out, and trampled until it was unrecognizable?

I looked over helplessly at Jimmy again. His eyes were still fixed on me. "Go find Sophie," he said.

"Where?" I struggled to control the impulse to reach over the table and throttle him. "Where would she be? Where should I look?"

Jimmy shrugged. "Don't know. Doubt she's gone too far, though."

I stood up, leaning my weight on my fingertips. I wasn't going to get anywhere with this guy, apparently. He had absolutely no intention of offering assistance. "Thanks for all your help," I said.

Jimmy tipped his hat forward. "Anytime," he said softly. "And Julia?"

"What?"

"Let me know when you find her."

chapter
48

Someone said the night is darkest just before the dawn.

But they lied.

Night is dark the whole way through, from the beginning all the way to the impossible, interminable end.

I went from room to room again inside the house, turning off the lights, searching behind the doors, but it was empty. When I called Sophie's name, it reverberated against the walls, a sad, frantic echo. At least my car was still in the back, parked next to the garage. Still, when I thought about it, Sophie could have gone anywhere. This was her territory, not mine. Where had she disappeared to? When would she return? And where.... The thought made me shudder, bringing hot tears to my eyes.

Where was Goober?

Suddenly, I remembered the phone number on the refrigerator. Racing down to the kitchen, I grabbed it and then dialed the number with trembling fingers. It rang once, twice, three times.

"Hello?"

"Greg?"

"Yes?"

"This is…" I pressed my hand gently along the hollow of my stomach. "This is Sophie's sister. Julia."

"Oh." He paused. "Hi, Julia."

"Hi." A nervous laugh escaped my lips. "How are you? I mean, how are things?"

Another pause. I knew how weird this must be. I'd only met Greg once. The day Goober was born, he had shown up at the hospital just as Mom and Dad and I were leaving, holding a bouquet of sunflowers. Sophie had made the awkward introductions, shifting uncomfortably in her bed as Greg set the flowers down carefully on the windowsill. I remember just watching him, how he moved with unease around Sophie, kissing her stiffly on the cheek, avoiding her eyes. And then, how his whole face changed, flushing pink, as he leaned over the bassinet and stared down at their daughter. "I'm…fine," Greg said now. "And you?"

"Oh, I'm good." I coughed lightly. "I'm actually at Sophie's place. In Poultney."

"How's that coming along? She get it fixed up yet?"

My heart skipped a beat. So he knew about Poultney. He knew she was down here. Okay. It was a start.

"Yeah. She's working hard on it. I've been sort of helping." My eyes fell on the wall across the kitchen. My mural of Main Street. There was the Laundromat and Perry's with the wooden tables out front and the pizza place too. They were all there, set back a little against the street itself. A wrought iron lamppost stood in the left corner, and next to it was the chokecherry tree, its leaves small and pointed like elf ears. Just like outside. I had done that.

"Are you staying for the summer?" Greg asked.

"Yes. I mean, no." I turned away from the mural and leaned against the butcher block. I didn't know anything anymore. "I mean, I'll be here for a little while."

Greg didn't say anything for a moment. I could tell he was trying to guess the real reason for my call. Suddenly, in the background, I heard a little voice.

"Daddy, come finish your picture."

My knees buckled at the sound of Goober's voice. I pressed my knuckles against my lips as Greg answered her. "Hold on, baby. Daddy'll be right there."

"That...that's Goober?"

"Yeah." Greg answered. "We were just coloring."

I began to cry. "Then she's...okay? Goober, I mean? She's okay? She's safe?"

"Julia." I could hear the sound of Greg's footsteps as he moved out of the room, out of Goober's hearing range. "What's going on? Why are you calling me?" His voice was considerably softer, but firm.

I struggled for the words. There was no possible way I could begin to explain things to Greg. "There's just been some stuff... going on. Sophie's been making all these excuses about why Goober isn't down here with her, and I didn't know where she...really was. And I..."

"Sophie didn't tell you?"

"Tell me what?"

"Goober lives with me now," he said simply. "Sophie and I are in the process of getting the whole custody order changed so I'll be the primary custodian."

"What?" I could feel the breath leave my body. "Why? Why would you do something like that to her?"

"I didn't do anything," Greg answered. "Sophie came to me with the idea, not the other way around."

"But...that doesn't make any sense! Goober's her whole *life*, Greg! You know that! She loves her more than anything. Why would she do something like that?"

Greg was quiet for a moment. When he spoke again, his voice was unsettlingly calm. "You know, Sophie and I have never really been close. I mean, aside from the fact that we had a child together." There was a pause. "It's been five years since we met, and I still don't know a lot about her. She doesn't share anything with me. Never has and, I realized quite some time ago, never will. So when she came to me a few months ago and told me that she was having nightmares about hurting Goober, I knew better than just to blow it off. It was the first time she'd told me anything real about herself. Anything honest. And when she followed it up with the custody discussion, I kept listening."

"Hurting Goober?" My voice was faint.

"She's never laid a finger on Goober," Greg said. There was an edge of defensiveness to his voice. "I'm not accusing her of anything, okay? She just said that she'd been having these nightmares...and that she didn't think she had it in her to be the kind of mother

Goober deserved." He paused. "She's not totally out of Goober's life. She comes up when she can—sometimes for the weekend, sometimes not. And they talk every day on the phone."

I sank down along the wall. "How is Goober?"

"She's... adjusting," Greg answered. He cleared his throat. "I'll be honest. It's not easy. She asks a lot of questions."

"Yeah." Would I ever get to see my baby niece again?

"She'll be okay, though." Greg's voice sounded wistful. "Kids are resilient, Julia."

"Yeah," I said again. "I know."

chapter
49

It was impossible to stay inside, to sit still anywhere, after I hung up with Greg. I walked rapidly along Main Street on legs that somehow managed to keep me upright and moving. The fact that I had no destination did not enter my mind. Just the act of breathing was enough. A swell of black sky, perforated with electric bits of stars, stretched out above me. The street lamps threw yellow halos of light down the sidewalk, but everything else was dark. It was almost midnight. Even the Dunkin' Donuts at the end of the street was dimmed, the store emptied and shut tight until morning. I pushed on, up the little hill, past the high school, and stared down at the fork in the road. I didn't want to go look at the yellow house. I didn't want Aiden. I didn't want Milo. I didn't even want Sophie at that moment.

What *did* I want? The question reverberated back and forth inside of my head. "What do I want?" Had I ever asked myself that question before? Even once?

I want the truth.

I kept going, heading down the road Sophie and I had walked only a few weeks ago when I had first come to town. Had it really only been a few weeks ago? It felt like years now, a lifetime. The smell of rain drifted out from the grassy field we had stood in front of just before she had told me. Or had tried to tell me.

What had she been planning to say? Was she going to tell me she had drowned Maggie that day? That she had held our little sister underwater to stop her crying, to shut up the incessant, nerve-racking noise? Had that been it? I sank to my knees, staring toward the inky horizon. For a long, long time I looked, peering through the shadows, but there was nothing to see.

Nothing at all but black.

———

After a while I reached into my back pocket and took out my phone. I stared at it for a few minutes before flipping it open, then dialed the number and pressed the phone to my ear.

"Milo?"

"Julia! Everything all right?"

"I didn't wake you, did I?"

"No, I'm just up reading." He paused. "So what's up? What's been going on? How are things with you and Sophie?"

"It's…" I caught the word "fine" on the tip of my tongue and drew it back in. "We're still going through some things," I said instead.

"Good things?"

I hesitated. "Maybe eventually. Right now it's pretty hard."

"Okay." I could hear him adjusting his position. "Julia?"

"Yeah?" My voice cracked.

"What is it?"

It was such a simple question, such a short, tiny question. But for some reason, I remembered the old story about a little boy who noticed a leak in the dike that separated his town from the sea. The boy blocked the leak with his finger until help arrived, ultimately saving the town from a flooding disaster. I felt like that little boy right now. Except that I had withdrawn my finger and was standing there, watching the water rush out.

"Milo," I whispered. It was right there. Everything, about Sophie. The mental hospital. Maggie. Drowning. My mother's ear. But what I said was, "That night in the car…when I leaned over and kissed you." I closed my eyes, safe again, remembering how soft his lips had felt against mine, how his skin smelled up close, like heat and musk, how our noses had bumped at first and then fit against each other, side by side, perfectly. "Why did you pull away from me?"

I waited, hoping he had heard me. I knew I would not be able to ask again.

"I've played and replayed that moment a million times in my head," he said finally. "I'd do anything to take it back."

"You would?"

"Yes," Milo said. "And everything I said after Melissa's party too. About not wanting to lead you on, and just wanting to be friends. That was all crap. It wasn't the truth."

"What is the truth?"

"I was trying to tell you the truth, that night of the prom…"

"What was it?"

He cleared his throat. "How I really feel. About you." He took a breath as if the words had been choking him for months. "And how much it scared me, because for the last two years, I've been watching my parents turn into these two crazy people. I mean they used to love each other more than anything in the world, but now they can't even be in the same room together. And I don't know. Seeing them change so much made me scared when I realized how I felt about you. I guess maybe I thought it was too risky, or . . . God, I don't know. I tried to figure it out from all those poems I read, but none of them gave me any answers. But Julia." He paused. His voice was louder, as if the words, exposed now between us, were not so frightening after all. "I love you."

"You do?" I whispered.

"More than anything." Milo's voice was steady. "I've loved you ever since the first day of senior year when I read that line of poetry out loud and I turned around and you were looking at me from the backseat of Zoe's car."

I closed my eyes. I remembered it, Whitman. *I am to wait . . . and to see to it that I do not lose you.*

"You had your hair pulled back," Milo continued. "And you were wearing a blue shirt that made your eyes look like little pools of water. Except that I barely got to see them, because you looked away so quickly."

I was speechless. I had been staring at Milo from the safety of the backseat, my eyes roving slowly over his hair, which hung down in little rivulets behind his ear, the blue denim of his shirt, and his baggy khaki pants. And when he had said that line—as he had done countless times before—I whispered it back, to myself, silently.

"Why didn't you ever say anything?" I whispered.

"I tried to, I guess, after I gave you the Christmas card with the e. e. cummings quote. But you didn't really seem like you were into it."

"I have it taped to the top of my desk," I said. "I read it every single night before I go to bed."

"You do?"

"Yeah. I do. I love it, Milo." I pulled on my bottom lip. "How could you not think I was into you after I kissed you on prom night? I mean . . . I've never done anything like that before. With anyone!"

"It couldn't have been that terrible," Milo said. "Especially since you were thinking of someone else."

"Oh, Milo. No I wasn't. I just said that so I wouldn't look like such an idiot. There wasn't anyone else."

"And I guess I kind of freaked, thinking it was gonna be real."

"But . . ." I pushed. "Isn't that what you wanted?"

"Yes," Milo answered. "Definitely. But I guess I was just kind of . . . Jesus, Julia, I don't know. I think I was afraid that I wouldn't be able to live up to your expectations after that."

"What expectations? I never put any . . ."

"The ones I imagined you'd have," Milo interrupted. "I never really thought I had any kind of a chance with you. Cheryl and Melissa, well, they're pretty, but that's about it. But you . . . you're such an amazing person. Smart. Beautiful. Kind. *Smart*. The valedictorian! I don't know. I guess I just thought I'd never be enough next to you." He coughed lightly. "It was stupid."

"No," I whispered, struggling not to cry. "It wasn't stupid. I know what you mean." There was a long pause. I lifted my hand up in front of me and stared at it. Then I put it down again. "What about Cheryl?"

Milo was quiet.

"At the party," I insisted. "I saw you there, sitting with her, letting her touch your shoulder and everything…"

"I'm embarrassed to say this," Milo answered. "But as long as we're finally saying everything…" He cleared his throat. "The only reason I sat down next to her was because I knew she still liked me. I was betting on the fact that she would do something like that. I don't know; I guess I wanted to make you jealous."

"Jealous?" I repeated. "Why?"

"It was a crappy move," Milo admitted. "I thought I needed to do something drastic, you know? Something that would tell me how you felt about me."

"Letting your ex-girlfriend manhandle you was your idea of getting me to pay attention?"

"I know," Milo's voice was miserable. "It was dumb." He paused. "But it worked a little. Didn't it?"

"Yes," I said reluctantly. "It did."

"This is so much easier, isn't it?"

"What is?"

"Just saying it like it is," Milo answered. "Being straight with each other. It's scary telling the truth."

"It is," I said. "But it's worth it, don't you think?"

"Absolutely."

"I miss you, Milo."

"I miss you too. When I think about the fact that you're so far away, it actually hurts—physically. I must sound like a total dork, but it's true. I hate that you're not here. I think about you all the time, Julia."

Neither of us said anything for a moment, basking instead in the warmth of the moment.

"Julia?" Milo asked finally.

"Yes?"

"Come home soon."

part
three

chapter
50

I sat on the side of the road for a long time after Milo hung up. I might have been too stunned to stand. Or maybe I was afraid that if I did, the warm, safe feeling inside my chest would disappear.

Milo.

All along, he had felt something for me—something real!—and I hadn't known.

Me, the "most intelligent" girl in the senior class. The valedictorian, who got a 1680 on her SATs, but couldn't read between the lines of all the silly, stupid gestures a boy who adored her had made.

How was it that the truth about one thing could make you feel so good—and that the truth about something else threatened to destroy you?

Something—a dog? a coyote?—howled in the distance. Above me, the sky split open as a half moon slid between the shadows. The howling sounded again, a low, mournful cry of someone waiting to be found. In front of me, the field grass rustled with movement. I stood up quickly. I didn't know what kind of wildlife lived in Vermont, but I was not interested in finding out.

Turning around, I headed back down the road, toward town. A breeze began to blow, rustling the grass on either side of me. The smell of wet asphalt and jasmine filled the air. And then I stopped, remembering the gorge. It was the only place Sophie had ever mentioned to me. Where she went when she needed to think. How would I find it, though, from here? In the dark? I had no idea how far along this road the gorge was. But there was someone—actually, two people—who would.

———

WELCOME TO EAST POULTNEY.

I peeked out of the side window of Jimmy's truck as the sign—a wooden placket planted on the edge of a circular-shaped road—glowed under the headlights. In the middle of the circle was a beautiful white clapboard church. Its steeple cut through the darkness like a glowing needle, and its doors were bright red.

"Park over there, Dad," Aiden said. "By the bridge. Then we can just run down to the gorge."

Aiden had opened the door when I'd rung their doorbell, looking surprised and then frightened as I burst into tears. "Julia? What is it? What's wrong?"

Jimmy had come up behind him, baseball cap off, his white hair comfortably mussed. He'd been the one to pull me inside as I began rambling about Sophie and the gorge, leading me into the kitchen with slow nods of his head and a soft, steadying hand along my back.

It wasn't until I sat down at the table—a roughly hewn slab of wood, complete with real tree branch legs—that I realized I was inside the little yellow house. It didn't smell like apples or cedar. It smelled like guys' deodorant and burned toast. There was no wide window in the kitchen or any jelly glass full of wildflowers on the table. The table was cluttered with tools: wrenches and screwdrivers, small drilling bits, and a hammer. It was a mess. And it was lovely too.

Now Jimmy swung the truck around the wide gravelly arc and parked. I got out of the car and stared around at the houses skirting the edges, straining forward, as if Sophie might appear magically through the dark. But there was no sign of her. I stayed close to both men, grateful for their presence, as we passed the East Poultney General Store. Next to the general store was a smattering of clapboard houses with white picket fences and weather vanes, and beyond them, a stately brick home labeled the Horace Greeley House. I bit down on my tongue so I would not yell Sophie's name. Despite my panic, I knew that breaking the silence in that tiny town would have been like standing up in the middle of SATs and screaming at the top of my lungs.

Jimmy and Aiden turned abruptly past the Horace Greeley House, heading down another road, more of a path, really, heavily forested and pitch-black. I moved with them, my chest tightening like a fist. Loose gravel crunched under my feet and the wind blew through my hair. I shivered. In the dark, I could see part of the small makeshift bridge Aiden and I had stood on just a few days ago, and then the sound of rushing water. I ran to it, clutching the sides of the bridge as I looked over into the belly of the gorge. It was as dark as ink.

I leaned over farther, squinting desperately for some sign of Sophie.

"Sophie!" I called hoarsely, trying to keep my voice low. "Sophie! Are you down there?"

A sound, small and faint, drifted up from a spot next to one of the birch trees. It was indecipherable, but there was no mistaking Sophie's voice.

"She's hurt," Jimmy said grimly. "Let's go." The three of us raced to the end of the bridge until we reached the tattered path that led down the side of the gorge.

Aiden turned around then and grabbed my arm. "You stay here. It's dangerous down there. We'll get her."

I shoved him back. "No way."

He let go. Slipping and sliding, I half fell, half crawled my way down behind both of them, until I reached a level part of the ground.

"Sophie!" I called again. "I can't see where you are! Say something and I'll move toward the sound of your voice!"

"Uuunnnhhh…" The voice came again out the dark, pleading, desperate. I struggled toward it, pushing past the thick scrub and hanging branches, steadying myself carefully along moss-covered rocks. But Aiden and Jimmy had already found her. Through the dark, I could make out the shadow of two shapes hovering over a third.

"Sophie!" I was next to her all at once, clutching her around the shoulders, pressing my face to her cheek. She was shivering violently, but her face was burning hot. Her braids, damp with mud, clung to the sides of her neck, and her bandanna was missing. "Sophie, what happened? What are you doing down here?"

She pointed toward her foot, which was lodged in between two rocks. Jimmy and Aiden were already examining it. "I came down…" Her voice, which was barely a whisper, slipped out between her chattering teeth. "Just to sit. And think." She pointed to her foot again with a shaking hand. "I tripped and fell. My cell phone fell out of my pocket, and my foot…got stuck. I think it's broken." She tried to balance herself up on her elbows, but winced from the movement and sank back down again.

"Hold on," I said, looking up at Jimmy and Aiden. "They're going to get you out, Sophie."

"We need a flashlight," Aiden said. "I can't see anything."

Jimmy nodded urgently. "And a blanket. In the trunk."

Aiden disappeared into the blackness, his shoes making heavy scraping sounds as he crawled back up the side of the gorge.

I leaned over to get a better look at the rocks trapping Sophie's foot. The one on the left was as large and wide as a mattress, but the other was only about half that size. Both of them, however, were half submerged in water. The space in between, where Sophie's foot was caught, was frighteningly narrow. I moved directly into the water, gasping as the frigidness swirled around my knees. It could not have been over twenty degrees. My body had already started shivering. Sophie had been down here, her left leg submerged to the knee, for God knows how long. How was she still conscious? And talking?

I stared down at my sister. For a split second, I wondered how much more of her I didn't—and might not ever—know. And in the next second, I realized it didn't matter. What mattered was how much I loved her. Right now.

Wrapping my arms around her again, I leaned in and cradled her head in my arms. "Hold on, Sophie, okay? We're going to get you out of here. I promise. Just hold on."

She reached up and grabbed my elbow and she did not let go.

chapter
51

Once we had the flashlight, it took Jimmy less than ten seconds to assess the situation Sophie was in, grab Aiden's cell phone, and call the fire department for help. They arrived minutes later, springing into action as Jimmy, Aiden, and I stood by. One of them added another blanket to the growing pile on top of Sophie, but her lips still trembled violently. A wide, glaring beam of light had been directed down from the top of the truck positioned at the edge of the bridge. Under this light, two firemen were busy tethering a rope to the smaller of the two boulders, while the other two attended to Sophie. An ambulance screamed its arrival, sidling in next to the fire truck with a screech of brakes. Two attendants jumped out and joined the firemen in the gorge. One of them began taking Sophie's vital signs while the other covered her with heated blankets. Above us, the red siren lights flashed back and forth, in and out, in a dizzying display of urgency.

I listened with one ear as an attendant began barking out Sophie's statistics. "Heart rate is forty! BP is eighty over sixty and we got a temp of ninety-one! Any chance you guys can hurry up with that rock? This girl is in serious hypothermic shock."

I turned to Jimmy, my eyes wide with panic.

"Let them work," he said steadily.

I turned back, straining to see Sophie behind the swirl of moving bodies. My whole body began to shiver again, weakened from the strain of the last few weeks, terrified at the thought of losing Sophie. Jimmy took off his jacket and draped it around my shoulders while Aiden patted me gently on the back. The three of us stood very close to one another for the next thirty-seven minutes, until at last, with a roar from the firemen, the earth released its hold and, with one enormous, groaning, sucking movement, set the rock free.

———

We followed the ambulance to the Rutland Regional Medical Center, which was the closest hospital. The twenty-minute drive seemed interminable. I sat close to the window on the passenger side of Jimmy's pickup truck, an ancient, rumbling vehicle that rattled whenever we hit a bump, and prayed that we would make it to the hospital without breaking down. The inside of the truck smelled like pipe tobacco and home fries. A thin coating of dust covered the dashboard and the floor mats were worn through with holes. We probably would've been better off taking the quad.

We drove for a while in silence, following the deep glare of red ambulance lights as they cut through the fading night ahead of us. To the right, the sky was turning the faintest shade of pink, like morning glories wakening. Jimmy drove with just the inside of his right wrist resting on top of the steering wheel; next to him, Aiden sat quietly. He had taken his hat off and was rubbing the edge of his hairline with his fingers.

"She'll be okay," Jimmy said finally, as we passed a sign that said RUTLAND——2 MILES.

I turned to look at him. "You really think so? Even after everything that guy back there said about hypothermia?"

He nodded. "They got her in time. She's a little broken up is all. They'll fix her."

Hot tears spilled down my cheeks suddenly, as if Jimmy had turned on a faucet with his words.

Next to me, Aiden reached his arm across my shoulders and squeezed.

———

The emergency waiting room was filled to capacity. I was surprised until I remembered that it was Saturday morning. I'd heard somewhere that Friday and Saturday nights were the busiest in every emergency room all over the country. Why should Vermont be any exception?

Blue-cushioned chairs, shoved together to make one long couch, were pressed up against one side of the room, while the middle was taken up by three separate rows of backless seats. Nearly every seat was occupied, mostly by sleeping people, their coats bunched up in makeshift pillows, heads bent at unnatural angles. Two girls, who looked to be my age, were curled up in fetal positions at the feet of an older couple. With their hair splayed out behind them and their faces slack with sleep, they could have been at a slumber party, not in an emergency waiting room. Another woman, dressed in a pale green suit, nude pantyhose, and black heels, was slouched in a chair at the very end of the wall. Her hand covered her face, but her shoulders shook with sobs. The cuffs of her suit sleeves were covered with blood.

"I'm going to go find some coffee," Aiden said, nodding at me. "You want some?"

I shook my head.

"Dad?" he asked.

Jimmy nodded. "Cream only."

"Back in a few," Aiden said.

Jimmy pointed to a small space in the middle row between two sleeping people. I followed as he settled himself down, crossed his legs at the ankle, and stared at the TV. It was 5:20 a.m. An early morning show blared out a series of morbid headlines. Inflation was up, the stock market was down. The whole world as we knew it was burning, and none of it mattered because the only thing that was important was in the next room, a wall away.

"You knew about Goober?" I heard myself say. "With the custody and everything?"

Jimmy nodded. He did not take his eyes off the television.

"Why?" I asked softly. "Why would she do something like that?"

"She didn't tell me." Jimmy shrugged lightly. "And I didn't ask."

"Why not?"

"Some things aren't ours to ask."

I stared down at my feet.

"I don't think she'll go through with it, though," Jimmy said.

"You don't?"

Jimmy shook his head. "They haven't signed the papers yet. I think this is a temporary thing while she's been trying to figure some other things out."

My heart pounded. I'd already leapt to the conclusion that it was a done deal. That I'd only get to see Goober on one of Sophie's weekends. Which would probably be close to never. "Oh God, I hope so."

On the television, a woman was crying. Her hair stuck up straight off her head and she was dressed in a pink housecoat. Behind her, the scene was a slate of water, punctuated with small, bobbing houses.

"God," I said, looking away. "There's just so much…awfulness in the world. Nobody gets a break, do they?"

"Nope." Jimmy stared straight ahead, watching the woman as she continued to wail.

We both stared at the television screen as the camera panned to another view of destruction. The whole side of a house was gone, gutted like a fish. Inside, a large family portrait still hung on one of the remaining walls, and a living room lamp was upright in a corner. "People get through," Jimmy said. "You don't got much choice, really. You either get through or you get stuck. That's about it."

I looked over at him for a moment. Little white hairs stuck out from inside his ears, and the lobes were wide and fleshy. "Jimmy?"

"Huh?"

"What were you doing in church that day? With the rocks, I mean?"

He squinted, as if there was a glare on the TV. Then he said, "I put them out in front of the Blessed Virgin. It's just a thing I do."

"What's it mean?"

He paused. "Did Aiden tell you about his mother?"

"Yes."

He nodded. "It's for her. Mostly. She liked them. Rocks and things. Whenever I see one, I pick it up. Usually, I make things out of them. It keeps me busy, now that I'm retired. But sometimes when I feel the need, I go into the church and sit down and try to listen for her."

"For your wife?" I asked softly.

He shook his head. "For the Blessed Virgin." He turned his head finally, and looked at me. "Don't worry, I'm not some crazy old guy who hears voices." I smiled. "But sometimes, when I wait, she comes. She does. I can feel her. And when that happens, I know Theresa is close by too. And that's when I leave the stones." He shrugged. "They're sort of a thank you, I guess. And a hello too."

I wasn't sure if I understood.

But I knew that it was true.

I knew that it was good.

I slipped my hand inside his big rough one, and left it there.

chapter
52

Sophie's injuries included a fractured femur, a shattered ankle, and extreme hypothermia. When a nurse finally came to retrieve us hours later, Sophie had already been moved to a room upstairs. Her leg, which had been set and cast, was propped up in a sling, and two IVs were dripping warm liquid into her arms. Someone thankfully had cleaned the mud out of her hair and wiped her face so she looked almost normal, even healthy, when we finally got a chance to see her.

I went over to her bed. Jimmy and Aiden hung back by the doorway.

"Sophie," I whispered, hugging her tightly. She smelled like antiseptic. Her fingernails still had mud under them, and there was a tiny cut above her left eye. I straightened back up and turned around, beckoning the two men in, but Jimmy shook his head.

"Just wanted to lay eyes on you," he said to Sophie, touching the brim of his cap. "You two take some time alone. We'll be back in a while."

Sophie gave him a grateful look and then blew him a kiss.

Aiden gave me a little nod and then disappeared down the hall.

I started to take a step back, when Sophie reached out suddenly with two fingers and pulled on the belt loop of my jeans. "Wait," she whispered.

"What?"

"I want to tell you." She closed her eyes. "About Maggie."

I swallowed with enormous difficulty. "You don't have to. It's okay, Sophie. You don't have to anymore."

She shook her head, lolling it heavily from side to side. "Just listen, okay?"

I stared at her, remembering Lloyd's words: *You don't go easy on someone when they're just startin' out. You go easy on someone when they've got blisters on top of blisters and they're about ready to throw a hammer at someone.*

Sophie looked back at me. "If I don't tell you now, I'll never do it. Okay?"

"Okay," I whispered.

"It was a Saturday," Sophie began. "Mom was away for the weekend. I don't remember where she was. Maybe at Gram's. Anyway, she left us both with Dad." She draped the crook of her arm over her eyes. Beneath it, her mouth spread into a smile. "We had such a great day, the three of us. It was really warm out. Dad took us to the park and then to Hillside Farms for ice cream. Then later, after Maggie's nap, we went miniature golfing. On the way home, he stopped at the supermarket because he wanted to get stuff to grill hamburgers and hot dogs for dinner. Maggie loved hot dogs.

He told us to wait in the car while he ran in. We were both practically jumping out of our skins from all the excitement and fun we'd had—with even more to come."

Sophie removed her arm from her eyes. "Except that as Dad came back out of the store, I saw the blue cans sticking out of the top of the bag. And suddenly, you know, it was like all the air went out of a balloon or something. I knew what was coming."

She was staring straight above her now, past my face, looking back.

"Dad went upstairs and started a bath for us. He put in some strawberry-scented bubbles that Maggie loved and helped us undress and put us both in. Maggie was splashing around and laughing, but I remember just staring at the blue tiles on the wall."

Sophie began shaking then. At first I thought she was having a seizure, until I realized it was just from the memory. She struggled to restrain herself.

"Stop," I said. "You can tell me the rest later. I'm going to go get a nurse."

She clutched me around the wrist with freezing fingers. "Not saying anything to you all these years was my first lie," she whispered fiercely. "And I haven't stopped since. Whenever Mom or Dad—or anyone else—ever asked me what was wrong, I told them 'nothing.' Everything was always fine." Her face contorted. "If I had just told them then, right at that moment, maybe none of this would have turned out this way."

"This is so much easier, isn't it?"

"What is?"

"*Just being straight with each other. Think of all the time we've wasted doing everything except this.*"

"I've done it too," I whispered, stroking Sophie's cheek with the tip of my finger. "It's not just you, Sophie. We all do it."

She winced. "But not at the expense of someone else." She struggled to get her breath. I slid myself alongside her in the bed, wrapping my arms gently around her shoulders and drawing her toward me. She rested her cheek against my collarbone.

"He said he was going to go downstairs to start the grill," Sophie started again. "Five minutes. That was all." Her eyebrows narrowed. "But I knew where he was going. And all of a sudden, thinking about it, I got really, really pissed. Boiling mad. Red mad." She paused. "All I could think about was getting rid of those blue cans. So I got out of the tub."

"You left Maggie?" I asked faintly.

Sophie nodded. "I told her I'd be right back. I told her to sit down and be very quiet. And then I left. I went downstairs. Dad was outside in the backyard, already drinking out of one of the blue cans. He had one of Mom's aprons on, and he was whistling. I could smell the charcoal. And then real quick, before he came in, I opened the fridge and grabbed the stack of cans. I had one under one arm and was just reaching for the other when I noticed something different."

"What?" I asked.

"They were blue, but they didn't have the white stripe on the side like his beer usually did."

Her eyes roved the ceiling above her, searching, searching.

"I remember there was a red stripe on the side, and little black letters that spelled out C-O-L-A." She blinked. "I was so confused that I didn't even hear Dad come in. He gave me this funny look and asked me what I was doing. I couldn't even answer. I put the cans back in the refrigerator and told him Maggie wanted a drink.

" 'Where is Maggie?' he asked me.

"When I told him she was in the tub, he said, 'By herself?' and then he rushed off.

"I followed him up the steps. I could hear water running for some reason. And then I heard this yell..."

Sophie closed her eyes. I had not realized how tightly clenched she had been until she released herself suddenly against me. "She'd turned the water back on, maybe accidentally, maybe to make it higher, and she'd gone under. The doctors said later that if she hadn't had asthma, she might have lived."

An anguished sound came out of her mouth suddenly, and she brought her fist up and bit down on it hard. Her eyes were wide, wild with fear and memory. I knew what she was feeling now was more painful than any of her injuries.

I bent my head over hers and wept.

chapter
53

I was still in bed next to Sophie when Jimmy returned. He was holding two plastic packages of cream-filled oatmeal cookies and a large container of orange juice. He stopped when he saw us, tears still running down our cheeks. "Should I come back?"

"No, no," Sophie wiped at her face with the heels of her hands. "Come in. Where's Aiden?"

"He went back into town to get something." Jimmy walked in hesitantly, nodding at the items in his arms. "It's all I could find this early," he said apologetically, dumping them on the little table next to Sophie's bed.

Sophie smiled wanly at the cookies, and then looked away, embarrassed. "I'm so sorry...," she started.

I took her hand in mine. "No more apologies," I whispered. "It wasn't your fault."

She stared past me, out the window.

"It wasn't your fault."

She sat motionless, her eyes empty and riveted.

"It wasn't your fault." I said it louder this time, and squeezed her hand.

She blinked.

Jimmy came over and took her other hand. We exchanged a look across the bed and I knew then that she had told him about Maggie, that maybe he was the only one in her entire life up until this moment who had known. And that he loved her anyway. Just as I did.

"It's not your fault, Sophie," I said again.

"It's not," Jimmy echoed.

She broke down all at once. Her body strained forward, even as her hands clutched ours, as if they were the only things left in the world holding her up. Moans drifted out of her mouth, and her thin frame shook under their weight.

We held her tight, Jimmy and I, and let her cry.

———

Afterward Sophie fell asleep. Jimmy walked over to the window across the room and stood in front of it. I pulled up a chair next to Sophie's bed and just watched her for a while. Her face looked more peaceful than I'd seen it in a long time; the tight muscles along her jaw were relaxed. Her skin was regaining some color too; a little bit of pink had bloomed under her cheeks and her lips had lost that awful purple shade.

"Now what?" I thought. "Does this mean she's all better inside? That things will be different? Is it all over? Am I supposed to go home now?"

Aiden walked in with a little white box in his hand. "Hey," he said softly. "How's she doing?"

I stood up. "Better. She's sleeping now."

"Can you come outside for a minute?" he asked. "I have something to give you."

Jimmy was still looking out the window.

We walked out into the parking lot, which was starting to fill up with more cars. It was light out, the air pale and new. "This is for you," Aiden said, pushing the little white box into my hands. "I wanted to make you something, after that day we talked about my mother. Open it."

It was the tiny bowl, the one the size of an orange, the one I'd said was too small to eat out of. Except now it looked different. Before, it was just a pale brown color. Now it was a rich honey hue, the surface burnished and glossy, with a rough, pebbled texture. "You salt glazed it?" I asked.

He nodded.

"Thank you," I said. "It's beautiful. But I still don't know what I'm supposed to eat out of this."

"It's not for eating," Aiden said. "It's for your earrings, so you don't lose them anymore."

I grinned and then moved in for a hug.

His arms tightened around my shoulder. "I'm gonna miss you, Julia," he said softly.

"Me too." I squeezed him around the waist, tucked my head under his chin. "I'm so glad I met you, Aiden. You have no idea—"

"Actually, I think I do," he said, cutting me off gently. "Because I feel the same way."

I took a step back, let my eyes drift over his face. "You do?"

Aiden nodded. "Being able to talk about my mother again…" He shook his head. "You know, I told myself that I was done with the whole grieving thing after that night at the gorge. It was time to move on, be a big strong man." He shook his head. "But being able to talk about her again with you…" He took my hand. "It was something I didn't realize I needed to do until I did it." His thumb moved gently over the tops of my knuckles. "And I'm just so grateful. I feel like I can go off and really start the rest of my life now, you know? Without feeling like I'm leaving her behind."

I moved in for another hug.

He was right.

We felt exactly the same way.

chapter
54

Jimmy and Aiden left a few hours later, Jimmy promising Sophie that he was going to get to work on a little stepstool for her to get in and out of bed when she got home, and Aiden promising me that he would put my little earring bowl in a safe place. I watched them leave from the window, Jimmy slinging his arm around Aiden's shoulder, drawing him in close before they got into the red truck. I felt lucky to know them. Both of them.

"It's none of my business," I said to Sophie. "But I really think you should let the Table of Knowledge guys help you with the rest of the house." I nodded toward her foot. "Especially now. I know you think you're Wonder Woman and all, but—"

"I know." Sophie cut me off abruptly. "I've been thinking about that a lot. It's so stupid of me to push them away when they want to help so much. Besides, if I keep going the way I am, even with all *your* do-it-yourself expertise…" She stopped for a moment and laughed. "I'll never open the place!"

I grinned. "Good," I said softly.

Behind us came a light tap on the door. I turned as Sophie sat forward and then I stood up, almost knocking my chair over.

"Mom! Dad!"

Mom rushed in first, her face streaked with old tears. She clutched me to her wordlessly and held on, as if she might never let go. Dad waited patiently behind her, his hand resting lightly on her shoulder. Something twisted inside me as I watched him with new eyes, as I felt her, and I pulled away. Mom looked startled for a brief second, and then her eyes moved to Sophie. "Honey," she said, her voice breaking. "We got into town this morning—we wanted to surprise you, both of you—and when we couldn't find you at the house, we went across the street and they told us…"

"Who told you?" Sophie asked.

Dad shrugged. "Some big guy with suspenders," he said. "But everyone in the place seemed to know that you were here."

Sophie grinned. "It's a small town."

I took a step back. "I'm gonna go outside for a minute. I just need some air. I'll be right back."

"Honey," Mom said, stretching out her arm. "Stay…"

I nodded. "We'll talk. I just need a minute, okay?"

The sun was soft on my arms as I strolled outside and sat down on one of the visitor benches. I didn't know what to feel about Mom and Dad, now that I knew everything. The only thing I did know was that it hurt to be in the same room with them. How was I supposed to move past the fact that they had kept so much from me, for so many years?

Where, along a road so thickly shrouded with trees, was I supposed to take the next step?

I leaned against the trunk of a tree and flipped open my phone.

"Julia!" Zoe said when she answered. "How are you? Why haven't you called?"

"Zoe, listen. I need to ask you something really important."

"Okay. Shoot."

"It's personal."

"Okay."

"And you can tell me to shove off if it's none of my business."

"Are you *trying* to annoy me?"

I swallowed. "Do you think your mom is still cheating on your dad?"

I bit my lip hard as the silence reverberated through the phone. The sound of birds chirping grated on my ears, and for a moment I felt the urge to pee.

"Yeah," Zoe said finally. It came out as an exhale, a breath. "I do."

"And ..." I hesitated, stepping on my toe. "And do you love her anyway?"

Another pause. "Yeah," Zoe's voice trembled. "I wish I didn't, because it would be easier, but she's my mom, you know?"

"Yeah," I said. "I know."

———

I stood in the same spot for a long time after hanging up with Zoe. I didn't want to go back inside. Not yet. If I knew Sophie, she was probably telling Mom and Dad right now, right this minute, that she had finally told me everything. All of it. The *real* all of it. Who knew what would happen now? You either got through it, or you got stuck. We had moved through some of it. But there was a lot more to do. And I wasn't sure about Mom and Dad, but I knew I didn't want to get stuck.

Not again.

Not with so much ahead of me.

Maybe later, some night at dinner, we would be sitting around another table, talking and laughing, and wonder how we had gotten there from where we were now.

epilogue

The sound of feet came pattering down the hall just as I slipped on my dress.

"Aunt Julia!" Goober gasped. "Are you ready?"

I lifted her under her arms and swung her around as she screamed with joy. Her blond hair, cut in a pageboy style, floated like a little mushroom around her face, and the blue polka dots on her dress matched her eyes. "Almost! Are you?"

"Yes!" Goober shrieked. "Put me down!"

I obeyed. "I just need to fix my hair," I said, picking up the brush from the bed.

Goober put her hands on her hips. Her shiny black patent leather shoes were planted firmly on the floor. "I don't want you to leave," she said suddenly. "I want you to stay in my room forever."

I finished smoothing my hair into place and knelt down next to her. "I've been here all summer, Goobs. And now I have to go to school. But don't worry. I'll come back to visit on my breaks. And I'll write you letters, okay? Would you like that?"

Goober nodded. "Yeah. I like letters. With pictures! Will you draw me pictures like the one you did in my room?"

I nodded. After Sophie and Goober had seen the finished mural on the kitchen wall, Sophie had offered to pay me to do one in Goober's room. Goober—who was back for good—spent a long time telling me what she wanted me to paint. Finally, she settled on an underwater scene, complete with mermaids, dolphins, jellyfish, even a shark. It took me a lot longer to do the ocean wall than the kitchen wall, but when I was finished, I hadn't felt that excited in a very long time. It was good. I knew it was good.

Goober threw her arms around me. "But I'll miss you. Like to Pluto and back and around again to infinity miss you."

I held her tight. Her hair smelled like soap and sunshine. "I'll be back before you know it."

Goober pulled out of my hug and grabbed my hand. "Mama needs help buttoning her dress." She steered me down the hallway into Sophie's bedroom. Sophie was sitting on the bed, fumbling awkwardly with the buttons in the back of her dress. Her walls had been painted a beautiful lemon color, and the curtains were pale and sheer, letting in a lake of light.

"Here," I said, kneeling on the bed behind her. "Let me."

"I'm so nervous," she said. "I can't do anything today."

"Of course you're nervous," I said, finishing up the last few buttons. "You're standing on the edge of a dream come true. You've worked your whole life for this moment. I'd be nervous too." I leaned in over her shoulder. "Just don't forget to enjoy it."

"I couldn't have done it without you, Jules." She put her hand over mine.

I smiled. "I wouldn't have wanted you to."

———

A small crowd had gathered in front of 149 Main Street. I recognized many of the faces—Mom, Dad, Walt, Lloyd, Jimmy, Aiden, Miriam, Greg, the lady from Dunkin' Donuts, even the guy from the delicatessen, still dressed in his white apron and biker shorts. And Zoe, who was on my right, wriggling with excitement, and Milo, who was holding my left hand. They had come up last night, as a surprise.

But there were some unfamiliar faces too, people I had never seen before. And I thought for a moment how unlucky they were, to see the beautiful building before them with its new roof and freshly painted siding, its new porch with a sturdy set of steps, and its freshly landscaped lawn, complete with rhododendron bushes and lilies-of-the-valley. They probably took for granted that the place had always looked like this.

It was the rest of us who were lucky, the ones who had witnessed the building before its renovation; the ones who had stayed in the broken-down mess of a thing until it turned into the proud, durable structure in front of us now.

And I was one of them.

———

The crowd erupted into cheers as Sophie and Goober appeared on the front steps. Sophie ducked her head shyly as the applause grew, but Goober beamed out at the crowd and hopped up and down. After a moment, the crowd quieted and Sophie lifted her head.

"Thank you all for coming today," she said. "I'm so excited to be opening this beautiful little bakery, which, as some of you may know, is a lifelong dream of mine. And as long as I don't mistake the flour for the salt, I think you'll be very happy with some of the things that I have to offer you."

Sophie's face eased some more as a loud ripple of laughter came from the street. Goober began to swing her mother's hand back and forth between them. "I could never have gotten here, though, without the help of my friends," Sophie said. Her eyes began to tear up as she looked over at Walt, Lloyd, and Jimmy. I bit my lip. "The Table of Knowledge!" Sophie said, extending her arm, as the crowd cheered again. "Without whom this place would never have come together."

She brought her hands to her mouth, forming a little steeple with her fingers. I could tell she was trying not to cry. I got a little teary myself. Walt, Lloyd, and Jimmy had outdone themselves over the last month or so, working every day until late at night until the place was finished. It was still as much their house as it was Sophie's. Or so I liked to think.

"And my sister," Sophie said. "My little sister, Julia, who came all the way up from Ohio and stayed with me all summer until we got this place done." Her voice was strong. "Julia," she said. "I love you so much."

I waved to her and cried as Milo squeezed my hand.

Sophie bent down and whispered something to Goober. Everyone laughed as the little girl raced off the porch and stood anxiously next to a small sign covered with a black cloth. "Okay, Goober!" Sophie said. Goober reached up and pinched the edge of the cloth with two fingers. "When I count to three!"

"One! Two!" The crowd roared with her. "Three!"

Goober snatched away the cloth.

And there, in the sunlight, stood the Three Sisters Bakery.

I sat as close to Milo as the seat belt would allow. It was not close enough. His right hand was between us, holding mine tightly, while he steered with his left. I could smell the peppermint Cert between his teeth, and the heat from his skin warmed my palm.

"That bakery is gonna go through the roof," Zoe said, popping up from the backseat. She leaned her long arms down between us and looked at me. "You know that, don't you? Your sister is sitting on a total gold mine." She shook her head and adjusted the barrette in her hair. "And I'm totally, totally digging the name."

I grinned and glanced at her. "I still can't believe you two surprised me like this."

"We wouldn't have been able to, if your parents hadn't told us," Milo reminded me.

"Yeah, how about that?" Zoe said, scooting forward a little more. "I almost shit a brick when your mother called. I thought for sure she was going to ream me out about something. And then she tells us about the whole deal about the opening, and that we could follow them up if we wanted to!"

Milo raised his eyebrows. "It was pretty nice of them."

I ran my hand through my hair. "They're good parents," I said.

"Man," Zoe said. "I woulda paid a million bucks to be a fly on the wall during the conversation you had with them about Pittsburgh."

"It wasn't nearly as dramatic as I'm sure you would have liked it to be," I said, grinning back at her. "Besides, they both calmed way, way down after I told them about Plan B. They're meeting us there, too, by the way."

"Plan B isn't exactly shabby," Milo said. "Speaking of which..." He pointed out the window to a sign on the highway: WELLESLEY COLLEGE—4 MILES.

I shuddered with joy. I still didn't know what my dream was, but I knew this was going to be the first of many steps toward finding it. Deciding to apply to the college of my choice, enlisting my major tentatively as art history, and taking out loans might not have been as practical as accepting a free ride and prelaw, but in a way, it felt like standing in a kitchen with a head full of ideas. More important, it was me.

One hundred percent me.

———

That night, as the five of us were sitting around the table inside the fancy Japanese restaurant Mom and Dad had taken us to for my eighteenth birthday, Milo looked up at Dad.

"Do you mind if Julia and I go for a little walk?" He dropped his eyes nervously. "I just... I want to tell her..."

Mom leaned forward, putting her hand on his wrist. "Go ahead," she said softly. "We have plenty of time before the cake."

She and Dad exchanged a look as Milo and I stood up, and Dad nodded slightly.

"Don't be too long!" Zoe called out as we made our way to the door. "I'm not exactly on a first-name basis with these people, you know!" She looked over at Mom and Dad, held up a can of Dr Pepper, and grinned. "Just having a little fun, guys. Just having a little fun."

It was dusk. Downtown Wellesley was abuzz with Saturday nightlife.

"So this will be home for a while," Milo said. "This and your dorm room, of course. Which, by the way, I have to say I am glad we're done with. I didn't think we'd ever get your computer hooked up. I thought your Dad was gonna lose it when we had to start all over again—for the third time."

I smiled. "He's a big fixer-upper kind of guy. He gets frustrated if it doesn't come together right away." I paused. "He's learning, though. And you two worked well together."

Milo nodded. "Rachel seems nice." He looked at me. "You like her, right?"

I shrugged. "So far." My roommate had seemed nice. A little nerdy, like me. Quiet. A biology major. Awed by my shot glass collection. She had already asked where she could get a tiny bowl like the one Aiden had made for me.

"You're gonna do great," Milo said, slipping his hand into mine. I looked up at him briefly and smiled as the warmth of his fingers traveled up through me.

"You are too."

After waiting until the last possible moment, Milo had finally decided to attend Boston University, which had not only offered him a scholarship but had one of the best English programs in the country. He was going to major in creative writing. It didn't hurt that I would now be only twenty minutes away.

He shrugged. "I hope so."

"You will. And you'll come here? To visit me?"

Milo stopped walking and turned to face me. We were still on the sidewalk, facing Washington Street. I glanced at the couple walking toward us on my right, and then at the girl wearing a tight, bra-like top coming closer on our left. But Milo didn't seem to see any of them. Instead, he cupped my face in his hands, holding it the way the sky holds the moon.

"Julia," he whispered. He bent his face toward mine and kissed me so gently that my knees buckled. "Always."

Everything around us fell away—the street with its throng of cars, people rushing by, even the storm clouds swirling overhead—as Milo lowered his face again and, holding the back of my head with his hand, pressed his lips against mine.

acknowledgments

Thank you—always—to my family: my husband Paul and my beautiful children, for being so supportive of the long hours I sometimes need and the meals I occasionally skimp on because of those hours. (Let's hear it for pancakes!) I love you all so much.

My editor and publisher, the luminescent Melanie Cecka, took this project on despite the amount of work it still needed. For taking the leap of faith, as well as seeing me through to the end, I remain eternally grateful. Special thanks also to Caroline Abbey of Bloomsbury, for all her hard work and attention to this book, as well as the incredible arts and graphics team at Bloomsbury for devising such a beautiful cover. You're the best!

For finding this book—and all of my books—a home away from home, I am forever indebted to my agent and true friend, Jessica Regel. You stand out far above the rest. I am so lucky to have you.

I had lots of help along the way, especially when it came to getting the facts about Poultney, Vermont. To that end, I would like to extend my appreciation to Kitty Galante, who is without a doubt Poultney's most ardent fan; my dearest friend, Kemi McShane (who checked on the maple syrup statistics at least three times); and all the fabulous patrons at Perry's Main Street Eatery, especially the Table of Knowledge. (Let's hear it for creamed chipped beef!)

Roland Merullo gave me invaluable advice when I was stuck, something that I return to again and again. Thank you, friend. Rachel VanBlankenship read at least eight drafts of this book—and found new ways to encourage me every time. You're one in a million, girl.

My final—and most important—debt of gratitude goes to someone I met only once. Let me explain:

Two-thirds of the way into this book, I lost it. Literally. My bag, which contained my bright blue flash drive (which contained the only draft of the book), was stolen out of my car. In less than five minutes, my wallet, driver's license, a small chunk of money, my high school students' grade books (all 109 of them), and 256 pages of the newest novel I had promised my agent had disappeared. I wept and ranted, swore and cursed. I called the police department and filed a report. Over the next two days, I wrote down as much of the plot as I could remember (not as easy as one might think) and all the bits of dialogue I could still place. (Again, not so easy.) I prayed to Saint Anthony, patron saint of lost things. And I made a promise to myself to back up everything I wrote in the future on my hard drive.

On the third day, I received a phone call from the police

department. They gave me the name and phone number of someone who had found my bag in a ditch. It had been rummaged through, and it was wet, but the caller said that it looked as if everything was still in there. I drove to the address like a bat out of hell. A shoeless older man, dressed in a blue flannel shirt and jeans, opened the door. He had a lazy eye and a garbled voice. His name was Thomas. He walked every morning across the mountain behind his house and then back again. Yesterday—he pointed to my bag—he had found this. I leaped toward it, yelping, and pawed through the contents. Every single thing was in there—except the bright blue flash drive.

I turned to Thomas, desperate, and begged him to take me to the place on the mountain where he had found the bag. If I could just look around myself... maybe the flash drive had fallen out. Maybe, somehow, I could find it. Thomas—who I guessed to be in his late seventies—had never heard of anything called a flash drive. He had no idea what one looked like. But he said he'd take me. He had a red beat-up truck. Between us, chunks of foam peeked out from beneath the split upholstery and Doritos bags littered the floor. We drove eight or nine miles along a rutted, desolate road without talking until he finally stopped and pulled over.

It should be noted here that later on, as I relayed this chain of events to a few family members and got to this part of the story, they gasped and shook their heads. What was I thinking, getting into a strange man's car and driving up the side of a mountain on a deserted road? I could have been murdered! Chopped up into a million little pieces! And no one would have ever found me! In hindsight, I guess they were right. But at the time all I could think was this: my book was out there. Somewhere. And I had to find it.

We got out of the car. The sky was a sheet of white above us. It was so cold that I could see my breath. I wrapped my arms around my waist and ducked against the wind. In my haste to get to Thomas's house, I had run out without my winter coat. Thomas pointed to the ditch running along the left side of the road. It was filled with decaying diapers, rusted doorknobs, Burger King bags, and split tires. There was even an iron buried under a pile of weeds. Side by side, we looked for a tiny, ChapStick-sized instrument, kicking garbage over with our feet, pawing through mounds of dirt and leaves. After twenty minutes, I was shaking so badly from the cold that I told Thomas we had to go back. By then, something had resigned itself within me. I had my skeleton of retrieved notes back at the house. A few salvageable pieces of dialogue. As hard as it was going to be, I would just have to start over.

I said good-bye to Thomas, thanked him profusely for everything, and went home.

I worked until very, very late that night, trying to get the story started again. It was a laborious, agonizing process, made even more difficult by the fact that Julia and Sophie seemed to be a hundred miles away. My head was crowded with other things, namely an old man who took long walks and didn't speak very much. I stopped trying to find the girl's voices that night and began to write about him instead.

Two days later, the police called me again. Someone named Thomas had found something of mine and wanted me to call him.

Dumbfounded, I made the call. "It's blue," Thomas said. "And I don't know for sure, but it might be."

My husband insisted on going himself this time to retrieve the item. Twenty minutes later he returned, my flash drive in hand. He said Thomas had told him he'd looked every day on his walk until he'd finally spotted it, beneath a thin pane of ice in the ditch. He'd stomped on the ice until it broke, and then fished it out. There was no way the material on it was still retrievable. Except that when I plugged it into my computer, it was. The whole book was still there, as intact as it had been before.

I still don't know Thomas's last name. And I doubt that we will cross paths again in the foreseeable future. But Thomas is in this book. He became the inspiration for Jimmy, who, like Thomas, takes long walks and speaks only when spoken to.

I think the story is better for having him in it.

I know I am.

of a loner, even when I was real little. I just kind of preferred it that way. It wasn't Dad's fault. Or Mom's."

"Okay," I said.

Sophie sat back again in her chair. She looked exhausted suddenly. "Anyway, I don't even know if I answered your question. About what she looked like." She leaned forward. "But that's all I can do for today, okay?"

"Yeah," I said softly. "Okay."